Filigrane

By

Y. L. WIGMAN

Bella
BOOKS

2014

Bella Books, Inc.
P.O. Box 10543
Tallahassee, FL 32302

First Bella Books Edition 2014

Editor: Katherine V. Forrest
Cover Designer: Judith Fellows

ISBN: 978-1-59493-417-9

About the Author

Emerging from a career in research and public service, Y. L. Wigman has turned her skills to the art of telling heartfelt stories. Her passions for studying the human condition, spirituality and astrology are evident in her work. With extended family nearby, she lives in Bandicoot Hollow, a cottage in the hills above Perth, Western Australia.

Acknowledgments

My first thank you goes to the universal intelligence that writes through me, the next to Kelvin Cruickshank for inciting me to just get on with it.

To my loving family and dear friends: my sister Annette, cousin Christine and her wife Annelies, Jan Jamieson, and Rebecca Czajor—thanks for your keen support and priceless advice.

Poppy MacLean granted me the pleasure of meeting her champion Bouviers, Eepie and Harpo.

Claire McNab generously led me to Katherine V. Forrest whose fine editorial skills have enhanced the quality of this novel immeasurably—thank you.

PART ONE

1995

CHAPTER ONE

Kreyna Katz stilled herself in a single breath and thinned her energy to assume the full white state. To the casual observer, she appeared to be slightly out of focus, the air surrounding her shimmering like a heat haze. Positioned in the shadows at the edge of the Rotterdam Seaport Police interrogation room, she steadied a notepad in her lap and held a pen over the page as if it were the focus of her attention. In truth, she altered her essential frequency and moved within the room, an unseen thought form.

Five men sat hunched over a bare, steel table bolted to the concrete floor. Sitting with their backs to opposing walls, Kreyna and her colleague, Robert Varazslo, were acting as observers, ostensibly. Chief Inspector Versluis of the Rotterdam Criminal Intelligence Department and his fearsome second-in-command sat facing Robert. Kreyna faced Victor Deprez, an Inspector with the Antwerp Gendarmerie and Investigation Brigade.

Both Dutch and Belgian police were investigating an unlikely story from a snitch named Piet Van Whalen. He had told the Dutch police of a drug organization headed by some of Belgium's most senior law enforcement officials who were helping notorious Dutch and Belgian drug barons to import drugs through the port of Antwerp. One of those officials, Inspector Deprez was alleged to have masterminded illicit schemes that trafficked drugs across the globe as far as Australia.

Interpol had alerted Australian Customs who briefed the Australian Security Intelligence Organisation, otherwise known as ASIO. As ASIO's senior remote viewer, Robert had been brought in to evaluate the truthfulness of Deprez and two Public Prosecutor's Office clerks during interrogation. Kreyna had accompanied him in a final test of her telepathic skills.

Kreyna's mission was to mind-scan the suspects, record their thoughts into a quantifying matrix and to measure to what extent they were lying. How well she performed would determine her admittance to ASIO's Non-Physical Surveillance Team of remote viewers who were trained to gather military intelligence at any distance. Competition for a role in the team was strong and Kreyna was determined to earn her place.

Sitting at the table on either side of Deprez, the two Public Prosecutor's Office clerks were accused of sabotaging all attempts to investigate the Belgian inspector—an accusation they had denied. Instead, they had implicated Antwerp's highest official in the PPO, the Prosecutor General himself. In response, the Belgian parliament had gone into meltdown, met behind closed doors and called for the Dutch authorities to provide further proof. Chief Inspector Versluis was in charge of the investigation.

With casual menace, Chief Inspector Versluis addressed the younger PPO clerk, "We have documentary evidence that shows thousands of francs being deposited into your bank account in Antwerp. What is your explanation?"

Kreyna heard little beyond the first question. She was working. Answering evasively, the clerk grazed fingernails across his lips and spoke softly. Kreyna slipped into his thoughts. He would have felt her as a waft of fresh air, or a pleasant coolness. Oblivious, he continued. She appraised the volume of his varying emotions, peeling them aside like lasagna layers: at the top, uncertainty about the way the interrogation would go and concern as to what Versluis thought of him. Down a layer to his worry about the other clerk, his close and equally corrupt friend—how much would he say? Down another layer to the long-gone bribe spent on his family. And down to where lurked his crawling fear of being caught, his zero chance of escape and the sickening threat: could he survive an extended jail term, if Deprez let him live?

With pen to paper, Kreyna sketched out a matrix that supported her assessment of the young man's sincerity. There was a ninety-six percent probability he was lying.

Versluis turned his attention to the sweating, gray-faced older PPO clerk who tugged at a jacket that failed to button across his belly. Within seconds, Kreyna had all the information she needed and recorded the verdict of ninety-eight percent—he too lied as if his life depended on it. She looked up in an attempt to catch Robert's attention, but saw only the top of a bowed head topped with plentiful blond curls. He was deep in concentration.

She considered Inspector Deprez. A tall man wearing a perfectly tailored black suit, he surveyed the proceedings with a sly, contemptuous smile. Despite the petty arrogance, he seemed innocuous enough. Would he prove more challenging? She narrowed her eyes, inhaled deeply and homed in on him.

Deprez picked up her intrusion. With lightning speed he closed his seven energy centers, the chakras, like a sequence of doors to a vault crashing shut. Surprised, she shifted a fraction too slow. A moment's indecision and she hovered in stillness— an unreadable quietude. Feeling him try to get her measure, she suppressed a little jolt of excitement at finding a worthy adversary. He was a competent intuitive, albeit a criminally corrupt cop. Interesting.

Chief Inspector Versluis turned his attention to Deprez. "How much did you pay De Vries to lose the warrant for Van Whalen's arrest?"

Caught off guard, Deprez's concentration faltered. "Assuming I know either of them and I don't."

No time to lose. Again, Kreyna scanned his chakras and found a sliver of an opening at the solar plexus. Startled by this new intrusion, his shock soon turned into fear, then anger and rage. Instantly, she grasped his hostile energy and used it to sneak in the back door—his sacral chakra directly below.

Deprez's pupils dilated. She visualized her fingertips caressing his scrotum. Within a second, he was erect and ready to explode. He lurched, grunted and dropped his hands to his groin. Beside him, the young clerk stared in confusion. Between the four men, gazes met, heads shook and shoulders shrugged.

Unimpeded, Kreyna shot up to Deprez's crown chakra, mined his thoughts at will and fled back to emerge through his solar plexus. She wrote fast, recording his memories, conversations and shady deals, mercenary cruelties and bribe-fueled indulgences. Deprez thought he was invincible.

In her haste, the pen clattered to the floor—with a quick glance up, she stooped to retrieve it. Teeth bared, Deprez shot looks like bullets. Her psychic flak jacket held him at bay.

For the remainder of the interview, she closed down her hyper-senses. There was nothing more she could do and she needed to save energy for the next subject. Soon, Deprez and the two clerks were bundled out of the room. A few minutes later, another man was escorted in and sat down at the table.

A slight, bespectacled thirty-five-year-old Belgian, Piet Van Whalen was a known drug trafficker and police informer. He'd been supplying details of clandestine drug movements to Deprez who protected him from prosecution, in return. According to Piet, Deprez had made good use of the information Piet fed him and built a mini drug trafficking empire. More and more audacious deals had made Piet fear for his life until finally he wanted out. With the help of three other drug runners who were former accomplices of Deprez, he put together multiple dossiers bulging with trafficking details. Then he had contacted the Rotterdam CID and asked Chief Inspector Versluis for protection in return for information.

Under interrogation, Piet Van Whalen sweated—it reeked of stale nicotine. From her vantage point in the gloomy interview room, Kreyna could detect its rankness too easily. But she smelled another unfamiliar substance that she strained to identify.

When Chief Inspector Versluis barked questions, Piet's heart rate surged and faltered to unnatural extremes. He was high on something, definitely. Sticking to the routine of her job, Kreyna plumbed his halting answers and found truthful motives jumbled by mortal fear.

Piet described his connections to well-known drug traffickers, citing names that the chief inspector's second-in-command jotted down in a casebook. Detailed accounts of Inspector Deprez's criminal activities implicated the two Belgian clerks, as well. By the end of the interview, Kreyna didn't doubt the truth of his story. However, he had a drug problem. What kind of drug was another question—crack or ice? She couldn't be sure, but that he concealed a habit was certain.

Satisfied that everyone had been thoroughly assessed and her conclusions were accurate and verifiable, Kreyna withdrew and stabilized her senses. Her job complete, she sat back and switched off from the remaining dialogue. Across the room and ignoring her, Robert wrote sporadic notes.

Kreyna was drained, yet well pleased with her performance here. For days, she'd been in and out of planes, taxis and hotel rooms, with no opportunity to explore Rotterdam, Europe's busiest harbor city that celebrated a diverse culture and busy nightlife. Regrettable as it was to have missed out on being a tourist, it would be a welcome relief to get home to Canberra.

* * *

Despite the extra width and legroom of the 747's business class seat, Kreyna found it difficult to settle down and catch some sleep. The cabin crew had dimmed the lights, and handed out blankets and pillows soon after they had reached cruising height, thirty minutes out of Bahrain. In keeping with the airline's world-class reputation, the Qantas flight attendants anticipated her every need by supplying quality food, fine wine and comfort.

By now the subdued hum of engines and discreet conversations between the crew should have been background to her peaceful sleeping. Yet she hovered on the edge, trying to doze, trying to block the intrusive, agitated thoughts of someone close by. She didn't usually have this much trouble. When she'd boarded the plane at Heathrow, she'd checked immediately for possible threats and found nothing discernible.

Once again, she scanned the energy. A disturbing signature, oddly skewed—strange yet familiar—it made no sense. She knew no one on the aircraft, she was sure. Whatever the origin, she accepted it as neutral, yet it warranted ongoing monitoring.

She studied the passengers in the gloom, sending out a sigh of thought that wafted past each shadowed form, unnoticed except for one who stirred briefly, looked around and repositioned some limbs. Kreyna noted the seat and began counting the seeds in a very large imaginary sunflower, clearly visualized. With a smile, watching a worker bee stuff pollen into bulging yellow sacs on its legs, she slipped into sleep.

* * *

Polite fingertips on her shoulder roused her. The neatly uniformed attendant offered fruit juice and a hot, perfumed towel. She smoothed her face with its refreshing luxury and scanned the cabin with well-trained ease, paying lengthy attention to the person who had been so agitated earlier. Timed right, she would gain a proper look. How about a comfort stop?

She made her way back from the toilet suite, just as the flight attendant's trolley blocked the aisle. Alongside the lone woman's seat, she was forced to loiter. "Are you on your way home, too?"

Disturbed from a distant mental scene, the woman's eyes steeled and relaxed, appraising Kreyna's charcoal sweatshirt over the flattering black Versace jeans. "Yes, still a long way off, aren't we?"

Kreyna registered the cultured English accent—not as plummy as Received Pronunciation but definitely public school. "From Singapore, about five hours or so, I think. But I'm guessing home's not Australia? I'm heading for Canberra myself. How about you?"

"I've been visiting family in the UK. My husband has a two-year posting at the High Commission in Canberra." The

Englishwoman speared her fingers through the thick, dark blond hair that brushed Nordic cheekbones. "It's a lovely city, really it is. But I've left my children in boarding school in England, you see."

Kreyna saw—the woman's distress pierced her brain like a drill bit. "That must be difficult. I'm sorry. Leave you to it." She returned to her seat, regretting the intrusion into the woman's sorrow, yet satisfied it had been a necessary precaution.

Reseated, she shook loose her hair and massaged the tension from her scalp. Exasperated by fatigue, she wrestled the mass of long dark curls into a plain gold clip—a few rebellious strands sprang free around her hairline and neat ears. The persistent ache in her lower back attested to lack of weight training. She hadn't had a chance to exercise in the five days she'd been away, at least three of which had been spent in aircraft. With her watch reset to Singapore time, she calculated the flying hours beyond Changi Airport and onward to Melbourne—yet another six, conservatively.

Had her boss, Adrian Frode, gotten her phone message confirming her arrival at 7:20 p.m., as scheduled? And where was Robert? They were supposed to have flown from London together. The empty seat beside her exacerbated a sense of foreboding. It was vital to debrief with Adrian alone at headquarters, to present her report with confidence. The information gathered during the interviews in Rotterdam was convincing, yet she was uneasy. Robert's version was a potentially treacherous unknown.

As an ex-boyfriend who wanted her back, Robert could be, by turns, charmingly persuasive or bullying with a vengeance. He knew her vulnerabilities and did not hesitate to exploit them when he felt so inclined. At her insistence, they were now merely colleagues and both working for the Australian federal government's top security agency in Canberra.

Early last year, like many university graduates, Kreyna had applied to join a graduate program or internship with several government departments, including the Department of Foreign Affairs and Trade. With a bachelor's degree in international relations, she'd progressed to an interview and then a psychological assessment. At yet another interview, she was asked if she would consider joining ASIO. The psychologist had noted her exceptional intuitive ability and recommended her for training as a remote viewer, authorized to gather intelligence at a distance. Kreyna had thought her natural talent, considered perfectly ordinary in her family, would be of little value to her prospective employer. ASIO management thought otherwise and fast-tracked her recruitment into the Strategic Surveillance Division.

Adrian Frode managed the division and Kreyna, being proud of her familial abilities, was determined to impress. He would be pleased with her work. Of this, her first assignment in Europe, she was quietly confident. Once she was a member of the Non-Physical Surveillance Team, she would have plenty of opportunity to hone her remote viewing skills.

With a start, she remembered the research article her remote viewing trainer, Pankaj Corea, had instructed her to study and rummaged through her briefcase. John Gribbin's latest book, a guilty pleasure, somehow made its way onto her lap instead and fell open at the tenth page.

"Excuse me, sorry to bother you." The Englishwoman hovered in the aisle. "I couldn't help notice the title. Is that his sequel to *In Search of Schrödinger's Cat*?"

Kreyna flicked the book shut to examine the cover featuring a blue-eyed puss. "It's called *Schrödinger's Kittens and the Search for Reality*. I think it's an attempt to tie up a few loose ends, plus it explains his views on string theory—not bad so far. Are you familiar with his writing?"

"The world is a construct of our sensations, perceptions and memories, so he says. I think Schrödinger's a fine read. Though he's written plenty I haven't found…"

Without warning, the aircraft dropped in altitude. The woman lurched forward and grabbed the seatback, bracing herself. Hurriedly, Kreyna snatched up her briefcase and moved over; the woman reeled into the rocking seat. For a few juddering moments, they fumbled to fasten seat belts and waited for what seemed an age for the turbulence to subside.

"Phew, glad my stomach's already empty. I'm Frances, by the way. And quantum theory is a fascinating subject. There's so much yet to be discovered. Exciting, wouldn't you agree?"

Taken aback by Frances's enthusiasm, Kreyna shook the extended hand, clasping warm, tapering fingers. "The name's Kreyna. Pardon me asking, but have we met before? You seem familiar."

The woman's gaze met Kreyna's with sudden coolness. "Excuse me? Not a chance—I would remember you, I'm sure."

Kreyna tried again. "Where did you cultivate this particular interest? It's not exactly standard fare."

"Cambridge. Ten years ago. When I was an undergraduate in the Physics Department—the Cavendish Laboratory. Have you heard of it?"

Kreyna shook her head and sat back to listen. Next to her, long legs stretched out under a gored denim skirt, their owner reaching a height of about five foot nine—no wonder Frances was in business class. A plain white blouse suited the kind of skin that relished the sun. The woman had a curiously open face with ample lips, the corners upturned in a permanent half smile, even when she wasn't smiling. She spoke with a restrained passion, reminiscing over her time as a student.

Kreyna had to ask, "You didn't finish your degree?"

Wide set, pine-green eyes cast a sweeping glance over her, lingering at her mouth and throat. "I met my future husband, Bryce. Not long before, he'd been appointed to the Diplomatic Service. I had to make a choice—either fulfill an interest in physics or satisfy my wanderlust by marrying a diplomat. Traveling the world won out."

"Any regrets?"

"I don't know that I would have made a great physicist. Hard to say." Frances spun the rings on her left hand. "Made the right decision, I should think. I've been abroad for years, off and on, and have two *bootiful* children. I'm very lucky." Her smile flared and extinguished like a match.

Shifting into an opaque state, Kreyna sent out a tiny surge of energy that barely grazed the mind of the woman beside her. Resignation covered a layer of regret mixed with resentment, beneath which crept anger at herself and others, mostly at herself. And something else, carefully guarded—what was it? Taking too long. Retreat.

"Excuse me, ladies." The flight attendant leaned over them. "Would you prefer a Thai chicken green curry or beef Wellington?"

Frances made to get up and hesitated. "Would you prefer to be alone? Or may I keep you company over dinner?"

"You're welcome to stay. Although I've reading I must do for work once we've eaten."

A quaffable Shiraz accompanied the meal, prompting them to debate the merits of Australian wines as they ate. Margaret River whites were agreed upon favorites.

Afterward, Frances chose to amuse herself watching the in-flight film, *Babe*. Kreyna dug out the research article Pankaj had given her. She studied the results of a recent experiment confirming the significant effects of intention. With the knowledge that thought has a physical effect on perception, could she set up favorable conditions solely by intent, thereby easing her access to highly secure environments? It was something to bounce off Pankaj when she got back. She glanced at the film's credits rolling on the screen hanging from the bulkhead.

"Would you study again?" Kreyna asked.

"Too late for that." Frances shook her head. "Besides, I'm not long enough in one place to attempt it. I have a part-time job at the Australian National University. Doing administrative support for the Centre for Consciousness. Part of the Physics Department. I enjoy the work."

"Don't you envy the researchers?"

"Sometimes. I'm involved without getting too involved. I've met a few fine people there. My boss has brains and drive. They're all good sorts, but I know I'll lose touch with them, probably—goes with the territory. In the end, we all move on. The Centre's putting on an end-of-year party soon. I shall miss them."

Abruptly, Frances added, "I think I'm supposed to be organizing it. Oh, hell. At this time of year venues will be in short supply. Better have it at home." She swiveled to face Kreyna. "Would you like to come? There'll be some likeminded people there. May I tempt you?"

Could be out of the country but can't be sure. Kreyna tentatively consented, which seemed to please Frances. The Englishwoman relaxed back into her seat, stretched one arm over her head and stifled a yawn. Kreyna tried not to stare at a birthmark just above Frances's left collarbone. Following her gaze, Frances adjusted her blouse to obscure the café-au-lait splash.

At Singapore's Changi Airport and after umpteen total hours in the air, it was a relief to find shower facilities that gave Kreyna the opportunity to freshen up. Frances said she needed something to read and went looking for a bookstore. Two hours later, with the plane cleaned and restocked, passengers straggled back on board and settled down to another chunk of their lives spent in the singularly unnatural activity of hurtling across the face of the earth in a cylinder, five miles up.

Through heavy-lidded eyes, Kreyna watched Frances wander off to the toilets. The woman moved well for her height. And was strong—neither as compact nor as athletic as herself, but definitely fit—she'd make a good squash partner. As per routine, Kreyna extended her senses and gauged her environment. The other passengers were equally tired, yet relaxed and comfortable.

Frances approached, still three rows away. A distinct golden halo radiated from her figure, brightest at her head. It swirled and shimmered in hues of deep yellow, orange and gold that intensified as she drew near. Startled, Kreyna took some seconds to react, to gather in her clamoring senses and dampen down her chakras. With an awkward attempt at humor, she said, "Not you again."

Frances grinned and sat back down. "Can't stay away." Arranging a blue blanket around her shoulders, she held Kreyna's gaze, smile receding. In a low, richly mellow voice, she said, "Best get some rest."

Kreyna turned away to the window, warmth permeating her stomach and her pulse gathering speed. Yet not as fast as her thoughts that raced from sensation to explanation, unable to make sense of what had just happened and her response.

How often was an aura that strong, that bold? What on earth was going on? Note to self: must ask Pankaj. Later. Sleep now.

* * *

In Oma's kitchen. A plate of croquettes and a bowl of hot mustard sauce wobble in Oma's arthritic hands. She offers the croquettes to her namesake, who sits at the high wooden table. The excited child claps her hands and reaches to take one. Oma holds the plate just out of reach and says, "Listen, meisje, *hold fast to him who saved me, the one behind you."*

* * *

Cabin lights brightened; the plane had begun to descend into Melbourne. Kreyna came fully alert and peeked over her shoulder. Frances was stirring. They would change planes to pick up the next flight to Canberra, but they'd have to clear customs first. Kreyna was fed up with air travel. Just a few more hours— nearly home. Briefly, she ran through the dream with Oma who only ever turned up with good reason. There would be more time to analyze the incident when she closed her own front door.

Ninety minutes later, a half-empty 737 climbed steeply out of Tullamarine airport to cruising height. Through the left-hand window, the red sunset shifted to mauve, then indigo. Kreyna went looking for Frances who was ensconced near the front of the aircraft. They agreed to exchange contact details.

Frances stretched her legs into the footwell between the seats. She examined a business card. "Kreyna Katz. Eastern Europe?"

Kreyna nodded her thanks to the flight attendant who had brought a perfect Campari and soda. "I'm named after my grandmother, a Dutch Jewess."

"Australia's about as far as you can get from Holland. Post-war immigrants?"

"Yes, much like many new Australians. When war first broke out, Oma was working as a translator in Berlin. She could mimic any accent, including High German which saved her life often." Kreyna took a sip of the drink that refreshed her palate with its tangy complexity. She continued, "Her family in Holland was trying to get her home, but she refused to believe she was in any danger until too late. With the help of a Dutch resistance fighter, she crossed the border at Arnhem."

She tore open the bag of nuts on her tray and offered them to Frances. "So the family story goes, Oma found herself pregnant courtesy of her gallant savior. Nobody cared enough to be scandalized—everything was such a mess by war's end. Europe was in ruins and thousands of homeless people struggled to find their families. Fortunately, she met Valk Katz who accepted her son, my father. She married Valk and they migrated to Australia in nineteen fifty-one."

Kreyna inhaled a waft of hot cooking oil. Oma was close. "She made perfect croquettes, a Dutch specialty. Most people think they're disgusting because of the consistency: overcooked, pureed chicken and vegetables coated in breadcrumbs and deep-fried. I used to love them almost as much as I love—loved her. She died suddenly in nineteen eighty-four of a heart attack. She was more than a little bit gypsy, which I seem to have inherited via my father. It's a family trait that has its uses."

"Not something I know anything about. I'll stick to quantum physics." Frances's keen gaze traced Kreyna's profile. "Do you have your grandmother's ear for languages?"

"Only passable French, but I'm fluent in clog-wog." Kreyna added, "Sorry, that's Aussie slang for Dutch. And you, where are you from?"

"Originally, Norwich. It's northeast of London. Do you know it?"

"I've heard of the Norfolk broads—marshy countryside riddled with canals." With a smile, Kreyna said, "May I take you for a Norfolk broad?"

Frances raised a laconic eyebrow. "The wetlands drain to the North Sea. A few centuries ago, marauding Vikings landed their boats on the coast. Raped, burned and pillaged. The locals didn't stand a chance. But they're my ancestors. Wouldn't be here without their wicked ways—mustn't be churlish." She repositioned a pillow under her neck. "I assume you're in the public service like most of Canberra's workforce?"

Kreyna trotted out a well-rehearsed spiel. "At AGs—the Attorney General's Department in Barton. I'm their conference organizer. And you can see from my address I have an apartment nearby."

Frances passed across an embossed card. She'd annotated the back with her home address and private phone number. Kreyna turned it over.

"Oh, you're living in Garran? No surprise there. Standard British High Commission style of abode, I presume Mrs. Parrey?"

"Four bedrooms, huge living areas, too big for two. But we do a lot of entertaining—it goes with the job. I cook when I can. And I'm always looking for new recipes. A passion is desserts, especially chocolate. My specialty is yuletide logs. Speaking of Yule, Bryce's posting ends in two months. We should be home in London for Christmas."

Frances reached for the salted cashews. She wore a ring bearing a weighty, princess-cut emerald flanked by two single diamonds that nestled behind a plain gold wedding band. The pairing of hand and rings was unusually beautiful, reminiscent of Dürer's sixteenth century drawing.

Kreyna felt Frances studying her and met her gaze. Behind the smiling green eyes was a challenge that made Kreyna catch her breath. Mrs. Parrey was a very handsome woman. And she knew it.

Why was her psychic signature so intrusive and familiar? And the vivid gold aura? The Sentinels would let her know, at the right time, in the right place.

Kreyna leaned toward her potential new friend. "Would you be interested in a game of squash next week? I'm quite experienced so consider yourself warned."

CHAPTER TWO

Rising nearly six hundred feet above the summit of Black Mountain, the city's telecommunications tower dominated the skyline. Its familiar shape eased Kreyna's tension and fatigue only marginally. At least she was in Canberra, if not quite home. The chauffeured Holden Statesman car, one of the Commonwealth fleet that ferried bureaucrats and politicians around the city, cruised out of the wasteland called an airport.

The car traveled past low-lying farmland milking the Molonglo River, choked with water-thieving willows on its way to Lake Burley Griffin. Along broad avenues of perfectly kept asphalt, a succession of traffic roundabouts controlled the major intersections and remained a source of untold grief for tourists attempting to navigate the city.

On this warm spring evening, public servants and support staff leaving late created sporadic road traffic. The four lanes making up the Kings Avenue Bridge were prettily lit from under its handrails, casting reflections into the lake below. At the approaches to the bridge, rows of pole-borne vertical banners announced Floriade in Commonwealth Park, the southern hemisphere's largest display of spring flowers. On the other side of the lake and to the right, the National Gallery and the High Court buildings rose high above a skirt of artfully positioned native trees and shrubs. Throughout the national capital millions of trees, both exotic and native, had been hand-planted since the early 1920s.

They drove past new and not so new office buildings until they reached State Circle and turned left toward Kreyna's destination, the recently opened Department of Foreign Affairs and Trade edifice. Officially named the R.G. Casey Building, it had been had nicknamed Gareth's Gazebo by the locals—a snide swipe at the grandiosity of the department's minister, Gareth Evans. Lit up like a Christmas tree for the horde working late, it was large and imposing.

The sleek, white Statesman pulled up at the main entrance. Kreyna climbed out and inhaled a delicious scent like ripe apricots sharpened with citrus—sweet olive shrubs in full flower. Once inside, she took a lift down two levels. When the basement door opened, the overwhelming stench of new concrete was eye watering. Trailing down a chain of featureless corridors, she found the Operations debriefing room.

Daylight fluorescents purposefully dazzled its occupants. High in the corners, security cameras bristled and microphones would record her every word, destined to be replayed and analyzed. She sat across from her boss, the Strategic Surveillance Division's Director, Adrian Frode, who slouched on an inadequate chair like a disjointed orangutan. Expression noncommittal, he leafed through stapled papers open atop a blue file on the desk. Speaking with authority, Kreyna presented her report.

"I'm ninety-eight percent certain Piet Van Whalen was truthful. Once his thoughts and behaviors were entered into the matrix, it became obvious that he spoke honestly. Yes, he was nervous and wary which is only to be expected, but he stuck to the facts. He showed absolute conviction when he named Inspector Deprez and the PPO clerks. In conclusion, I can state Piet Van Whalen's testimony is reliably factual."

In bureaucrat mode, Adrian was careful to confirm the parameters that underpinned her report. "Did you apply the same matrix when you assessed Victor Deprez?"

"Affirmative."

A frown deepened. He scanned the document and flicked through the few white pages, agitation palpable. Abruptly, he sat upright and peeled the massive steel watch off his wrist, a testament to his enthusiasm for deep-sea scuba diving. The watch body jerked back and forth against the bracelet between his fingers. She knew the gesture all too well—Adrian was displeased.

"Robert's waiting for us over at the House."

"He's back already? Can't be—I left Rotterdam for London before him."

"Last-minute change of plans. He took the train down to Antwerp and flew from there, before you left London."

He held the door open for her, the blue case file under his arm. "Come on, let's move it!"

Stark lights illuminated the broad underground passage to Parliament House. The maze of tunnels was so uniformly confusing that they had been signposted with street names. The lengthy journey by electric cart gave her precious time to think.

Robert had been with her at the Rotterdam meetings. Why had he gone to Antwerp? What wasn't she being told? Weary and apprehensive, she was in no mood to confront Robert—exactly the scenario she'd been trying to avoid. She tightened her chakras to shore up protection. But she knew full well it would be useless in the presence of her nemesis.

In Conference Room B53, Robert's gaze locked onto her. She sat on a chair, rather than in it. How had she ever fallen for this man? Simply because she hadn't known any better and she'd been attracted to his sensuality. Emanating charisma and self-assurance, his body was a classic V-shape with broad shoulders and narrow hips. Beneath masses of flaxen curls, his pale blue eyes became iceberg white with contempt when he was angry. He had a square, cleft chin and a mouth that was the only clue to his inner nature: no lips to speak of.

They had been arguing about Piet Van Whalen for fifteen minutes. Kreyna was adamant Piet had told the truth. Robert thought otherwise.

"He lied, Kreyna. And you missed the fact. It's a serious failure of both skill and judgment." Robert turned his powerful back to her and shook his head at Adrian. "Your first attempt in a foreign environment was an abject failure."

Dismay threatened to overwhelm her. "I'm not wrong. I measured Van Whalen's input against the matrix. I checked and double-checked. He wasn't totally honest about everything, but he was about Deprez. I had Deprez wide open…"

"Wide open?" Robert sneered. "You were too busy having a psychic grope to measure anything. Or are we supposed to believe what you were doing was work?"

Her skill aided by her gender had granted access to Deprez that had been denied to Robert—he hadn't the benefit of knowing what she'd discovered. And he was loath to let her take the credit. With effort, she moderated her heart rate and breathing, deferring to his authority with resentment. Humiliation cornered her. Perhaps he wouldn't notice? His smirk confirmed he had.

In a voice strained yet steady, Kreyna said, "What I learned from Deprez concurs with, *verifies* the information I gathered from Van Whalen. You've read my report, the observations inserted within the matrices and my conclusion—it's self-explanatory."

"Blind Freddy on a galloping horse could see…"

"Enough, you two!" Adrian smoothed his matted fringe. Repositioning thick glasses, he surveyed them both and addressed Robert. "Greater experience and seniority takes precedence, no contest."

To Kreyna, he instructed, "Report to Pankaj tomorrow. We'll review your status from there. Now go home."

* * *

The bleeding heart vine had wilted. Alone in her Macquarie Street apartment, Kreyna tilted the watering can and decided to sleep on the complications of the day. She had too much to think about. Robert's derision had rattled her and Adrian pulling rank made it even more galling.

Determined to salvage some peace from the day's events, she sat cross-legged on a low stool, hands loosely held in a mudra position with thumb and index finger touching. Before her, a small shrine featured a vibrantly colored, eight-inch high statue of Quan Yin, a delicate pastel drawing of her Sentinels, a silver-framed photo of Oma with her Bouvier des Flandres, Wodan, and a freshly lit votive candle.

I am surrounded by the pure white light of Infinite Living Spirit through which nothing negative can penetrate. The pure white light flows through me and fills me, surrounds and protects me at all times. Namu Quan shir yin pu sa. *I offer respect to She who hears the sounds of the world, being of wisdom.*

Following a series of deep belly breaths, she opened her forehead chakra and pinged the Filigrane. An echo came, followed by seven more—familiar ripples heralded her secure connection to the global astral network. Scores of trained sensitives, their psyches vibrating in unison, shared their intelligence and energy. Palpably in the room with her, Kreyna acknowledged the Sentinels—her ever-present, personal retinue of non-physical beings.

Kreyna soaked it all in and restored her inner equilibrium, halfway to being human again. It took ten minutes to meditate before a brief hot shower and the welcome slide under the bedclothes.

* * *

Involuntarily, the down on her left thigh responded to the warm palm sliding up to her hip. She shifted sensuously and a mouth moistened her left breast. Hugo Boss aftershave wafted past, astringent, yet sweetish. A familiar voice murmured a jumble of obscenities, some of which appealed. Her response escalated enough to awaken her—she lurched upright, touching herself where she had been touched. Eyes strained to focus in the gloom. About 3:00 a.m.? She tapped the touch lamp and swung protesting legs out of bed.

A fumbled journey to the kitchen, lights slapped on along the way, a stab with a finger fired up the kettle and turned on the FM104.7 radio station. Annie Lennox sang a wrist-slashing song with sentiments too close to the bone. She turned the radio off and, with attitude, doused a tea bag. How tired would she be in the morning, with yet another night's broken sleep? It had become a pattern from which she desperately needed respite. She'd tried every which way to block her ex-lover's unwanted attention. In a sudden burst of anxiety, she doubted she ever would.

To the kitchen made safe only by light and sound, she commanded, "Get out of my head, Robert. Leave me alone!"

CHAPTER THREE

The worn tread on her much loved white Reeboks let her down at the critical moment. She careened into an ugly skid and slammed against the glass back wall of the squash court, sweat leaving a new smear amongst the many fingerprints. Frances stood over her prostrate body, offering a hand up. They grasped thumbs and Kreyna hauled herself upright, her shattered racket dangling.

Mopping her face with a towel, she noted Frances's toned biceps emphasized by a sleeveless blue cotton top. The woman had barely raised a sweat. "If this is you taking it easy on me, I'm not sure I want to see your best effort. Where did you learn to play so well?"

"Cambridge." Frances holstered her racket in its carry case and straightened up, hands on the waistband of her cropped denim shorts. "And Abu Dhabi. There's not a lot for diplomatic wives to do in Abu Dhabi. Food, fashion and sport, both indoors and outdoors."

Kreyna tossed the mangled mess of strings into a bin ten feet away. "Game over!" She waved to Helen, the Lycra-clad Deakin Health Spa aerobics instructor who gestured a greeting.

In the foyer, the building's air-conditioning system failed to disguise the rank air which was permeated with stale sweat, smelly socks and soggy running shoes. They walked out into markedly fresher air and the parking lot.

"Indoor sports in Abu Dhabi. Sounds diverting. I suppose you're no slouch with a tennis racket either?"

Frances chewed a lip. "I have a reach advantage in squash and must run more to win at tennis. You'd be in with a chance, I should think."

Kreyna looked askance and opened the car door. "Let's meet at Regatta Point in Commonwealth Park at six fifteen. Don't forget the insect repellent."

* * *

Wodan had wiped snot all over both rear windows, as usual. Kreyna bundled him out of the backseat and slipped the chunky choke chain over his black woolly head. He pirouetted and whined, eager to set off. She adjusted her backpack and scanned the half-empty parking lot, coaxing the Bouvier to sit at her left side. Coal black eyes, barely visible under huge ferocious eyebrows, glowered at her. She met his gaze and he thumped his stumpy tail on the asphalt.

"What on earth kind of a dog is that?"

She spun around. Wodan bounced to his feet, neck craning to sniff an outstretched hand. With feigned formality, Kreyna announced, "Frances, this is Wodan, my parents' Bouvier des Flandres. Wodan, this is Frances, outstanding squash player. Odds on, she can outrun you."

Frances hooted. "Not a chance! Look at the size of this beast—he could carry a saddle. Quite probably a jockey too." With his teeth, the dog gently tugged the leather loop handle of his chain from Kreyna's hand and moved to lean against Frances's left thigh. When he nuzzled her hand, the women exchanged surprised looks.

Kreyna said, "Well, who's the chosen one? I think he just laid claim to you. Are you up for it?"

With casual aplomb, Frances extricated the handle and headed for the gates of Commonwealth Park and its current display, Floriade. She walked on her toes which caused her head, held high, to bob characteristically. Beside her loped a magnificent, happy dogs-body. A perfectly ordinary picture except Wodan was usually anything but friendly to strangers. Kreyna jogged to catch up.

The heady scent of a thousand hyacinths hung heavily at twilight. The flower gardens were past their best this late in the season. Even so, there were enough determined bloomers to maintain an impressive display, with row after row of color-coordinated tulips, daffodils and irises interspersed with early flowering annuals. Meticulous planting designs glamorized the million bulbs, enhancing their intrinsic beauty. Groups, couples and individuals strolled along paths between the manicured beds. Strategically placed colored spotlights made a feature of select trees and shrubs.

Kreyna and Frances chose a site near the rhododendron grove, in view of the waterfowl and black swans cruising an elongated pond in preparation for nightfall. Next to the tartan car rug and cane picnic basket, Kreyna spread a large mat of faded canvas onto which Wodan folded his long legs and assumed the Sphinx position. Paws out in front, he studied the wildlife with mild curiosity.

"Is he allowed any of this roast chicken?" Frances peeled off some tasty-looking skin.

"I have raw chicken necks for him, but only when we've finished. He chugs them down like sweets and practically eats my parents out of house and home. Not that they mind, he's such a sweet-tempered brute."

"Seems an odd breed to own in this climate." Frances licked her fingers and searched for a napkin.

"It's a family tradition started by my grandmother. She bought a black male Bouvier puppy soon after she got here and named him Wodan. When he died, she bought another, and so on until she died too. They've all been named Wodan."

Frances drank white wine from an acrylic goblet. "From what you've told me, I should think she had more imagination."

"She believed he reincarnated each time," Kreyna explained. "The same dog soul reborn over and over again. My dad likes to maintain the tradition because we can't bear the thought of him being lost to us. Yes, I know it seems irrational, but we're pretty convinced it's him."

"Why the same breed—couldn't he come back as a Pomeranian?"

Kreyna guffawed, fell about laughing helplessly and slopped wine on the grass. Frances beamed at her, enjoying the effect. Wodan stood to join in. He alternated licks between Kreyna's neck and Frances's ears.

"Wodan the Pomeranian? Yup, right!" Kreyna shoved the dog away and gestured at him to sit back on his mat. With a bottle-green scrunchie, she resecured some unruly curls that had made their escape. "Remember the resistance fighter who helped Oma? She said he had a black Bouvier des Flandres with him. The breed was a Flemish cattle dog originally. Nowadays, because of their intelligence and fearless nature, both the police and the military use them. Anyway, Wodan was his dog, you see?"

"Uh-huh, sure—it all makes perfect sense to me now." Frances's mocking smile gave Kreyna pause. Confiding a piece of family culture was not something she did easily. Had she been too forthcoming? A surreptitious mind scan could verify the woman's actual thoughts. However, beyond the requisites of security and without justifiable cause, Kreyna reminded herself it was forbidden by the Filigrane's rules of conduct. No, Wodan's behavior had been unambiguous—she would rely on the animal's superior instinct.

Frances reached out a hand and said in a resonant, English timbre, "I'm just teasing. Your grandmother's reasoning makes sense, in context. I believe there're only ever two possible explanations for everything—the rational or the divine. This sounds like the latter."

The older woman's fingertips had lingered on Kreyna's forearm. Perhaps she was being an overly suspicious Scorpio.

Her dear friend and confidante, Morwenna, chided her often enough. *Okay, friends for now.*

"What was Abu Dhabi like? And did you participate in the indoor sports?"

With a wry smile, Frances took the bait and swam with it. "Diplomatic families lived in compounds. Segregated from the general populace. It was isolating, especially for the women. Our husbands would look forward to going to the office. We looked forward to them coming home. Dozens of westernized women living in a mass of buildings, spread out over a few acres. And with nothing to do and all day to do it in. Can you imagine?"

Kreyna shook her head once. "It sounds like you were virtual prisoners."

"We could go into the city. But only with an ironclad reason. And a safe male escort."

"I don't know how anyone could live like that for any length of time, especially with no real work to occupy you. How did you amuse yourselves?"

"Gossiped, mostly." Frances stretched out on the rug and slipped off her shoes. "It was a hotbed of gossip, of course. We did the usual cooking and playing cards. A dash of tennis and squash. Mostly, we talked about our husbands and children back home. Or which couples were having affairs. And who fancied who. Some wives swapped more than recipes, out of sheer boredom. Husbands, I mean..."

High in the nearest gum tree, a kookaburra burst into raucous laughter. Frances searched above. The brown-winged bird was difficult to spot amongst the gray-green foliage at twilight.

"I found it unfunny at the time. Newly married, I was full of the prim righteousness of youth. Thought it all too sordid for words." Her gaze came to rest on Kreyna's small hands with their sensitive spatulate fingertips. "I had to toughen up, quick smart. It was our first posting abroad. I learned everything I had to know about my husband's mistress, the British Foreign Service. A rude awakening to a harsh reality."

All at once, she got to her knees and busied herself collecting their crockery and debris. "Sorry to drone on. I must sound frightfully jaded. It has its pluses. I've seen myriad places and met every kind of character. And forged some friendships, albeit fleetingly." Brightly she said, "Shall we?"

"Just a minute." Kreyna pulled a broad, clear plastic container out of her backpack. She removed the lid and put the fleshy necks in front of the dog. Under a minute later, the empty container was repacked.

They meandered back through the park, grateful for the insect repellent; the evening patrol of hungry mosquitoes was out in force. Light dwindled for the few souls dawdling to admire the flowers. Once back in the parking lot, the two women stopped beside Frances's small cream Mercedes bearing distinctive blue diplomatic corps number plates. Wodan sniffed the wheels and christened one with a golden stream.

"I've arranged drinks and a meal for the Centre's staff and friends. It's two weeks from this Saturday," Frances said. "Is there someone you would like to bring along? A boyfriend, perhaps?"

The Southern Cross materialized in the blue ink sky. Black Mountain Tower blinked a warning to a jet on its way to Melbourne, its lofty vapor trail fading fast. Kreyna hammed it up. "Damn, I knew there was something I'd forgotten to do—get a boyfriend."

Frances stooped to unlock the car door and cast back an amused glance. Smiling benignly and with arms folded at the waist, she said, "When you're ready."

"No, wait—I had one and lost him. Must have left him at the mall. Instead, may I bring my friend, Morwenna? She's interesting, eloquent and kind, although she may analyze you mercilessly, being a mad-keen astrologer. That said, she actually knows what she's talking about which can be very helpful, plus she's the most positive soul I know."

"She sounds a treasure. But I want to hear about the mislaid boyfriend. Another time—promise?"

* * *

Kreyna accelerated out of the parking lot. She stroked Wodan's beard, his massive head nudging her left shoulder. "You recognize her, don't you, young fella? I wonder where from. It's a pity I don't speak canine well enough to understand if you told me." Good-natured, he snuffled prickly whiskers in her ear.

Could she explain Robert without revealing her work? Only if she omitted a good deal of detail. But she wanted to get to know Frances. She was very good company, sharing a similar sense of the absurd, plus a special interest in quantum physics—a rare find. A normal friendship would have been nice, one uncomplicated by Kreyna's heavily cloaked job. Much as she loved what she was doing, close friendships with people outside of the organization were nigh on impossible to sustain, not without being an exceptional liar. And being a consummate liar was highly ranked in the job description.

During the ASIO induction process, she and the other trainees had been told they would have to conceal every aspect of their jobs. Their friendships would be monitored, even vetoed. The rule was, if she made a new friend, she must notify management so the person could be vetted, as had happened to everyone who got close to her. At the time, she had agreed to the conditions of her employment. But she grew weary of the constant need for subterfuge. Did she need to tell the boss about her new friend?

Not necessary. Frances would be leaving the country soon which left insufficient time for their burgeoning friendship to become an issue.

CHAPTER FOUR

Pankaj's ASIO office faced east toward Mt. Pleasant. At about fifteen hundred feet high, it was more hill than mount, though it made an attractive backdrop to the cluster of utilitarian buildings in Canberra's military suburb of Russell. A two-hundred-and-twenty-foot high column topped by the likeness of an American bald eagle, the Australian-American War Memorial dominated Field Marshal Sir Thomas Blamey Square. The memorial boasted a variety of nicknames coined by the locals: the phallus in blunder land or the chicken on a stick—more politely, the eagle.

On the other side of Mt. Pleasant, newly green from spring rain, sprawled the Australian Defence Force Academy, Duntroon, the national military officer training facility. Behind it stood an ugly curve of concrete Department of Defence buildings, Campbell Park. To the west, Kings Avenue bridged Lake Burley Griffin, an artificial body of water named after Walter Burley Griffin, the visionary landscape architect from Chicago who designed Canberra. At the end of the avenue, the new federal Parliament House with its outsize flagpole and giant flag crowned Capital Hill.

Shielding her eyes from the strong morning sun, Kreyna turned away from the window and toward Pankaj Corea, Doctor of Physics, specialist in quantum theory and cosmology, a master remote viewer and the Non-Physical Surveillance Team's Training Officer. Like the other trainees, Kreyna referred to him as The Guru when out of earshot.

"Your grandmother is in the fourth Bardo of becoming, faced with the prospect of rebirth and all it implies, you see." Pankaj spoke with a softly lilting accent through his black mustache, liberally sprinkled with gray to match his temples. "It's not easy, you know, to make the decision to return. She must give up so much, farewell all the others to come into this, the first Bardo, the birthplace. Each transition between the four Bardos is frightening, you understand?"

"Could she be preparing to return soon?" Kreyna asked. "She seems to be around more than usual. As I said, she was too cryptic in my dream on the plane."

"Soon could mean years yet. Do you know anyone with child?"

"Nup! In case you're thinking of me, it's definitely not on my agenda. I'm completely uninterested in any kind of relationship. Robert's nocturnal intrusions could turn me off sex for eons. I've tried everything I know to block him and nothing's working."

"Kreyna, you have only yourself to blame." Pankaj sat back and laced his long fingers. "You're only approaching twenty-five—still young and liable to make mistakes. But it was a major blunder and cannot be undone. As part of your induction training, you were forbidden to become involved with other operatives. What were you thinking?"

Her shoulders rose and slumped. "I didn't understand, not really. Don't you see? I was awestruck by his abilities and experience. He's very talented."

His bushy eyebrows met in a frown. "You haven't answered my question. Why did you? With the knowledge that mutual orgasmic sex would give him an imprint of your psychic signature, potentially to grant him access to you for life. Perhaps even eternity?"

She mumbled a short, inaudible phrase.

A hairy hand slapped the desktop. "Answer me! You have jeopardized yourself and him. And your critical roles as operatives—something the Division can ill afford."

She shrank back. "Because I was in love with him. I thought we would be together forever. He seemed so spiritual. Did I know 'spiritual' doesn't necessarily mean either ethical or honest?"

"In love? What foolishness is this? How can you love someone you do not know thoroughly? This is a misguided romantic notion. You have much to learn about life and authentic love. As to spirituality, now you know better, hmm?"

"Right now, I believe 'spiritual' means manipulative, egotistical and full of bull."

"You're indulging in dramatics, Kreyna. He is a senior member of the team and you must put aside your antagonism." Pankaj seated himself and wagged a finger. "You see, if you live in the river, you should make friends with the crocodile."

"I'm trying, but he won't leave me alone at night—it's exhausting. Maybe it would have been easier if I'd taken up with someone else. Nobody likes to be dumped without a seeming competitor, least of all Robert, but I had to get away from him."

"You're wishing for a lover to bear Robert's wrath? Am I to take you seriously?"

"No, no—I'm just desperate for a peaceful night's rest." She looked down at her crimson blouse under the black suit—she had put it on in a futile attempt to lift her spirits. The same went for the tapering, twenty-four carat gold fob chain inherited from her English grandfather. Neither was working.

"My apologies, sir. I thought I knew what I was doing and didn't. From now on, no more complaints—he's my personal problem."

"Let's keep it that way." He turned his attention to the papers in front of him. "But we still have the conflicting reports from your work in Rotterdam. Robert asserts you misread Van Whalen. He says the man was implicating Deprez to cover his own criminal activities. Why the discrepancy?"

Could she say Robert wanted her back and, if he couldn't have her, was intent on sabotaging her career? Would that sound anything less than paranoid? Neither could she see the point in mentioning Piet Van Whalen's probable drug problem, sorely tempted though she was to declare Robert's. Better not. So far, it had not impeded his ability to do his job and remote view distant targets. Or had it? Difficult to be sure and it was only a suspicion. Against the superior weight of his reputation as an experienced performer, her opinion stood little chance.

"I gained complete access to Deprez which I believe Robert did not manage, therefore I had more information than Robert. You are going to have to take my word for that. As to Van Whalen, he was hiding something—nothing of significance, or so I thought. Perhaps I misunderstood through lack of experience. I don't think so, but that's for you to judge."

He formed a steeple with his fingertips, his gaze flicking between Mt. Pleasant and his young trainee. A decision made, he arose.

"The whole point of you going to Rotterdam was for you to work under pressure, in a foreign environment, reading suspected criminals. The result is mixed and a little discouraging. Irrespective, I've spoken with Adrian and we've agreed to advance your training."

He stepped over to a combination lock-fronted cabinet and hauled out a blue case file splattered with yellow sticky notes. Loose papers spilt across the desk. The file registry staff would have a fit, if they could see it. There was not a folioed page in sight, which made it highly likely the contents were less than official.

"We're arranging a remote viewing exercise with two highly experienced intuitives for this Thursday at forty-one Blackall Street. Because of time differences between their locations and ours, it is scheduled late evening. This exercise is complex to set up, so you must make yourself available at short notice. You understand?"

Kreyna bowed her head to The Guru.

"Life is not a continuum of pleasant choices, but of inevitable problems that call for strength, determination and hard work." He bent forward across the desk toward her. "Personally, I have the utmost confidence in you. I believe you to be more naturally gifted than any of our previous trainees. While you have my support, be advised it would be unwise to disappoint me."

Luminous black eyes mirrored her image back to her. She held his gaze, knowing it to be a privilege.

* * *

Windows painted black obscured the lights inside. Behind eight-foot chain fencing topped by three strands of barbed wire stood a row of wooden temporary buildings, originally used as public service offices. Compared with other structures in the vicinity, the buildings were glaringly anachronistic. To the west rose the Edmund Barton Building, memorable for wheat silo-style service shafts at each of its four corners. Over the road, the Attorney General department's towering facade of glass and concrete was brightly lit, legions of lawyers hard at work. But at 41 Blackall Street in Barton where the Remote Surveillance Centre operated at night only, all signs of activity were undetectable.

Inside, Kreyna lay on a modified recliner in the viewing room. She had adjusted it to support her comfortably, dimmed the lights and positioned her pen over the target sheet. Wires from her head and chest connected her to the monitoring apparatus on an adjacent desk where Pankaj sat at the ready.

"When I give you the coordinates, I want you to shift from here to that location. As you know, you must put yourself into a very deep theta brain state—four point five cycles per second. Then take it down to delta, just under four Hertz. While your body sleeps, you will remain fully aware, fully conscious and make the shift. When you find you're at the non-local site, you will have three-sixty degree vision, a bird's-eye view and the ability to zoom in on the details. A solid amount of verifiable detail is required to confirm your success beyond all doubt. Please remember this is science, not a party trick. After all the training and those boring rote drills, here's your chance to impress. The coordinates are latitude twenty-five degrees twenty south, longitude one thirty one degrees zero two east. Do it now, Kreyna—go!"

As trained, she stilled her thoughts, slowed her breathing and halved her pulse rate in a matter of seconds. To a sound like ripping carpet, she separated from her body and entered the astral plane. Rising straight up, she gathered speed, hovered in midair, and plummeted like a hunting falcon down a tunnel of light, accelerating in a deafening roar.

"Acquiring target now," she gasped, barely conscious of the two master intuitives who shadowed her like friendly porpoises. She hurtled into an invisible net. It stretched wide and broke like a bubble against her face. Utter silence.

She stood on the cool, red dirt floor of a shallow cave. "I've locked onto a place with a huge amount of energy. I think it's a cave under Uluru." It was almost dusk at the sacred site in Central Australia. An orange glow from the west indicated the setting sun behind her. The monolithic mass rose nearly 1200 feet overhead.

"You are doing very well." Pankaj sounded like he was talking underwater. "Now, I want you to relax, focus sharply and describe what you see."

"The paintings—they're stunning—done mostly in ochres with bright yellow, red and white dots, circles and lines—like tram lines. There are some figures with radiating white halos, animals and what must be mythical creatures."

"Can you see any people?"

"No, I just have a feeling of a very strong homogenous presence, like thousands of people as one. This must be a place for initiations. Wait—I feel people close by, perhaps encamped here. I can smell water and vegetation, eucalypts."

Without warning, she soared straight up at mind-numbing speed through miles of cloud. Fear made her heart hammer and she fought to slow her ascent, nausea threatening to take her consciousness. She came to an unexpected halt in a wide clearing where twelve of the great rock's Anangu aboriginal ancestors danced and sang, "*Ah-oo, ah-oo, doo, doo, doo.*" The mob stamped and whirled around and around on nothing discernibly solid. She risked a wave and they grinned cheekily, showing off blindingly white teeth in dark faces decorated with white symbols. Lightning crackled, the tang of ozone laced the air and she plunged back down to the cave. Staggering to stay upright, she gulped air and rubbed her ringing ears until she could clearly hear the rain outside.

"It's sufficient. You must return now. Lock on to the others. Return now."

She poured into her body stretched out on the recliner. Starry-eyed, weak and wobbly, she said, "Wow! What a buzz! It was—wow! Amazing. I got the feeling if the others hadn't directed me, I might have spun off into all sorts of fascinating places."

"Yes, you were in part of the Bardo, the astral plane. Without guidance and experience you—well, the expression 'my father's house has many mansions' is an understatement. The discipline of your training grants a measure of safety only."

She lurched to her feet and steadied herself to remove the wires from her body. Pankaj studied her, fingertips measuring the pulse at her wrist.

"Give yourself a few minutes to recover before you move, please. Every bi-location will be taxing. We allow no more than two out-of-body experiences in twenty-four hours."

"Yes, but I nailed it, didn't I? I could feel the earth solid under my feet, see the marvelous rock art, smell the rain and vegetation—it was all real. I was there in all but body."

Pankaj rocked his head from side to side. "Very pleasing. Congratulations, Kreyna, you have achieved a fully controlled OOBE. Now you're a trained remote viewer, capable of going anywhere at will. Well done! You are all but ready for promotion to the Non-Physical Surveillance Team. There's paperwork to process, but we should be able to confirm your appointment by early December. I'll let Adrian know."

* * *

Rapidly approaching footsteps echoed down the corridor. Spooked, Kreyna hastened toward the dimly lit exit stairwell. Bruising fingers grabbed her arm and swung her up against the wall with a sickening thud. Robert crushed his mouth to hers, tongue worming its way between her teeth, spreading sour spittle. He was unshaven and his whiskery growth scoured her lips. She fought to release pinned arms, kicking at his shins and finally hitting home. He removed his mouth with a grunt.

"Let go, you bastard! Get away from me!"

He released her, then lunged and slapped the wall above her left shoulder. She flinched and he grinned. "Afraid? So you should be."

She retreated until she had her back hard up against a locked office door. He loomed, fists clenching and unclenching, his usually ruddy face pale with anger, the deep blue eyes turned glacial.

Her own anger making her bold, she said, "Go on—hit me. See if it makes any difference this time."

His eyes widened. Thin lips curled with mirth, he cuffed her ear. "Nah, small fry—I'd crush your pretty head before I'd begun to really enjoy myself. Who is he? Tell me who you're screwing. Is he hung like a horse? A real stallion? Is he as good as me?"A wheedling whisper, "We had some fantastic nights, remember babe? Remember how you came like a freight train? We don't have to remember, we can do it again. And again. Until we're bowlegged. C'mon Kreyna!"

She unleashed a menacing no-nonsense look, eyes becoming intense black pools. "Not a hope in hell, trust me, there's no one else. I'm not interested in you, Robert. It's not happening and never will again, so just leave me alone. And please, will you quit trying to do me in my sleep? I'm way over it. Can we move on?"

He straightened up and raised a fist, smiling smugly when she shied away. "Fine, I believe you. But you're missing out on a great opportunity, babe. What do you think you'll get out of the organization, huh? They'll train you, for sure, but they'll dump and disown you when you lose your marbles. You *know* how risky this stuff is."

Kreyna's jaw dropped. "You're trying to tell *me* how risky this is? Oh, Robert. Listen to yourself, will you? You've got company. I know a good deal of what you've done to me in the past wasn't you, not really. You've *got* to stop using."

"I can handle them." Robert shoved his fists in his pockets.

"Don't give me that bull! No matter how often you clear yourself of entities, if you keep using drugs, they'll just keep coming back. They can only be there with your permission, tacit or otherwise."

"I told you, I've got it covered."

"Really? You haven't so far. Your inability to manage your habit has already cost us both this relationship. I can't be around you when you're high and full of them. I won't be bashed and abused anymore, Robert, I've had enough."

"Babe, give me a break. I've got a handle on it, mostly. It's only been a couple of times."

"And the rest. I can neither sleep nor have sex with you because they get access to me through you. I refuse to be a haven for parasitic beings. You have the choice, had the choice—you chose and I left." She held his gaze, stony-faced.

"That's not the point. Listen to me, will you?" Robert tossed his blond mane. "ASIO will suck you dry for a shit salary and wipe their hands of you. You'll have an empty CV and nowhere to go. C'mon Kreyna. You've nearly finished your training. We can set up shop together. There's heaps of work out there for people with our skills and talent. And a bunch of coin for the taking. Trust me, I've done my homework."

As if she were perfectly calm and in control, she said, "What part of the word no don't you understand? We've had this conversation before and I *told* you it isn't my style. Nothing's changed, nothing will. Give up, won't you?"

He backed away. "I thought you were smarter than this. Correction, you *are* smarter than this. You'll come around, I know you will. See you later!"

A shoulder thumped open the exit door and he disappeared down the stairs.

Kreyna rubbed her arms against the sudden cold in her bones. Ignoring prickling tears, as much for him as herself, she wiped her mouth on a sleeve. A search in her bag found a lip gloss. Fingers trembling, she smeared some on, thankful that its wild tropical flavor was sufficient to mask the smell off his grass-laced spittle.

Robert's behavior was getting worse. From what he'd told her when they first got together, he became a sensitive after a near-death experience as an eleven-year-old. He'd contracted whooping cough and gone into hospital where he went into a coma and died. Once resuscitated, he assumed a very different personality. With great excitement, he told his parents of traveling through a tunnel, encountering loving beings of light and visiting a great city filled with wondrous sights where he was perfectly healthy again. Too relieved to care, his parents paid scant attention.

But Robert was never the same again. Where he had been brash, he became thoughtful and shy; where he had once barreled along in joyous oblivion to the world, he became aware of others and their feelings. He saw and heard things no one else did, and dreamed of events before they happened. But his parents soon tired of his stories and scolded him for a too vivid imagination.

Entering his teens, Robert had found the world a harsh and uncompromising place. He'd taken to substances that numbed reality and emboldened his shyness until he appeared confident and strong. However, the drugs weakened his already thin auric shield and made openings through which aimless beings could creep and hide within. Drugs made him unaware of their presence; drugs made him their easy target.

The disembodied spirits attached to him had a terrifying influence on his behavior which he chose to discount. Kreyna could barely stand to be near him when he was in such a state, their presence was so sickening. When he became abusive, she could see them in his eyes, knew it wasn't him landing a punch or shouting obscenities at her. She feared and hated them, not him.

In the corridor of the Remote Surveillance Centre, Kreyna held her breath, pushed down the handle of the exit door and peered out. Must be gone by now, mustn't he?

The gravel in the car park crunched too loudly under her feet. She scanned every shadow, checking each and every car she passed, waiting for a figure to leap out of the darkness. Once safely in the car, she hit the central locking button and started the engine, thankful she'd been running late and had decided to drive the few blocks from home.

The problem remained: what to do about an obsessive guy who wouldn't take no for an answer and was as equally single-minded and persistent as her? More worrying, his escalating drug use served only to fuel his obsession with possessing her all over again. The vibrant man she'd once loved was becoming increasingly servile to drugs and their creatures. She'd allowed too much. Now, she must protect herself.

Fresh out of effective strategies to deter him, she needed urgent advice. Morwenna. She would talk it over with Morwenna on the weekend. She'd know what to do. Probably. Maybe.

In the past, the creative lateral thinking of Ms. Morwenna Brodribb had saved Kreyna from many a tricky situation.

PART TWO
1986

CHAPTER FIVE

Kreyna wasn't sure if she liked the new girl. As directed by her biology teacher, Kreyna had gone to the front office of Telopea Park School, collected her charge and brought her back to the Year 10 classroom. The two sixteen-year-olds had made the trek through the school grounds in an awkward silence, punctuated only by Kreyna asking brief, polite questions by way of conversation.

"Do you like Culture Club?"

"Why would anyone?" From behind a screen of long, dark brown hair, the girl glanced sideways, battleship-gray eyes thickly kohled like all the other goth chicks.

"Boy George has a great voice. And I love his clothes and makeup. He really can sing you know." Kreyna held open the door to the classroom. "What's your name?"

"Morwenna," drawled the girl as she slipped past Kreyna. "Don't wear it out."

* * *

Two weeks passed before they spoke again, even though Kreyna often spotted the goth in the library, a place that "ash people" were not supposed to frequent if they wanted friends of a similar ilk. Not that Morwenna seemed to have many friends and those she did attract were all male, especially gangly young men with tousled hair wearing ripped acid-washed jeans. One in particular wore a row of silver studs and tiny rings in his left ear and, when he passed by with his choir-boy face cast down, wafted a mixture of incense and stale cigarette smoke. Once, Kreyna caught his glance and was startled by a feeling of fragility that took her breath. More often than not, he hung around with Morwenna at lunchtime in the quadrangle.

"He's a total burnout—gets weirder every time I see him." Sandra passed a hand through the crook of Kreyna's arm, as was her right as Best Female Friend. She'd walked up to Kreyna and noticed her friend studying the guy who was sitting and talking quietly, intensely, with Morwenna.

"I reckon he's a flamer." At Kreyna's puzzled frown, Sandra continued, "He hates being near girls. I was in the same history class as him last year. A few of us used to try to touch him. He'd flinch like he'd been hit and rush away. It didn't take long for us to lose interest because he got upset. And I mean *really* upset and told the teacher. We didn't mean any harm, didn't realize how serious he took it."

"He doesn't seem to have a problem with her."

"Yeah—what's with that? She'd be the first female to get anywhere near him, ever. But then, I hear she's got a kangaroo loose in the top paddock too."

"I get the feeling something's not quite right with him," Kreyna said.

Sandra shook her head. "Couldn't have said it better myself. Gotta go."

Unusually, Kreyna barely noticed Sandra's departure. Instead, unease shortened her breath and tightened the pit of her stomach; she knew what she had to do. Since Oma died—nearly two years ago now—she rarely projected herself into someone else's headspace. As Oma had taught her, Kreyna closed her eyes and took three slow deep breaths. On the third breath, she rolled her eyes upward, looked through the chakra located between her eyebrows and saw the boy's left inner forearm with translucent skin covering blue-green veins, flesh and sinew. Gaping slashes from a razor blade oozing dark blood, running, dripping, congealing at the wrist. Bitter tears falling, diluting the red snaking across the white.

Pain sliced through Kreyna and she inhaled sharply, a hand coming to her throat to still its racing pulse. As usual, the exercise had proven an uncomfortable experience. But necessary. A free period was scheduled between 2:30 and 3:30 p.m.—ample time to visit the study room in the school library.

* * *

"Sorry to interrupt."

Morwenna looked up from the dense notes she'd been writing on a lined pad. She leaned back, tapped her purple fingernails with a ballpoint and pointed to the chair beside her. Kreyna sat down.

"Your friend's in mortal danger."

Morwenna gaped for a moment, and snorted. "How *very* dramatic. Am I supposed to know who you're talking about? Go away, little girl. Come back when you've something intelligent to say." She grabbed an open textbook and made herself look studious.

Kreyna persisted. "I don't know his name but you know who I mean. I'm not prone to dramatics, I'm deadly serious. He means to hurt himself, permanently. He's been practicing. Soon, he'll get it right."

Morwenna slammed the book shut. "And you know all this how?"

Kreyna dropped her gaze. "If I explained you wouldn't understand. And you wouldn't believe me."

"Try me."

A heavy silence stretched and thinned. For the first time since they'd met, Kreyna looked straight into Morwenna's eyes that gleamed like black diamonds—equally ancient, alien and extremely rare. Kreyna recognized a kindred spirit and began to smile. For the first time ever, she told an apparent stranger.

"I'm psychic."

"Spectacular." A grin dawning, Morwenna said, "I do astrology."

"Then we're both nuts." Kreyna's smile faded. "I mean it—he's not well."

"I know Simon's stressed. His parents are getting a divorce." Morwenna puffed air in and out of her cheeks. "And other stuff. What can we do?"

"Maybe talk to the school counselor?" Kreyna shrugged. "I don't know what help is available, only that he needs it. And fast—he's not coping. He's putting on a brave face for you. Do you think he might listen if you suggested counseling? Obviously, he trusts you. The thing is, if we do nothing and he does something awful, it will be on both our consciences forever. Not my first choice."

"What exactly did you see when you were doing your psychic thing?" Morwenna asked.

"Nothing you want permanently seared in memory, trust me."

"Seems I'll have to."

* * *

The girls sat on a wooden bench under mature spreading English oaks that marked the perimeter of Telopea Park School grounds. The bilingual French and English teaching facility was located near the center of Canberra, about half a mile from Lake Burley Griffin.

Across a grassed area and in the near distance from where they sat, the annual end-of-year school fete, Le Burp, was in full swing. A crowd of several hundred milled around food stalls and patronized the entertainment—music distorted by distance became an aimless bass beat. Somewhere in the crowd, their respective parents and siblings mingled. Morwenna had lured Kreyna away by begging her to be lookout while she smoked.

"Do you want a ciggie?" Morwenna asked.

"No thanks, don't like them." Kreyna watched Morwenna spread crumbly tobacco into a cigarette paper and fashion a torpedo shape. "Tobacco's like coffee—smells a whole lot better than it tastes."

Once the creation was lit, Morwenna exhaled and picked strands of tobacco off her lips. "Can't afford tailor-mades—bit of a bummer."

"Have you spoken to Simon?"

Morwenna grimaced. "He's not happy about being pulled out of school on medical grounds. That might be the end of our friendship, especially since he's not moving to Narrabundah College with us. I think he thinks I betrayed him."

"At least he's alive for now."

"For now? You're freaking me out. Do you know what's going to happen to him?"

"Sorry." Kreyna ducked her head. "Sometimes I say more than I should. No, I don't know because I haven't looked. And I won't."

"Christ on a crutch, how do you live with being you?" Morwenna blew on the tip of the rollie that was threatening to go out. "How did you get this way?"

Abruptly, Kreyna stood and started to walk away.

"Hey! What's got into you?" Morwenna caught Kreyna at the elbow.

Kreyna turned, shook off the restraining hand and glared. "I'm not someone to gawk at or bag out. If you don't want me around, it's easily fixed. I'll bugger off."

"Jeez Louise, I'm sorry, okay? Take a chill pill. Please don't go. I like you, really I do. I think you're way interesting. C'mon, now—sit back down. Talk about sensitive and paranoid. You must be a Scorpio."

Rubbing her arms, Kreyna regarded Morwenna from under hooded eyelids, one foot scuffing the dirt under their bench.

"Of course you are." Morwenna smiled wisely. "Tell me your birth details. No? Maybe later. Truth is, I'm jealous. It takes me hours of setting up and reading a horoscope to begin to understand someone, or something. You can grasp it in a nanosecond—it's not fair. But I'm absolutely fascinated. Please, Kreyna, talk to me. When and how did you get this way?"

Kreyna told Morwenna what happened when she was nearly eight years old. Immediately after one of the family's Sunday lunches, she gave her grandfather, Valk Katz, a long hug with copious damp kisses and said a tearful "Good-bye Opa." During the drive home, her father remarked on his eldest child's uncharacteristic sentimentality. The telephone rang early the next morning with news that the tall, mellow Dutchman had died in his sleep.

Every night for weeks, Kreyna would see Opa standing at the end of her bed and he would wave or blow a little goodnight kiss. Of course, she reported to her parents that Opa was well again— floating now, but well. She remembered a time before she was born when she had floated and felt very good, so he must, too. Once, he told her that her mother's lost wristwatch was actually in the pocket of a pair of slacks hung in the wardrobe—not lost at all. And another time that the car was going to have a flat tire and that her father must drive carefully. Eagerly, she related every message, received in silence by her nodding parents.

Oma came to dinner at their house, which was wonderful. Both Kreyna and Lydia, who had just turned six, loved their Oma's visits. Usually, she would read stories to them at seven o'clock—their bedtime. Always, the girls couldn't keep their eyes open for long and this night was no exception. But after a short while, Kreyna woke up very thirsty and, in the dark, found her way to the kitchen for a glass of milk. In the dining room, Oma was speaking.

"Tobias, she chose this path for herself before she assumed this incarnation. It cannot be undone. And you two agreed to parent her. Not that we remember these things."

"Can't we protect her—discourage her?" Her father's tone was clipped.

"Discouragement may make her think there's something wrong with her—that's outright cruelty. I can teach her to control the senses when she's a little older. It will only be a problem if she's not properly trained."

"But people will think she's strange, possibly dangerous." Kreyna's mother's voice was pitched high with concern. "They'll want to lock her up and medicate her. I simply won't allow that to happen to my daughter."

Grimly, Oma said, "People thought the same about me. She is unusually gifted—or afflicted, you might think. With guidance, she will mature perfectly fine. In time, she may grow out of this sensitivity altogether. We can't tell. But please, you must accept her as she is and not deny or repress what is natural and effortless. For the moment, she hasn't a problem—*you* have. Let her be."

Holding her breath, Kreyna crept back to bed, her thirst forgotten. Strange. Dangerous. Aff—mumble. There was something wrong with her, that much was certain.

* * *

"I thought I had some kind of disease," Kreyna said. She pushed back the black curls that fell heavily around her shoulders. "But Oma said things that made me feel normal and ordinary. And she coached my parents to do the same. The whole of my extended family knows I'm the way I am. No one cares and I'm not allowed to think I'm special, or I'd get too big for my boots, they reckon. Still, they come and ask me stuff. Sometimes I know. Mostly I don't 'cause Oma said I mustn't misuse my abilities, especially not for myself—I must never look just for me."

Morwenna was rolling another smoke. "Awesome. What I want to know is, how does it feel when you do whatever it is—that thing you do?"

"Which thing in particular? For instance, I can tell what people are thinking—I see the pictures in their heads, sometimes with words. Maybe what they're going to do next. If I want to be somewhere else, I can think myself there, sort of, though I need to practice more. I can vaguely see dead people, sometimes—certainly feel them too often. I try not to, 'cause it can be yukky. And I can feel energy coming from objects and places, plants and animals. Which thing did you mean?"

"Holy Jesus, Mary and Joseph." Morwenna's shoulders

shook with soundless giggles. She held out the lit cigarette to Kreyna. "Hold this for a minute." When Kreyna took it from her, Morwenna began to unlace one of her cross-trainers. "There's some grit in here that's annoying the crap out of me. You're something else, you know that? All right, let's start with you seeing in people's heads."

"I decide." Kreyna looked off into the distance at the school buildings and the people milling about. "It's kind of like being in a glass-bottomed boat or putting on a pair of Polaroid sunnies—I shut my eyes, focus through my forehead, pull back a screen and it's crystal clear."

"Can you tell what I'm thinking now?"

"Nup! But I can guess!" Kreyna grinned. "Look, I don't do it all the time—not at all. I'd go crazy if I looked and listened to all the stuff people are up to. When I was little, it did drive me bonkers, like constant loud noise all around me. But Oma taught me how to switch on and off and protect myself."

"From what?"

A girlish voice behind them said, "Boy, are you gunna get it!"

They turned together and Kreyna groaned. Grinning hugely, her younger sister, Lydia, folded her arms in triumph. "Mum's gunna go ballistic at you smoking. Sprung!"

"I am not!" Kreyna held the cigarette out to Morwenna, who snatched it and took a deep drag before grinding it out under her shoe. She followed Kreyna who was hurrying to catch up with her jubilant sister, the three girls forming a loose conga line that traipsed across the grass to Le Burp.

That evening, Kreyna was grounded. In particular, she was forbidden to spend time with a very bad new influence named Morwenna.

"But Mum," Kreyna had pleaded. "Apart from Sandra who hangs around with anybody and everybody, I have no friends, no life. Can't I have one decent friend? I like Morwenna because she doesn't treat me like I'm a freak show. She's different—she understands and puts up with me. You just don't get it, do you?"

As usual, the girls' father had cooked and they'd enjoyed garlicky, baked meatballs. Dirty pots and dishes cluttered the kitchen bench and sink. Her mother, who had been stacking the dishwasher, stopped and washed her hands under running water. "Lydia, take over." Smugly, Lydia stepped in and continued putting plates between the plastic racks.

"Your family are your friends, every one of them. That's enough with the princess routine, Kreyna. I don't want you hanging around with that girl and that's final. She's too strange."

"Oh, yeah? Like this family is so-o normal. If you're all normal, God help me, I *want* to be strange." Kreyna stormed off to her bedroom.

From the kitchen, her mother bellowed, "I am not the enemy!"

"With friends like you who needs enemies?" Kreyna muttered so no one could hear. She slammed the door and threw herself on the bed. Headphones rammed on, she began to listen to Boy George singing "Do You Really Want To Hurt Me?" Tears welled and slid slowly down blotched cheeks.

The door burst open and Lydia flounced in. "Daddy's pet's in trouble and—oh." Lydia stared for a few seconds and retreated, hastily shutting the door behind her. Teeth clenched, Kreyna threw a pillow at the door. Down the hall, the phone rang.

Risking another pillow, Lydia knocked and whispered, "It's Morwenna for you."

Kreyna ripped off the headphones and hurried to take the call.

Given the unlikelihood of Morwenna ever actually being hysterical, she sounded remarkably close to it. "We need to talk. I have to talk to you in person, right now. Can you come over?"

"What? No! Don't be silly. How the hell am I supposed to get there?" Kreyna hissed into the receiver, "I'm not even supposed to be talking to you, let alone seeing you—I'm grounded."

"Shit. Fuck. Poo, bum, bugger, shit, fuck!" Morwenna seemed to be wringing the handset. "Can you get out without being seen? I'll come by taxi to the end of your street and pick you up. In about fifteen minutes. Be there!"

"What's the big rush?" Kreyna asked. The line was dead. Cross-legged on the hall floor with the phone still in her hand, Kreyna absorbed the energy behind Morwenna's words and shuddered.

During the taxi trip to Morwenna's house, waves of guilt at defying her parents swept through Kreyna—she wished she wasn't where she was. Morwenna was mute until they were safely ensconced upstairs in her bedroom. Kreyna looked at wall posters dominated by shots of Madonna, while Morwenna went to the kitchen.

"Simon's in Ward 12B at Canberra Hospital." Morwenna handed Kreyna a glass of cola. "He slashed his wrists in the early hours of this morning. I only found out when I got home after the fete and there was a message from one of his friends. I rang the hospital and they said he's alive, but heavily drugged. I can't go and see him because I'm not family." Morwenna dissolved into anguished sobs. "I'm scared—to death—for him."

Kreyna sat her friend down on the bed and wrapped arms around her heaving shoulders. "It's all right—he'll be all right."

"Will he?" Morwenna peered through wet lashes. "Will he really? Would you find out for me? Please?"

"If you mean what I think you mean, you can't be serious. It's not allowed. Not without the person's permission. And he's not *compos mentis* enough to ask. I can't."

"Where's the harm? It's not like you stand to gain anything from it. He won't know—no one will know."

"*I'll* know," Kreyna said. "Besides, there may be consequences. It could be dangerous."

"Dangerous how? Just do your psychic thing, check him out and tell me how he is. Then I can rest easy until he's well again. Please?"

"There will be consequences." Kreyna exhaled heavily. "Be very, very quiet. Don't speak for the next few minutes and then only after I speak first. Complete silence is essential."

Three, four, five deep breaths, down, down to a much slower brain wave frequency on the edge of sleep. Slow, slower, speeding up again. Damn—stay focused. Slowing, very slow now. Eyes up and focused through the third eye chakra. Her eyelids fluttered, concentration rewarded effort and she slid into stillness, yet fully aware. *Imagine the place.*

Canberra Hospital, Ward 12B. The loony bin. Mentally ill

people were committed or committed themselves here for their own protection. It was the first stop for attempted suicides. Sour smell of vomit and sweat. Terror, panic, horror—pounding hearts and endless whimpering. Waiting for a drug to wear off, waiting to be rescued by another dose.

Kreyna found Simon in white bandages to his armpits, blue gown, white cotton blanket over stiff white sheets, both breath and pulse faint, yet steady. He was healing. The crowd thought so, too. She elbowed her way through the throng of disincarnate beings filling Simon's ward room. Did they all belong to him? No way of knowing. But they saw her and surged forward, pressing and clamoring for attention. She closed her eyes and left.

Back in Morwenna's bedroom, Kreyna hugged and rocked herself, "Oh, oh! There's so many of them, oh!"

"Is he going to be okay?" Morwenna asked.

"Huh? Yes, I suppose so—for now. But he's infested with entities. They'll drag him down, back to despair. He's drugged up to the eyeballs but, long term? Who knows?"

"What are entities?"

"Put simply, bodiless souls stuck on this earth-plane. They don't want to or don't know how to move on. Usually, they're frustrated and angry—sometimes hate-filled and vicious. They latch on to sensitive people and live vicariously through them. Look, I'm no expert but they're bad news—don't get your hopes up."

Morwenna stared, unseeing, at an image of Madonna frozen in mid-song. With an effort, she said, "Let's get you back home, with luck before anyone notices."

CHAPTER SIX

School had broken up for the year. In 1987 and 1988, Kreyna and Morwenna would be going to Narrabundah College to study in Years 11 and 12, as a precursor to sitting the Higher School Certificate examinations which would determine their eligibility for university.

Since Kreyna's telepathic visit to the hospital, her skin seemed to have thinned. The shopping mall had her gritting her teeth at the noise and multitude of ill-tempered Christmas shoppers—she sidestepped people who seemed to walk at her deliberately and stared at her in passing. Ugly, critical thoughts would pop into her head and she wrestled to negate them.

On coming home from the mall, she was sure Lydia had been in her bedroom and gone through her private stuff. Kreyna stormed into her sister's room and provoked a blazing row which had their mother berating them both for being self-absorbed, teenage princesses. Both girls burst into tears, doors slammed and silence prevailed. Worse still, although Kreyna cleansed her aura with white light in the shower every night, she would catch shadows in her peripheral vision. Despite all her protective rituals, she couldn't shake off seething anger, an awful sense of futility and of being watched.

Three Sundays before Christmas, Kreyna attended the Canberra Spiritualist Church's final service for the year. When Oma was alive, they'd gone together regularly. Without her grandmother's confident personality to hide behind, Kreyna walked into the rented room in the Griffin Centre in Canberra's central business district. Unsure how and if she still fit into the diverse congregation which was singing a jaunty hymn, she took a seat toward the back. Up front, three people were seated on the platform facing the congregation.

Eadie Ibbett and her husband, Alf, had formed the church many years ago and remained actively involved. Preparing to lead the service, Eadie sat in the middle, her long white hair drawn back in a neat bun. Peering through thick glasses, she spotted Kreyna and smiled brightly. After the service, Kreyna hung around while Eadie, who was notoriously fond of a homemade teacake, lumbered between the stragglers for a last-minute chat. A tall, older man was stacking the remaining chairs against the rear wall.

"Hello, lovely lass. We've missed you." Eadie's speech held a faint Yorkshire accent, despite her thirty years in Australia. Ill-fitting dentures clicked and whistled when she spoke. "My, how you've grown. But you look a little peaky—are you well?"

Shyer than usual, Kreyna said, "I'm not sure."

Eadie's smile evaporated and she examined Kreyna with an intense, unwavering stare. She began to hiss through her teeth. "Ssss...oh dear, oh dear, oh dear. Where have you been? No matter, you must come to see me as soon as you can."

"I'm free now if that's okay."

Eadie called out, "Stanislav, can you spare a moment?" At the back of the room, the man straightened and ran a hand through a shock of thick, white hair. "This lass needs our help."

Stan approached. Stroking a pointy gray beard, he fixed Kreyna with watery amber eyes. With a pronounced Polish accent, he said, "So I see." Kreyna knew him from regular platform work. The Spiritualist Church was founded on proof of life after death.

Consistently, he had demonstrated flawless mediumship ability by conveying messages from the dear departed to loved ones in the congregation. "The sooner the better. Your house, Eadie?"

Eadie took Kreyna as a passenger in her Honda and Stan followed behind to the house in Canberra's inner suburb of Hughes. Inside, the threesome settled into a small alcove off the dining room where Eadie kept a desk covered with books and papers.

"How are you feeling, young 'un?" Eadie pushed three chairs back to create more space.

"Heavy," Kreyna said. Stan had settled down and closed his eyes, apparently in a light meditation. With a touch of panic, she prayed he knew what he was doing. "It feels like someone is standing on the back of my neck. I can barely hold my head upright, the pressure is unreal."

Eadie nodded. "They're gathering at your throat chakra. Word has gone out through the ethers. There could be lots waiting for this opportunity. Many may have been hanging around for quite some time. It won't be long now, lovie. Don't you worry—Stan and I will clear you out completely."

Stan opened his eyes and spoke. "Are you able to go into trance by yourself?"

"Probably. I'm really nervous, but I can't bear this much longer."

"It will be champion, we'll protect you." With a reassuring smile, Eadie placed a hand on each of Kreyna's shoulders. "Stan has cleared the room and mustered all the protection our Sentinels can offer. If you listen, you'll hear the beating of a thousand angels' wings, gathered on your behalf. Now, let's begin."

Kreyna closed her eyes and slowed her breath to a lazy rise and fall. Warmth permeated her throat. Blinking, she found Stan before her, both hands held out with his fingers only a short distance from her skin pointing at her Adam's apple. Smiling faintly, he caught her gaze with limpid pools, so full of love and warmth that they captured her attention completely.

Using a voice deeply resonant with authority, he began to intone repeatedly, "I call on the Almighty to act in the highest interest of all here gathered. Anything not made of pure light and love must leave now, if not to the light, then darkness forever. Prefer the light. In the name of the Christ, I command you to leave. I release you with love. In the name of all that is pure, I send you to the light." Intermittently, he would flick his hands away and return to Kreyna's throat.

To her right, Eadie stood and spoke quietly, like a descant to Stan's tune. "You are surrounded by the pure white light of Infinite Living Spirit through which nothing negative can penetrate. The pure white light flows through you and fills you, surrounds and protects you at all times. You are safe and protected by an impenetrable shield of pure love and light. Perfect and whole, you remain permanently inviolable."

Kreyna lost count of the seemingly endless stream of souls who passed through the doorway between dimensions that she had become. She floated in the depths of Stan's devoted eyes. Although his lips moved, she heard little. When his eyes widened, whites showing, and his voice climbed louder and louder, sound finally penetrated her awareness.

"Who are you, what are you? I command you to leave this body!"

Kreyna felt her face contort and her lips move, but it wasn't she who spoke. "I am Pasquale from Milano. My ship, she sunk."

"Pasquale, you don't belong here. Get out."

A cruel laugh. "I do what I like, have fun."

Stan stepped forward and boomed, "Get out of her! Get out!"

"*Vaffanculo bastardo.* I stay."

"Sentinels! Through your presence, all power is given unto us who seek to free this girl from the lost one within. Sweep her clean."

Behind Kreyna's eyes a blinding rush of crowding colors bolted across her mind, searing hot then icy cold, black then rainbow bright. A surge of power struck the base of her spine and swept up until white energy seemed to erupt through the crown of her head. Bubbles of excitement ran up her chest and burst in her throat—she grinned ecstatically for no apparent reason, her heart fit to burst with joy and love. In the presence of pure love.

"It's time to go, young man." Eadie's tone was conciliatory. "You've had your fun, nothing to be proud of now it's over. You will be looked after, you will be safe, you have no choice. In the name of Almighty goodness, I command you to leave. You must move on. Go now."

Voices calmed and faded out of conscious hearing. Kreyna's awareness drifted peacefully until Eadie said to Stan, "Is that the last of them?" She led Kreyna to a couch and settled her to rest. Curled up under a colorful crocheted blanket, Kreyna scanned her body and found only peacefulness. Her relaxed throat buzzed with warmth. Gingerly, she lifted her head and thought it might float away. Eadie and Stan were talking quietly over cups of something, so she sat up.

"Feeling better, m'lass?" Eadie said. "That's a relief. In case you don't realize it, you've just done an enormous service for a bunch of wayward souls who must have been waiting a very long time for someone such as yourself to come along. I've never done it meself, but I believe the role of Gatekeeper is a rare sacrifice, granting both suffering and blessings."

"I don't recall volunteering to be a—what was it? A Gatekeeper?" Still shaky, Kreyna sat stroking her humming throat.

"But you must have," Stan said. "It's not something imposed on anyone. And it can only be done by someone with access to other dimensions—someone with a foot in both worlds, if you like."

"No. No, I don't like. Why me, why now?"

Stan glanced at Eadie and continued in a measured voice. "If you hold any reservations about continuing to live on this earth-plane, you are being shown that you can leave without question. The option is yours."

Kreyna spluttered, "But I want to be here! At least, I thought I did. I'm sure I do."

"Then you must politely turn down the offer. And you can resign from the role of Gatekeeper as well."

"Oh, please—I *never* want to do that again. Noble and self-sacrificing as it may be, no thanks. That was the pits."

Again, Stan glanced at Eadie. "What I said about the Gatekeeper role not being imposed upon someone wasn't entirely true. Rarely, it's a duty imposed on a sensitive who has intruded without permission. Eadie was telling me that your grandmother trained you well, certainly well enough to know not to transgress. You wouldn't have, would you Kreyna?"

Kreyna decided not to magnify her crime by lying. "A friend begged me to find out about her friend in hospital—an attempted suicide. I was trying to help..."

"Hellfire, you soft lass!" Eadie clenched her teeth. "That was very, very foolish and extremely dangerous. The way of the transgressor is hard. Your grandmother would turn in her grave if she hadn't been cremated. Stop smirking, you soft—bah!" Eadie swept Kreyna into her arms and squeezed tight. "I promised I'd keep an eye on you. Words fail me, much as I've failed her."

Speech muffled by Eadie's shoulder, Kreyna said, "I think I've learned my lesson. Please don't worry—I won't do it again willingly. I was just trying to impress a new friend, so she'd like me. Friends are hard to find."

"Oh, lass. Y'wouldna be human if you didn't slip up while you're young. But you're so vulnerable without ongoing training." Eadie released Kreyna who pulled a chair over to the desk and sat down. Eadie poured a cup of milky, overly brewed tea and handed it to Kreyna. "Speaking of training, you're invited to a special church meeting we're holding this Thursday night. I can't say much about it now, but there's a long-term project in which your grandmother was deeply involved. We think it only fitting that you be given the opportunity to be part of it. Participation could lift your skill as a clairvoyant to a whole new level, you might say. Now, drink up and I'll drive you home."

* * *

Morwenna's gaze devoured the sheet of paper in front of her. She sat at a desk in one corner of her bedroom. Surrounded by open textbooks and strange mathematical tables, she'd been making mysterious calculations and drawing circles with lines all over them for the past forty-five minutes. Kreyna was beginning to regret having handed over her birth details.

"Phwar—you *are* an interesting beastie. Look at that sexy Venus in Scorpio rising—rock and roll!"

"What does that mean?" Kreyna hardly dared ask.

"Since Venus, the planet of love and beauty, is just above the horizon and in the twelfth house of the hidden, it's obvious to everyone that you're intensely passionate and blindingly attractive. To which you're oblivious. Very odd."

"Rubbish," Kreyna snorted, bouncing on the edge of Morwenna's quilt-covered bed. "I look like a Muppet."

Ignoring her, Morwenna continued. "As a matter of fact, you have five planets in the psychic and secret twelfth house which gives you a Piscean overlay making you super-sensitive, compassionate and gentle." Morwenna waved the paper and pointed at a squiggle in a circle. "See how Neptune is rising? It's the planet of insight which just so happens to rule Pisces—it's in your first house of identity. Sandwiched in between is Mercury in Scorpio which gives you a mind like a steel trap and relentless mental discipline. Unbe-fucking-lievable."

"You're boring me." Kreyna fell backward across the bed and flapped her arms.

"A razor-sharp marshmallow—who'da thunk it?" Morwenna turned and said, "How can this be boring? It's all about you."

"I don't find me that interesting. Tell me something I don't know."

"Well, you have the sexual planet Mars next to Uranus which governs unusual innovation. You could be sexually adventurous with unexpected results. Then your Moon ruling the emotions is in Aquarius. Therefore, you're highly analytical and logical. Some people mistake you for a heartless robot manufactured on the planet IBM."

Kreyna stuck out her tongue and broke into giggles. "That describes me perfectly."

"And your mother's an ice cube."

Frowning, Kreyna sat up and glared from under hooded lids—Morwenna visibly flinched. Kreyna dismissed the idea of a justifiable homicide and asked, "What about my father?"

"He's your white knight. But you knew that. What you don't know is that, as time passes, the planets keep moving and map out your destiny. Their progress shows difficulties and opportunities. As of now, your Sun has progressed to align with Neptune."

"Hm, Neptune. A gaseous giant orbiting the sun at a vast distance from our own tiny and insignificant flying rock. You really think that means something?"

"Ah. Well. Being Neptune, it is innately imprecise."

"Bo-ring—make sense soon, please."

"I...I don't know enough to say, exactly," Morwenna protested. "Neptune is about woo-woo, spooky stuff. It rules spirituality— um, cosmic consciousness and alternative dimensions— specifically, your psychic abilities. Taking a rough guess, with your Sun coming to the same position as Neptune, it's a golden opportunity to fully develop that part of you."

The words resonated with something Eadie had said. Slowly, Kreyna began to nod. "Could be true. My friend, you're pretty good at star signs and flying rocks. Thank you." She stood and moved to hug a startled Morwenna who grinned—embarrassed, yet inordinately pleased.

* * *

Kreyna bounded up Eadie's front steps and turned to wave to her father who accelerated the bulky, blue Ford Falcon away from the curb. She caught her breath and knocked tentatively— she was late because her father had been busy until the very last moment—she hated being late.

Eadie's husband, Alf, was shorter than his wife. Bespectacled, wiry and mostly bald, Alf let Kreyna in and led her into the lounge room where five grownups, three men and two women, sat talking animatedly. She recognized only Eadie, Stan, and one of the men whose name she'd forgotten.

"Here's our best lass, people," Eadie said. "Let's get down to business, shall we? This won't take long because things have progressed to the point of implementation. For the few of you who are new, I shall briefly recap." She turned and winked at Kreyna who had perched on an ottoman to Eadie's left.

"As you know, everything visible emanates from the invisible. Consciousness determines if, and how, we experience reality. For hundreds of years, monks and lamas in Tibet have worked collectively to raise the level of human consciousness so the world may experience a better reality. Some would say this has been a thankless task largely ignored by Westerners. Except for certain organizations, societies and associations of interested people, especially those like us with an acute awareness of something more than this obvious earth-plane. While we cannot hope to emulate the extraordinary dedication and sacrifice of those living in monasteries and lamaseries in Tibet, we can be trained to elevate our personal vibration to a similar level. From which we should be able to operate, collectively, toward the betterment of mankind.

"Some of us are better at attaining a higher vibration than others. All of you are here for precisely that ability. What we all have to be trained to do is to locate a precisely defined, narrow brainwave frequency, at will. At that particular frequency, a field is being established across the world, as we speak. From London to New York, Sydney to Vancouver, and all the way from Adyar in India home to Lhasa in Tibet—in numerous locations across the globe, intuitives such as yourselves are being trained to target this field that's come to be known as the Filigrane."

A murmur rippled through the group and Kreyna's eyes widened. Eadie smiled at her and continued, "Come the summer solstice, Australians will be welcomed into the Filigrane. We have to familiarize ourselves with the area in which we will operate, much of which we don't yet know. It's a tremendous challenge and a unique opportunity for which I think we're as ready as we can be."

Stan interrupted, "Have you heard anything from the Brisbane mob about the operating frequency?"

"No, but most likely it will be very low theta, just above delta. You can be sure it will be a stretch for us all. I believe it will take some doing to become adept. Only those who have mastered the techniques will be able to get anywhere near the field.

"It won't be a matter of simply dialing into a particular brainwave frequency. The process begins with activating and harmonizing the seven chakras, or energy vortices, which shift your entire being to a higher octave. Any imbalances will lower your overall vibration. It is a matter of practice and self-discipline to attain that state of perfect harmony within your physical body.

"Once that is achieved, then you will alter your brainwave frequency to enter the astral plane, the Bardo, and access the Filigrane. Be warned, any sinking of your core vibration will lock you out, indefinitely. As you know, it will be open to all invitees, regardless of their origins or beliefs—we'll be watching, policing each other. Misuse or abuse will mean permanent expulsion."

Kreyna blurted, "How will anyone know who anyone is?"

"Why, because of your psychic signature—it's embedded in your DNA and impossible to disguise. You know as well as I do that you can detect faces, names and places when you're a sensitive. You do this yourself. Do you think someone could hide in an astral field populated by highly talented, trained sensitives? You get the picture.

"When I know more, I will convene another meeting. Some of you have not yet received the training in Brisbane and that will be arranged very quickly to ensure you are ready. Kreyna, you will have to wait until the new year, providing your parents allow you participate. Do you want me to talk to them?"

"Do they have to know?" Kreyna said. Eadie raised an eyebrow and Kreyna pulled a face. "I guess so. I'll ask Dad."

* * *

Minutes from Queensland's Gold Coast, the Currumbin Bird Sanctuary had provided welcome reward after the Filigrane training in Brisbane. Both mentally and emotionally fatigued, Eadie and Kreyna were delighted by the sanctuary with its hundreds of native birds and particularly the rainbow lorikeets.

Kreyna had been transfixed by the sight of a tall, black female cassowary. She was glad for the fence between her and the azure-blue throated bird with its pink wattles drooping down a long neck. Weighing in at an intimidating hundred and thirty pounds and sporting a large, spongy, brown helmet, the cassowary gave the impression it was well prepared for any battle. The tour guide had explained that the flightless rainforest bird was actually fighting a losing battle with cars and dogs, and fast becoming endangered. At the gift shop, Eadie had helped Kreyna find a postcard to take home as a memento. Then they had returned to the Toyota hired by Eadie in Brisbane and headed inland.

Eadie told Kreyna that she was taking her to see on old friend and remarked how Queensland seemed to attract, if not breed the best intuitives in Australia—Kreyna being an anomaly, or course. After a forty-five minute winding drive through farmland and rising hills, they cruised into a village located on a plateau nearly two thousand feet above sea level. Tamborine Mountain was far less humid and cooler and greener than the coastal, urban areas they had left behind, but still cloying compared to Canberra's dry summer heat.

Eadie cruised along the main street where nondescript shops mingled with craftwork stalls and boutique art galleries. Tourist signs pointed directions to rainforests, waterfalls and scenic views in the surrounding areas. Down a narrow road bordered on each side by avocado plantations, Eadie slowed the Toyota, counted driveways until she turned onto a furrowed stretch of gravel meandering through the scattered trees.

Out of the car, sweetly pungent frangipani perfume greeted Kreyna. A low bungalow jostled with lush undergrowth and partly disappeared under branches laden with large, glossy oval leaves. Eadie had already climbed white wooden steps to greet and hug a figure on the verandah. Kreyna walked up behind them and waited. The person wearing a lived-in dark green tracksuit and brown ankle boots was painfully thin and evidently unwell.

"Jean, I'd like you to meet Kreyna Katz with whom you'll be working today." Eadie beckoned to Kreyna.

Kreyna clasped the surprisingly warm, emaciated fingers and stammered something polite, too distracted by the gaze from bottomless eyes that scoured her soul. Under the thick, cropped, wavy black hair, the woman had the bone structure of Egyptian royalty. She smiled, displaying neat white teeth and, before Kreyna's gaze, transformed into a strikingly handsome picture of androgyny.

"You didn't tell her much about me, now did you, Eadie?" Jean's lips twitched with amusement.

"I like to surprise her—she's not easy to surprise."

In a slurred, low voice, Jean said, "Then I don't suppose you've told her I'm going to draw and describe her Sentinels today. Did she tell you that, Kreyna? No? As a favor to this wonderful old friend of mine, that's what I'll be doing. Come into my studio, ladies." Leaning on a gnarled walking stick in her left hand, she led the way indoors.

Lit by two skylights, the studio was cluttered with leaning canvases, a workbench and desk, boxes of paints, brushes in jars, and milk crates full of small branches and twigs. Jean moved aside a large easel that supported a half-finished canvas. Dumping books off two tattered, red velvet covered easy chairs, she invited Eadie and Kreyna to make themselves comfortable. From a filing cabinet, she pulled out a piece of stiff A3-sized beige card and laid it on the desk beside a box of blunted pastel pencils.

"Please relax and keep quiet, if you would. This may take twenty minutes or an hour, it's hard to say. Then I'll explain so one of you can take notes. If you want to browse through my collection for something to pass the time, go ahead."

Eadie searched through the books on the floor. She extricated a large title on Australian landscape artists and settled back to read. Through a door that opened to the back of the house, a party-colored whippet pranced into the room. Kreyna put out a hand to the dog's elegant, dove-gray skull. Short whiskers and a moist, black nose nuzzled her palm.

"That's just Melody checking you out," Jean muttered, busily sharpening a pastel. Satisfied with the result, she resumed drawing. Melody retired to a shabby canvas bed and buried her muzzle beneath her paws, gaze flicking between Kreyna and Jean. Occasionally, Jean glanced at Kreyna who, in turn, tried to guess her age—quite old, judging from the lines around her eyes—at least forty. The woman was an odd mixture of vitality and sorrow, as if resigned to some terrible inevitability. Her sallow complexion appeared lit from within by an inhuman force beyond Kreyna's understanding. *Stop wondering, be patient and wait.*

Jean's voice sliced through the silence. "Do you have a tattoo on your inner left thigh?" Kreyna opened her mouth to speak.

"Of course not," Jean continued. "You're too young for such a thing—it must be a personal totem. From inside the top of your thigh to just below the knee, I see a bird of prey in flight with a scroll in its mouth which suggests you're a messenger. Of what, is for you to find out over a lifetime." Jean stepped from behind the desk and dragged over a paint-splattered, wooden stool so she could sit in front of Eadie and Kreyna. "I've finished the drawing—have a look."

Eadie slipped a stenographer's notebook and pen out of her handbag. Kreyna took the drawing and examined it. Central amongst the fine line work picturing beings and creatures was the serene face of a brown-eyed, faintly smiling person wearing a hooded garment. "Who's he—or she?"

"Spirit has no interest in gender, it's irrelevant. For ease of reference, let's say your primary Sentinel is female. Her name sounds something like Bright. She has and will always be with you to warn, advise and grant guidance. Be that as it may, she cannot make decisions for you and may not always communicate, if it is in your best interests that she doesn't. Moment by moment, you make choices according to your own free will."

"Why is she with me?" Kreyna said.

"That is something you and she would have agreed before you came into your present incarnation—it's pointless to ask until you are together again in another dimension, by which time you'll know anyway."

Kreyna was only half listening, absorbed as she was in the drawing. Four more faces smiled out at her from another world filled with detailed, enchanting scenes—a marketplace and a crop-filled field, riderless horses and soaring birds, and a vibrant rainbow arched over a mother and child.

"The young mother is Elisa. Centuries ago, she lost a child, descended into a catatonic state and passed away from grief."

"What's that on her head?" Kreyna pointed and Eadie looked up from her notes.

"She wears a small crown for you, as your name suggests. That muscle-bound bloke is from Ghana. His name is Kharto—he's with you to protect you from attack and to help you fight back, if need be. See the scar above his heart? He took a spear, a mortal wound. He'll guard your heart."

"Who's the dried up old fella?"

Jean laughed out loud. "Oh, he doesn't like that! He's Cedrik the wizard—very well-educated and experienced, an expert, you might say. See how he stands back from the others? He'll come to the fore when you're mature. For now, he watches and helps you learn the intricacies of the universe."

"And him—the Latin-looking guy with the mustache and goatee?"

"Ah, that's Stopha—he's around you a good deal of the time. He's not much older than you are now. At least, that's how he presents so you can relate. He took himself out on a motorbike in the fifties—still thinks he's pretty flash. What he is fantastic at is astral travel—he's fast, very fast. You'll learn much from him."

Kreyna looked up from the drawing. "I feel a bit funny, kind of self-conscious with these people watching me all the time."

"That's not how it works," Jean said. "These Sentinels will come and go as needed. If you truly cannot manage by yourself, help is at hand and you only need ask. However, if you've created circumstances for you to experience and learn on your own, you will be left to find the answers you need from within—from your Overself, best explained as the remainder of your consciousness inhabiting other dimensions.

"As you mature, some Sentinels may leave and others more suitable to your path will join you. But Bright is with you for life, joined to you at the heart chakra by a brilliant green rope of pure love. She—or he—loves you with a force beyond mortal description—the feeling is mutual. You don't remember now and that's as it should be. When this incarnation is over, you will once more."

Eadie said, "Is there anything else I should be writing down for Kreyna?"

"When you look carefully, there are other symbols in the picture that will gain meaning, with time. For now, take from it what you need. Know that you are always loved and never alone, as are we all."

When they were ready to leave, Kreyna sat in the car while Eadie and Jean chatted, hugged and said their final farewells.

Jean disappeared back into the house as soon as they drove away. Tears glistened on Eadie's cheeks and Kreyna remained silent while they dried.

On the other side of Tamborine Mountain village, Eadie said, "Sorry Kreyna. I know I won't see her again."

"What's wrong with her?"

Eadie heaved a heavy sigh. "Beggar me, what's right with her? A broken heart, broken repeatedly. I met her when she was living in Canberra, before you were born. She had come down from Queensland to get away from a bad marriage. Took her young son and ran away, she did. Financially, she struggled, barely managed. Things got better when she got a decent job as a vet's assistant. Then her son got meningitis after swimming in a river and died. The grief nearly killed her.

"But then she met someone. They moved up here for a new start and ran the motel near St. Bernard's church in the village. They worked hard together for twelve years until her longtime companion had a heart attack and passed over. Now, she's been diagnosed with multiple sclerosis and it's getting worse fast. I think she's had enough of life on earth. Can't say I blame her."

"That's so sad—she must miss both of them," Kreyna said.

"Jean knows their eternal souls will meet again. Consciousness always has been and always will be independent of the body. What you have perishes, what you are survives through time and space. However, there's only so much grief an earthly heart can bear. Sometimes I think those gifted with the sight are cursed by misfortune and heartache to compensate. Ah, pay me no mind, young 'un—I'm as daft as a brush—don't know what I'm saying."

"I thought she was a bloke when I first saw her."

Eadie looked sideways at her traveling companion. "You wouldn't be the first to say so. Jean says a person's spirit is more important than dangly-bits." Eadie guffawed loudly. "Begging your pardon, that was a wee bit rude. Jean also says that sensitives are less concerned than most with the mechanics of anatomy. Nothing you need dwell on. Let's get ourselves home in one piece, shall we?"

Kreyna immersed herself in Eadie's notes about the Sentinels. They seemed to have distinct personalities, parts of which she recognized in herself. Was that why they chose to be with her? And Bright was totally awesome—she emanated a powerful calm that seemed to channel an immense, endless intelligence. Cool— Morwenna will be so impressed. Way cool.

PART THREE

1995

CHAPTER SEVEN

Opportunistic redevelopers were picking off Barton's substantial double-brick 1920s residences to knock down and rebuild with apartment complexes like Kreyna's. Office buildings also encroached upon the inner leafy suburb, highly desirable by dint of proximity to a plethora of government buildings—even new Parliament House was a mere ten-minute stroll away. For Kreyna, it was a five-minute jog up the road to the office at DFAT.

Her ground-floor apartment was decorated in tasteful shades of beige. Long and narrow from front to back, the external walls were double brick to act as sound insulation between apartments. Two bedrooms and a bathroom led off a combined living and dining room. The whole apartment smelled faintly of her favorite citrus incense and votive candles.

Outside, a paved courtyard led off the living room and two slender silver birches lent it dappled shade. In the late afternoon, the photinia hedge was alive with bees gathering and carrying off their spoils from the cloyingly scented, bobbing, cream flower heads. Beyond the hedge and brush fencing, the traffic on

Brisbane Avenue hummed intermittently. Kreyna and Morwenna were having coffee in the courtyard.

"May I say you're looking particularly fetching today?" Kreyna slid a brimming cappuccino across the glass-topped patio table.

Morwenna was dressed for a soiree. At about five foot five, she stood level with Kreyna. A jet-black bob, parted exactly in the middle, framed thoughtful deep gray eyes set in a flawless, pale complexion. Her extravagant jaw rivaled that of Dame Joan Sutherland, Australia's most famous opera diva. Punky trails of red and blue hair mascara complemented an embroidered cobalt-blue jacket. It fitted loosely over her dark trousers that tapered down to black, patent leather Doc Martens with high blue laces. On her expressive hands, a medley of large silver rings, some with glossy stones, adorned every finger and thumb.

"You like the jacket? Another op-shop treasure. I thought I'd go all out. One never knows when a gorgeous man might cross one's path."

"He'll be a lucky man when it happens. By the way, I pulled off my first official OOBE at work."

"Your first what?" Morwenna exhaled and knocked the tip of her bidi cigarette into the ashtray. "You're not supposed to be telling me this, are you?"

"Of course not. Since when has that stopped me? An OOBE is an out-of-body experience, guided via the Filigrane, controlled and at will. Pretty impressive stuff."

"When was this, and should we alert the media?"

"Last Thursday, and I can't tell you where I went or I'd have to kill you, of course. But it was magical, a real buzz."

"Sweetie, you've had to kill me and I've been resurrected too many times to count." Morwenna sipped from her cup and licked off a creamy mustache. "Ah, delicious as usual. You should set up shop."

Settling into the padded cane chair, Kreyna smiled— Morwenna said the same thing every time.

"Pankaj is going to put me forward for an elite team. I've graduated, in effect. It means more challenging work and a salary hike. Not to mention it's a neat skill to have, although dangerous to do alone. I won't be doing *that* any time soon, at least not without assistance from the Filigrane."

"Pardon me if I fail to understand the whole Filigrane thing."

"Really? Well, you know how filigree is fine wire lace made from precious metals, with knots or tiny grains as complications? Let's use it as a metaphor for people, a particular type of people—intuitives who are more sensitive than normal. The Filigrane is a branching network on a global scale, via which intuitives communicate with each other. This network is not to be confused with the Bardo, which is any one of at least four alternate dimensions, but I won't get into that now. All you need to know is that for an intuitive, the physical body functions not only to originate thought and but also as an interface through which thought is received and sent. Only intuitives who can heighten their vibration sufficiently can access the Filigrane. It's neither privileged nor elitist and there are no secret handshakes or passwords."

She playacted a salute and continued. "Once people have access, names and locations can be communicated by telepathy alone and members can be identified purely by their psychic signatures."

Morwenna spooned foam off the coffee and into her mouth. "Is that how Robert tracks you down?"

"Yup, but he's finding it harder, I've noticed. The Filigrane functions on two levels. Altruistically, it elevates the frequency of human thought across the world. Mundanely, it acts as an amplifier for communication between intuitives. Mostly, members assist with channeling healing energy. We also fuel creativity in the form of genius insight. Ever wondered why ideas and inspiration occur simultaneously across continents? That's the Filigrane's influence. We assist imaginative self-expression of any kind, whether it's painting, writing, music, dance, invention—any of the sciences—anything requiring a flash of inspiration to come up with an original thought, or a new way of thinking."

"Spectacular. How many of you out there?"

"I don't know for sure." Kreyna swallowed the last dregs of coffee. "Less than a hundred worldwide, I believe."

A male fairy wren dropped down for a quick drink at the lion-headed wall fountain, only a few feet away. He flashed his bright blue cap and bib at his dull brown mate in the foliage above; she was not enticed and flitted away. He dashed after her, out of sight.

Kreyna wished she'd had her camera at the ready. "I should be working in the team by Christmas, just when the extra salary will be handy. Even though I pay Dad less than market rent for this, I'd like to buy a decent-sized piece of land soon, maybe out of town in Sutton, Wamboin or Hall, perhaps."

On the living room wall, Oma's Swiss cuckoo clock swung into action. A tiny demented wooden bird popped in and out, and blurted *cuckoo* six times—about the time they were expected at Frances's place in Garran.

"We'll have to go soon."

Morwenna stubbed out her bidi. "Sure, sweet cheeks. Before we go, have you managed to get Robert out of your hair yet?"

Kreyna made a face. "He bailed me up after the training exercise when it was after hours and nobody was around. He could have gotten away with anything he liked."

Morwenna's eyes widened. "Did he...?"

"Land a few punches? No, but I wouldn't put it past him, just for old time's sake. And he was off his face on some drug. It must be getting harder to function on a daily basis. He's always been able to control how much he used. Now, I'm not so sure. And when it comes to us getting back together, he's like a terrier with a rat—just won't leave me alone. I've run out of ideas as to how to get the message across. He thinks I'll come around if he nags me enough. I don't suppose you have any thoughts on how to handle him?"

"About the only thing that might slow him down would be you taking up with someone bigger than him. So, what did he want this time?"

"What do you think? He's still banging on about industrial espionage and how we would be a great team."

"Can't he do it himself? I thought you said he was an expert."

"At remote viewing, yes. I'm better at telepathy, which is getting inside people's heads and listening to what they're thinking. Anyway, he believes there's big money to be made as well." Kreyna gathered up the cups and stacked them neatly. "Sex, power and money—do guys think about anything else?"

"Not so you'd notice, though I'm curious about the money angle. Can he make any serious money that way or is he fooling himself?"

"Don't know, don't care—money's not a big motivator for me." Kreyna shoved fingers through her hair and leaned her forehead into the heel of each palm. "That said, it's probably true. If you consider the advantages of knowing what your business competitors are planning, I'd say there could be big sums in the balance. What worries me more are the prospective clients. One might have to work for some dodgy characters, just to make a buck. I know I couldn't."

"And Robert could?"

"I think he thinks he's smarter than most. He doesn't realize mercenary cunning will outsmart any other kind of genius. On the subject of Robert, I have a bone to pick with you, oh great guru."

"What have I done now?"

"You haven't *done* anything—it's what you *said* ten months ago. You checked out my horoscope for the year, remember?"

"About the time you were getting into him? I looked at the transits, plus your secondary and solar arc progressions. And your solar return too, which looked intriguing."

For a moment, Kreyna closed her eyes. "I got the distinct impression I was heading into a highly significant relationship. Any minute now, you said." She squeezed her eyebrows into a crest. "Did I misunderstand and if so, what was I doing with Robert?"

Morwenna blew air into her cheeks. "If it were only so clear-cut. I'm sorry, sweetie, it never is. The fault is not in the stars but in my less than perfect ability to interpret them. I can get it wrong. Give me a moment to think." She pulled a bidi out of its packet, wedged it between her teeth and flicked alive a miniature, red plastic lighter.

"If memory serves me, transiting Pluto is conjunct your natal Venus. It indicates a passionate, life-changing love affair, which fits the year thus far. But the solar return had Sun conjunct Venus square Uranus in the seventh house of partners. This kind of suggests two or three instances of said passionate affair—not sure what to make of that."

"So is Robert the one?" Kreyna asked. "Because he certainly doesn't feel like it now, if he ever did."

"Reasonably, he ticked all the boxes, but the heart trumps reason every time. Long story short, if he doesn't feel right he ain't. If it's any consolation, your Venus will progress to align with your Sun eventually, which indicates a great opportunity for lasting love. It's a once in a lifetime event that most people don't get to experience. Mind you, it's about fourteen years away so don't hold your breath."

"Meaning I'll get happy one day? Here's hoping." Kreyna carried the cups indoors. "Let's go, girlfriend."

* * *

Once past Parliament House, they took the ramp that skirted the Prime Minister's Lodge onto Adelaide Avenue. The setting sun shone dead ahead at a blinding angle.

"Two Scorpios together are like a cobra with a mongoose—someone's going to be lunch." Morwenna waved her hands to mimic the fighting animals. "What you need is a supportive Cancerian. Or a sweet Piscean."

Kreyna dropped the visor and squinted at the BMW's mirrors. She steered into the left lane. "I thought Cancerians were sentimental sooky-lah-lahs and Pisceans fall down drunks. Look, there's no need to worry because I'm out of the market, full stop."

"It's been six weeks!" Morwenna protested. "Time to build a bridge and get over it. You're free again. It's better if you find someone soon and have some fun, nothing too serious. You know I'm right. Remember, so many men, so little time."

Kreyna glanced across at her erstwhile friend. "You're making me wish I were an Aries like you. If I didn't know better, I'd think you have the depth of a mud puddle."

Morwenna pursed her lips. "Not every relationship is deep and meaningful. Lighten up."

Kreyna steered the car up the steep streets toward the more affluent part of Garran. "You don't really mean that, do you?"

There was a roll of wild laughter and Morwenna's shoulders shook. "Gotcha! You should have seen the look on your face." She grinned, all too pleased with herself. "Just yanking your chain, sweetie. I know you had it bad over Robert and things were intense. That's who you are and you're not going to change. I'm not suggesting you do."

They came to a halt behind a row of parked cars on Rusden Street. "All I'm saying is try not to fall so hard so fast. Practice discrimination, practice friendship, practice detachment. For Scorpio, easier said than done I know. Now, let's get this party started."

The lobby showed off massive entrance doors with stained glass sidelights featuring gum tree leaves, crimson rosellas and sprays of golden wattle. They scanned the room for their hosts.

Morwenna nudged her friend. "Grrrowl! Gorgeousness alert. Stand in line. Me first, you can go slops."

Kreyna frowned. She'd just caught a luminous smile of acknowledgment from Frances, striking in a tailored, gold-colored shantung suit with a distinctive mandarin collar. Morwenna must mean the sandy-haired man standing next to her. A forest-green shirt flattered his fair complexion. In one hand he clutched the stem of a champagne flute. With the physique of a rugby player, he would have looked more comfortable holding a can of beer.

"May I offer you a drink?" A cocktail waitress of Amazonian proportions came into view. Kreyna and Morwenna skimmed glasses off her tray. They made their way between the couples and groups cluttering the oversized, split-level lounge room. A disc jockey had set up sound equipment near a pair of glass doors that opened to a deck. Outside, mature trees dwarfed a swimming pool.

Frances's eyes tilted up in greeting. "You must be Morwenna. I'd like you both to meet my boss at the ANU Centre for Consciousness, Doctor Declan De Salles."

"Declan to my friends." The man's huge, warm hand engulfed Kreyna's. Bluish-gray eyes, set too close together above a prominent nose, held hers before they dropped to appraise her cleavage. He flashed a cheeky smile and almost a wink, and then turned to Morwenna and gave her the same treatment—she colored under his undisguised appraisal.

"I hear you're both interested in the extra senses we all share, you in particular, Morwenna. You're brave to confess to practicing astrology." He touched her wrist. "It was fashionable twenty years ago. You know—those days of love, dove, peace, brown rice, hug a tree and what's your star sign? People *must* stir you about it."

"It's not the first thing I mention, no. But I find astrology endlessly fascinating. And useful in ways you wouldn't dream of." From beneath sultry black lashes, Morwenna added, "Perhaps you would too if you bothered to learn, rather than dismissing it out of hand."

Declan laughed, a sonorous boom originating deep in his barrel chest. He bent toward her. "I would not dream of dismissing astrology out of hand, not at all. I grant you're vastly more erudite on the matter than I. And I admire those with the courage to defend their passions and stand up for what they believe to be true."

What an overbearing, self-appointed authority on everything he seemed. Kreyna was compelled to say, "Just because you believe something to be true doesn't make it so. Truth is an opinion."

He shifted his attention and considered her. She could hear him thinking. Literally. She reined in her mind scan. Had he noticed? "What I mean is, there's no such thing as an objective opinion. All observation of reality is subjective because the observer's mind determines what will be observed, so every opinion is subjective. We cannot escape the ego that colors our perceptions with our own rules, our personal belief systems."

Three pairs of eyes stared at Kreyna. She elaborated. "Science can explore and analyze what it finds, but it's on shaky ground when it asserts so-called incontrovertible facts about the world. Learning requires changing one's mind, which is something scientists are reluctant to concede. Science can only narrow down possible explanations for anything. And has no explanation for many things like the power of intention. Or faith. Or love." She waved her hands around vaguely.

"A fair summation," Declan conceded. "As a scientist, albeit working in a fringe field, I know the elimination of spurious explanations is essential. By challenging old theses, we can discover more logical explanations no matter how startling they may be. Truth, they may not be in your view, but they are the best rational thought can muster."

The DJ, who had been playing Enya or something equally soporific, chose that moment to change musicians—a blast of Mariah Carey broke the mood.

Frances stepped forward with a practiced smile. "Anyone care for a bite to eat? There's a spit roast set up in the garden. Should be ready by now. Come this way." She touched Kreyna's elbow and steered her through the red cedar French doors—Declan and Morwenna fell into step behind them.

"Sorry," Kreyna muttered. "Was I getting too intense?"

"A mite. He's equally as passionate. Not a bad thing. At least he cares about his job. Works very hard and does his best to make the Centre successful. Funding is uncertain at the best of times. With Declan in charge, money is surer than without him."

A garlicky, meaty aroma sent Kreyna's taste buds into overdrive. Beneath a spreading elm tree stood a stocky young man wearing a white apron. He basted oil on a taut-skinned beast rotating over white-hot charcoals. Satisfied with the result, he took a long, slim blade from a leather holster at his waist and sliced off a few chunks of meat, dropping them onto a large plate. He grinned hugely and held out the plate when they approached.

"Good evening everyone, I am Helios. You like to try roast lamb, Greek-style, yes?" He slipped a chunk between his full lips and, with the back of a hairy hand, caught the juices that dribbled down the stubble on his chin—he licked the moisture, unabashed.

Morwenna bit into a morsel studded with rosemary and obvious slivers of garlic, leaning forward to keep the drips away from her clothes. Aware of Helios's blatant admiration, she chewed and finally managed to murmur, "Ah-mm, delicious—*nosthimia!*"

He laughed easily, displaying large white teeth, and said with a bow, "My pleasure—*kali orexi.*"

They carried platters of meat to buffet tables positioned around the pool. On the tables, a generous array of Mediterranean-style salads, dips and breads lay ready for eating. Guests drifted out from the house, gathered plates and cutlery, and helped themselves. Kreyna and Morwenna found spare seats together at one of the long tables decked out with napery and tea lights. Frances saw them to their seats, lingering only to assure Kreyna she would catch up with her later. Stride sinuous as a big cat, Frances returned indoors to greet latecomers.

Kreyna ate pita bread smeared with hummus and forkfuls of Greek salad. She followed Morwenna's gaze that had drifted back to Helios, as if to a powerful magnet. Busily, he divested the cooked beast of its last remnants of flesh. Hovering around the roasting pit, he cleaned and tidied up after himself, muscular build obvious under the tight, white T-shirt. When he crouched down, the fabric rode up above his jeans to reveal olive skin covered by a thick, black thatch on his lower back.

Kreyna teased her preoccupied friend. "Which are you enjoying more: the food or the view?"

"You know I can't resist hairy men, especially a classic beauty like him." Morwenna sat back with a discontented sigh, swirling her chardonnay in its glass. "I think he's a bit out of my league though. Jailbait perhaps?"

"Nup, I don't think he's that young. In fact, Greek guys are deceptive because they have skin that doesn't mind our harsh southern sun. Nothing ventured, nothing gained, girlfriend—go for it."

Declan appeared and took the seat opposite Kreyna, just as the DJ cranked up the volume on a boisterous Greek melody. In between strums of bouzoukis, they discussed astrology until the conversation drifted to philosophy and quantum theory. They suddenly realized the sun had gone, as had Morwenna. Declan looked at his watch and announced he had to leave. Kreyna walked with him through the thinning crowd of guests. They hovered in the lobby until Frances made her way over to them.

"Are you both going?"

"No, no, I'm not, but Declan must," Kreyna said, distractedly. "I seem to have misplaced Morwenna."

Declan took Kreyna's hand and pressed it. "It's been a pleasure, one I hadn't anticipated from this evening." He met her gaze and leaned to give her a quick peck on the cheek, his complexion deepening. He turned to Frances. "See you Monday. And thanks for your generous hospitality." Then he was out the door and gone.

Frances said, "Let's see if we can find Morwenna. Would you like a nightcap while we look? I have a very fine aged Saint Agnes brandy."

After a cursory search of the main areas of the house and garden, they settled into deck chairs by the pool. Kreyna swirled the liquor around in a squat goblet featuring a curved gold wire embedded in the glass. Inside the glass, the alcohol slid down in random waves, releasing its woody caramel scent. Helios's equipment and van had gone. Still no sign of Morwenna.

"Do you lose people habitually?" At Kreyna's puzzled look, Frances elaborated. "First your boyfriend and now your best friend. Very careless."

"I can assure you that losing the former was a happy event. As for Morwenna, she's saved my sanity on many an occasion. Look, seriously, he's ancient history. Do you really want to know?"

Frances's eyes were dark, yet danced with reflections from the pool lights. She slipped off gold sandals to reveal shapely, well-kept feet. "Ouch, that's better. My hostess duties are all but over for the night. We won't be disturbed. Now, tell me about your lost love."

"That color flatters you. In fact, the whole outfit does. I'll bet you look good in olive green, too."

"Thank you." Frances straightened the jacket sleeves. "Dry clean only. What was his name?"

After a larger sip of brandy, Kreyna told what she remembered. At first, she'd been in awe of Robert's maturity and worldliness; he was self-assured, a natural leader who inspired others. He made her feel attractive and special, and proudly introduced her to his equally sophisticated mates when he took her to clubs and parties. They would drive up to Sydney or down the coast for weekend rages. For a while she enjoyed herself, until it dawned on her that much of their traveling revolved around either using or purchasing cannabis, sometimes hashish. Still, the sexual side of their relationship was too good for her to make it a big issue.

"Did he use anything harder than weed?" Frances asked.

Kreyna hesitated. "He said once he wouldn't try heroin in case he liked it. I thought that was very astute of him."

"The drugs came between you?" Frances looked over Kreyna's shoulder and her animated expression vanished. A slight, mouse-haired man stepped between the chairs.

"There you are, Frankie. I've been hunting all over for you. Who's this charming young thing you're entertaining so cozily?"

Kreyna secured her chakras and crossed both legs and arms.

"You're home late," Frances countered. "Did you get my message? There're two men waiting for you in the study. They've been there since eight thirty."

He glanced at her and barely nodded—he resumed his examination of Kreyna.

Kreyna jumped to her feet. "I should go."

"Please don't. Bryce, this is Kreyna Katz. I met her on the flight back from London. I did tell you, remember?"

He dropped his chin and peered over his glasses, metallic eyes flickering.

"She works in the Attorney General's department," Frances added.

With a finger to his forehead and a syrupy smile, he said, "Of course. The AG's girl. Very nice, my dear, very nice indeed." He turned on his heel and marched off toward the house.

Frances exhaled heavily and ran fingers through her hair. "I must apologize for Bryce's absence of manners. He has a heavy workload at the moment. Not that it's an excuse, but it is a reason. You were saying?"

"Coo-ee!" The voice came from the house.

"So much for not being disturbed," Frances muttered. She stooped to put her sandals back on.

Morwenna picked her way through the tables—they met her halfway. The three women walked back inside together. In the foyer, Morwenna headed for the bathroom while Frances and Kreyna waited.

"Would you be interested in going to the Melbourne Cup with me?" Frances sounded oddly brittle.

"Sure. I've heard the ANU puts on a great Cup luncheon. Is it the usual cold chicken and champagne?"

"I meant the race itself. In Melbourne. I've wanted to see it in person since I arrived two years ago. Haven't managed it yet. Bryce would take me, except he can't get away right now."

"Do you mean just for the day? Fly down, go to the race, and fly back?"

"I can get very reasonably priced air tickets for us. Courtesy of the consulate. Quite affordable. Shouldn't break the bank." She noticed Kreyna's hesitation. "Think about it."

Morwenna appeared at the end of hall. Briefly, Frances touched both of Kreyna's shoulders and caught her gaze. "I'm not comfortable going alone. If you could find the time, I'd be delighted to have your company. Let me know in a few days. No pressure."

* * *

Kreyna drove fast. It was late and she had to drop Morwenna at her house in Belmore Gardens, a few streets away from home.

Morwenna rummaged in her handbag. "A skinny guy in a blue suit snuck up behind me in the bathroom—fair scared me silly. He looked somewhere between thirty-five and a facelift— talk about creepy. My keys are here somewhere."

"That'll be Bryce. The husband."

"Yeah? They say that looks don't count for much, there goes your proof. You can stop looking, found them. Speaking of looks, did I catch our hostess looking meaningfully into your eyes? And what about Dr. Declan? Talk about bees around a honeypot. You had it all happening for you tonight, sweetie. You were smokin'."

"You what? What *are* you on about?" Kreyna slowed for a police radar trap set up on the median strip, waiting to clock lead-footed Canberrans. She retaliated. "Who disappeared midevening, hmm?"

Morwenna feigned coyness. "Helios invited me to the Hellenic Club for a glass of *metaxa retsina* and to meet his mother who runs one of the restaurants. She was nice to me—very generous and sweet. Helios showed me a few Greek dances. We—I had a lovely time."

"Sounds uncharacteristically chaste. Nothing else going on?"

Morwenna sat up straight and turned to Kreyna. "He did plant one on me in the driveway after he'd driven me back. Would you believe it was a magical moment?" When Kreyna looked askance, Morwenna continued. "Truly, he's different. This time is different. I've got a good feeling about him."

Kreyna pulled up outside Morwenna's house. "Yes, but did you get his number?"

"Does the pope wear a silly hat?"

"By the way, Frances asked me to go with her to Melbourne to watch the Cup in the horseflesh. She said she could get us a cut-price diplomatic airfare, up and back, and we could spend the day swanking about at Flemington. I'm thinking about it."

"You heard it here first." Morwenna shut the door with a satisfying thud.

* * *

Alarm bells jangled in Kreyna's head. She lit a candle and stared at Oma's image smiling back at her out of the photo. When they'd first met, something about Frances had stirred a memory of sound like the tune of a merry-go-round. She hadn't been able to figure it out, but Morwenna's remark had refreshed the memory. Now, she found a hint of it in Oma's smiling eyes—the sound of laughter.

From the bottom drawer of her desk, she pulled out an exercise book in which she recorded readings and dreams. She flicked back through the pages and stopped at an entry in March, over six months ago.

A woman laughing. Mellifluous voice. Bottomless eyes green. Lips on knuckles. Joy bubbles rising, blood singing. Name like answers.

Frances?

* * *

Eadie's house in Hughes was a red brick, three-bedroom box originally owned by the local government and sold off to its tenants. Bearded irises, ideally suited to the hot and dry Canberra summer, grew thickly along both edges of the dilapidated concrete path that led to the front porch. The irises were in full flower and formed a riotous pastiche of violet, blue, crimson, yellow and white.

Kreyna shaded her eyes from the glaring spring sun and waved at Eadie standing in the open doorway. The elderly lady had long battled Type 2 diabetes—her calves below the hem of the faded floral dress were puffy and inflamed. She rested awkwardly on a walking stick, steadying her heavy, misshapen frame with difficulty.

"You shouldn't have come out to meet me, Eadie. It's too hot out here." Kreyna strode up the path.

"I needed to move—fed up with sitting." With a forefinger, Eadie wiped sweat from under the frame of her glasses and leaned forward to peck Kreyna's cheek. "Let's talk in the conservatory where it's cool. Alf's making a cup of Earl Grey for us before he heads off to lawn bowls."

Eadie's face lit up when Alf appeared with a tray bearing two brimming Royal Albert cups and saucers—they kept the best china for visitors. Eadie leaned back in her recliner rocker, lifting one leg after the other up onto a brown, vinyl ottoman.

"It's been a long time between brews, m'lass." Eadie blew across the surface of the tea and took a big gulp. "But that's no matter. I'm right chuffed to see you, especially since I might be of use."

Above Eadie's chair, a drawing of an American Indian dominated the wall. Beside a depiction of a haloed Jesus Christ hung a photo of the guru, Sai Baba. Beneath him, more obscure spiritual pictures were pinned in a random collage.

Eadie fixed her watery blue eyes on her young visitor. "Hellfire, you resemble your grandmother all the more, now you're fully grown. Do you keep in touch?"

The bergamot flavor in the tea seeped sweetly throughout Kreyna's mouth. "In dreams. I can feel her better in the evening. More frequently of late, though she confuses me and often I can't make any sense of the things she says. But that's not the reason I'm here…"

"Hold it right there, lovie. Pass me that stable table. It's got me pen and paper ready to go. You be still and quiet. We'll see what comes through, shall we?"

Eyes narrowed to slits, Eadie rocked her head back and forth, side to side, tracing random patterns and stopping briefly to write and continue on. Kreyna stilled her thoughts and focused on the swirling energies in the room—peaceful warmth permeated her entire body. Time cruised to a standstill, measured only by Eadie's wrist scuffing paper. In reality, ten minutes passed, marked only by a blowfly buzzing from window to window, seeking to escape.

"Some of it's crystal clear and some of it's a right fuddle," Eadie tsked to herself. She sat back and examined Kreyna. "You're a fool for love, which surprises me. However, if one's going to be a fool for anything, it might as well be love. God knows, there are far less worthy subjects. What's more, you expect a lot from your lovers, but you give a lot."

"Lovers plural?"

Eadie glanced down at her notes. "Aye, a veritable queue. They're standing in line and sorting one from the other is a tricky business. I can see one's a straight talker, despite the emotional baggage. Then there's a pair of jokers, both guilty of romancing the truth. It's a wonder either of them can lie straight in bed, there's so much subterfuge."

She picked up the writing pad and peered at it. "There's danger here, lass. Not only is your heart at risk, but there's threat to you physically."

Kreyna's skin chilled. Could Robert's violence escalate beyond his tenuous control?

Eadie removed her glasses and rubbed her face vigorously. "There's death around you and by that I mean bloody murder." She lurched to her feet and shuffled about the room, walking stick in one hand, writing pad in the other. "What have you gotten yourself into, young 'un? Beggar me, if brains were currants you'd be a plain teacake. This line of work you're pursuing, this career with a capital 'C'—happy in your work, are you?"

"Happiness is not pertinent to the work I do. I'm proud to be part of an organization that keeps our country safe. And I'm training to be the best that I can be and developing my skill into a lasting expertise. Is there anything wrong with that?"

"Nothing, if that was all that's going on. What I'm getting is, you're being treated like a mushroom—kept in the dark and fed a load of."

Kreyna flinched at the septuagenarian's candid speech. "But I'm working within the Filigrane and trained experts are guiding me. Surely, I'm protected?"

"The danger comes not from the Filigrane, but from those manipulating you to their own ends. There are two people involved, maybe more. Please reconsider your choices."

"I don't know about all that, Eadie, it doesn't make any sense. I trust everyone I work with—well, almost everyone. But tell me about these so-called lovers."

Eadie sat down with a thump and fussed with her swollen legs until she was comfortable. "The one who breaks your heart does so for all the wrong reasons, believing them to be right. It's a mess of deceit, ulterior motives and espionage—an ugly agenda driven by secret authorities, conflicting priorities, jealousy and good old-fashioned lust!"

Eadie fell silent, her gaze flicking over her own spidery writing. "And yet..." Surprise crept across her face, offering a glimpse of how pretty she must have looked as a young woman. For the first time since beginning the reading, she smiled. "There is love between you—rock solid, indestructible love that has stood the test of millennia." She looked over her spectacles at Kreyna. "In a lifetime we have opportunities, but not all opportunities are possibilities, even for souls as deeply connected as you two. Put simply, it may not eventuate this time round."

"Definitely not this time, I'd say." Fatigue mixed with information overload got the better of Kreyna. "We had our chance and it didn't work out. In fact, he's the reason I came to see you. We've broken up, but he continues to harass me psychically and I have to find a way to block him."

"Him?" Eadie blinked. "Oh no, you soft lass—I speak of a woman."

* * *

On the way home and urgently in need of an appropriate environment for some serious thinking, Kreyna took a detour at Red Hill roundabout and onto a steep, narrow road that climbed through grassland peppered with native trees and shrubs. A yellow, diamond-shaped traffic sign warned of kangaroos, notorious for taking fright and jumping in front of passing cars— at dusk, usually.

At the summit, the car crawled into a spacious, gravel parking lot. Ahead, the Carousel Restaurant offered magnificent three hundred and sixty degree views over the city. Kreyna locked up and walked to the lookout point, grateful for a light breeze that relieved the late spring heat.

A shimmering haze made everything wobble. Atop Black Mountain, the telecommunications tower lorded it over the city. To the north, Parliament House dominated the parliamentary triangle with its plethora of offices and national institutions. Except for the Lakeside Hotel, all the buildings were less than six stories high.

Kreyna inhaled the distinctive scent of eucalyptus coming from the dense swath of gum trees descending the hill. A hint of smoke made her look for and find its source. To the west and in the far distance, the ACT Parks and Conservation people were burning off grassland as a firebreak, in preparation for the scorching summer ahead.

Around her, cicadas practiced their love songs, accompanied by courting pink and gray galahs, screeching and bobbing their heads in the trees below Kreyna. She loved the conundrum that was Canberra: on the surface, a haven for highly paid, well-educated, liberal-minded public servants; beneath, functioning as the heart chakra for the entire continent. In the presence of this city, she found solace.

Although she'd steered Eadie's focus away from her working life, the suggestion that she was being manipulated and lied to supported her own growing unease. Only yesterday, Adrian had mooted that she and Robert might be sent back to Europe, most likely Antwerp. To what end was unclear. They had already interviewed the prime suspects. What was to be gained by a repeat visit? A foreboding disquiet persisted.

Eadie had said Robert would have easy psychic access until she became involved with someone else. Even then, if a new connection was neither deep nor durable, in all probability he would always have access. Dread dragged at her stomach and prickled sweat under her arms. An error uncorrected becomes a mistake. No way to correct this one—get used to it.

What of her friendship with Frances? The Englishwoman seemed sincere, friendly, warm and interesting. Certainly, she was easy on the eye but also had an attractive personality to which Kreyna felt drawn. Sure, she held shadows—secrets and regrets, probably. Doesn't everyone? But was there more to it than friendship, as Morwenna had also implied?

Relationships happen between people, irrespective of gender—what did it matter? Not that she'd been down that road—well, not exactly. Did it count that she made out with Sandra at the school dance when she was thirteen? What about her reluctance to report her uncommon crush in the psychological profile section of her job application? It would have looked worse if she hadn't mentioned it and one of her relatives did, when asked. ASIO profilers had interviewed all her family and friends, as a matter of course.

Would a British diplomat's wife and mother of two young children pursue a same-sex affair with a single, Australian woman? Extremely unlikely, given the potentially hazardous consequences for Frances. It would be social suicide in the diplomatic community—instant ruination by gossip—fatal to the reputation.

It was a waste of time worrying about it because the whole notion was totally ludicrous. Obviously, Eadie was drawing too long a bow. Any psychic medium was doing remarkably well to achieve more than fifty percent accuracy. But which fifty percent?

It had been Morwenna's idea to consult Eadie. Kreyna wished she could sound her out, given what she'd just been told. But Morwenna was spending every spare moment with Helios with whom she was severely smitten. Nothing else for it—she would have to work things out without bothering her lovesick friend.

CHAPTER EIGHT

The first race train left Flinders Street Station at 8:15 a.m. Kreyna and Frances caught the 10:45 a.m., having taken a taxi from Tullamarine airport to the Grand Hyatt on Collins Street in the center of Melbourne. There, they'd unpacked and frocked up for a lavish champagne breakfast with other race-goers. Afterward, they made their way to the station.

In the packed carriage, Kreyna hugged an incongruously large carry bag. Rain lashed the windows all the way to Flemington where the Melbourne Cup race was scheduled to start just after 3:00 p.m.

Disembarked from the train, they picked their way across open ground to the nearest marquee. Frances's strappy shoes were muddied and saturated in minutes, but a flute of Bollinger and two hot roast beef focaccia fingers made the trip worthwhile.

Despite the abysmal weather, the crowd was enthusiastic and decked out in all manner of race-going finery. Outrageous hats and haute couture frocks were in vogue. A trio of handsome young men caught the eye in black top hats, bright white dress suits and black gumboots. Kreyna and Frances stood agog when a burly bloke pranced by wearing a pink tulle tutu and Blundstone steel-capped boots. A pinkie ring flashed a large diamond that matched his bejeweled Cartier watch. He twirled a gold wand in their startled faces and said, "Vanish!" in a simpering falsetto. To his immense satisfaction, they burst into laughter. Blowing kisses from ruby red lips, he disappeared into the throng.

Still chuckling, Kreyna said, "I thought it was just a rumor that the Cup's a daytime Mardi Gras for heterosexuals—well, mostly."

Cruising from marquee to marquee, the two women downed more fizz and savories, preferring to ignore the preliminary races in favor of people watching. Unofficially, they found seats at the back of an official marquee. Nobody seemed to care who they were.

Nearby, an Asian family had assumed ownership of a flotilla of chairs. From grandparents to teenagers and small children, they bickered loudly over their favorites and on which horses to place bets. Twin girls, aged about six years old and wearing matching bright yellow dresses, grinned impishly at them over the chair backs. Frances waved and they waved in return, giggling and batting short, black eyelashes.

"You must miss your children."

Frances was mute. She wiped her eyes with the back of her hand and gave a short laugh. "Sorry. I'm a mite wussy when it comes to my babies. I try not to think about them too much. Breaks my heart."

"I guess it's not forever."

"Feels like forever, I assure you. I keep telling myself it's best for them. Putting them in boarding school when we're overseas. They have consistent care and education. Bryce—we decided it would be too much to drag them all over the globe. Some countries simply aren't safe."

Frances searched for a tissue. "Do you want children at all?"

Kreyna sipped from her champagne flute, wishing it were hot coffee. "I haven't given it much thought, but yes. Although finding the right sperm donor is a challenge."

"Well, my husband's the perfect provider. I'm most fortunate."

"Is that all he is?"

Frances drew a sharp breath and Kreyna immediately regretted her tactless fishing.

Frances replied, "When I was a teenager, I yearned for children of my own. My parents divorced when I was eleven and my brother Mike, only seven. We didn't see much of my father. He began a new family. To make matters worse, our stepfather was a sleazy pig."

"Did he do something...?"

"Nothing overt—immature pestering, you might say. For instance, in summer he would parade about in his underpants with the tip of his penis poking out. Amusing and titillating for him, alone. Mother defended him constantly and put up with his behavior because he was very generous. She could have had anything she wanted, within reason. He was quite senior in the Foreign Service. When I was studying at Cambridge, he got me a part-time clerical job in his office where I met Bryce. I couldn't get away from home quick enough."

Frances shivered, all limbs crossed tightly. With an equal challenge in her eyes, she returned Kreyna's gaze. "Bryce was someone going somewhere fast. I found that compelling."

Silence stretched between them. Finally, Kreyna said, "Fair enough."

The public address system announced scratching after scratching when the incessant rain took its toll of equine hopefuls. Incoming helicopters increasingly droned *thunka-thunka-thunka* overhead—parking lots closed, having dissolved into dangerous quagmires.

"Would you prefer to be comfortable rather than fashionable?" Kreyna asked.

"I'm chilled to the bone. Not much one can do about it. Pointless complaining. I don't want to miss the race or I'd say let's crack on and go."

Kreyna hoisted her carry bag onto her lap and pulled out a pair of silver basketball boots and a white parachute-silk bomber jacket emblazoned with Canberra Capitals. She waved the boots at Frances. "These should be about the right size."

"You're a hero!" Frances headed for the nearest Portaloo with the race guide held above her head for meager shelter.

Kreyna looked down at her shot silk, sea-green slacks and black, Cuban-heeled boots, glad she'd made a last-minute dash up to the hotel room to change out of her navy dress and court shoes. She picked at the remains of a plate of Singapore noodles and peered out at her fellow race-goers. What were she and Frances doing here? What was anyone doing here, in fact? It was cold, wet and miserable, yet the crowd grew louder and more animated, thanks to a combination of copious amounts of bubbly and feverish anticipation as the time for the main race approached.

Frances dashed back into the marquee, basketball boots flashing. Kreyna clapped a hand over her laughing mouth. "How fetching, Mrs. Parrey." Frances feinted at her with the racing guide and flopped down, shaking droplets everywhere.

"Bloody hell!" Frances brushed down her jacket. "This race had better be good. A few winnings could assuage the pain of buying a new pair of shoes. Any hot tips?"

"As luck would have it, we have some possible winners, courtesy of the lovely Morwenna Brodribb. Having a tame astrologer has its uses, I can attest to that. The thing of it is, she's preoccupied at the moment so we're lucky to get any sense out of her. She drew an event chart for the race and used numerology, as well. How she came up with a couple of likely champions is beyond me, but there's an Irish horse called Vintage Crop and a young galloper named Nothin' Leica Dane in the running. She reckons either or both are worth a punt. You might prefer the favorite, Double Trigger, who's travelled all the way from Yorkshire. Feeling patriotic?"

Frances considered the racing guide. "Irish, Danish, Danish, Irish. I'll go for Irish if you're happy with Danish. Might put a few pence on the Yorkshire lad. The odds will be low, I should think. Not that I know much about horse racing."

She closed the booklet and studied Kreyna, an ironic smile curling her lips. "You Aussies are balmy. You stand around in a downpour, done up to the nines. And wait for a few nags to chase another nag across a sodden paddock. Crazy or possessed of a great sense of fun—I suspect the latter. I had to come and see for myself. I'm going to miss this country. And a few special people."

Kreyna dropped her gaze from a look too long and said, "If we want to place a bet, now's the time."

Once inside the main betting ring, they stood in one of many queues and discussed horses and bets with complete strangers as if they were old friends exchanging intimate counsel. By the time they got to the counter, Frances had been talked out of backing the Yorkshire horse. But she changed her mind again and bet five dollars each way on him for a win or a place. In the end, they both put ten dollars on Vintage Crop and Nothin' Leica Dane for a place.

"It sounds odd, but the colors feel wrong." Kreyna checked the racing guide again, comparing the jockeys' silks. "I keep seeing pink and blue out of the corner of my eye. It could mean the winning horse is a gelding. Never mind—too late now."

* * *

Running in fifth-last place and twelve hundred yards from the winning post, Damien Oliver eased the elegant chestnut wider and wider, passing horse after horse. Mud sprayed and splattered thick and fast, obliterating Damien's freckled cheeks and dulling the pink and blue of his shirt. Oblivious to the loudspeakers belting out a breathless commentary and the yells of the crowd building as they approached the home turn, the four-year-old with a mighty pump of a heart swooped down the heavy track past the last three contenders. Courage and class incarnate, Doriemus streaked into the lead and won the 1995 Melbourne Cup by a widening four lengths, ahead of Nothin' Leica Dane in second place, with Vintage Crop running a valiant third. Double Trigger turned up eventually, in seventeenth place.

* * *

They were making for the racecourse's turnstile, lagging behind a large crowd with the same objective. Three women, just ahead, all wore plastic bags over their sandals in a futile effort to keep out the mud.

"A gelding with pink and blue silks." Frances spied Kreyna through a small gap between her thumb and forefinger. "You could have spoken up a mite sooner, don't you think? I would have saved myself a whole ten dollars."

"Deciphering what I'm getting is no easy task at the best of times," Kreyna protested. "With thousands of people milling around, it's almost impossible. Anyway, we both won nearly a hundred each—not bad for a day's play. All the kudos are due to Morwenna for giving us the heads-up."

Over to the left, raised voices and muffled curses drew their attention. A large man dressed in a khaki Hypercolor tee under a gray Armani suit jacket pushed his way across the flow of the crowd. His mumbled apologies when an ingratiating smile drew only partial cooperation. People were wet and tired, and in no mood to be jostled. Coming closer, he glanced at Kreyna and Frances, his gaze flicking from one to the other. He stopped in front of them and grinned, eyebrows doing a jig that would have put Groucho Marx to shame.

"Ladies! I think we've met already. Any success on the gee-gees?" A hint of red lipstick on his generous mouth told a tale, confirmed when he drew a gold wand from a pocket and twirled it at them.

"The Melbourne Cup Fairy, I presume? Or have you lost your magic?" Kreyna said. There was something reassuringly familiar about this man, but it eluded her.

People pushed roughly past the threesome, now blocking the way. "Nearly froze and cracked my family jewels in that little pink number—it's perishing out here. Are you two heading back to the city?"

When they nodded, he continued, "May I offer a lift in my chopper? It's waiting now. That's why I'm trying to get over there." He stood on tiptoe, still wearing the Blunnies, and gestured way over to their right where the helipad was located.

Frances exchanged a querying look with Kreyna who nodded. "Yes, that would wonderful."

The helicopter rose into the steadily drizzling low cloud and headed for the city. Their benefactor shouted a few words at them—he gave up when they shook their heads uncomprehendingly. In a matter of minutes, they descended onto a helipad moored on the Yarra River, between King's and Spencer bridges in Melbourne's central business district. A tall, slim, fair-haired man waited under a rainbow umbrella. The three of them tailgated each other up the gangplank into Batman Park where the two men touched each other on the shoulder and exchanged a few sentences before turning to Kreyna and Frances.

"May I introduce my partner, Neil Beckridge? And myself, of course. I'm Artimus Hansen. Please call me Arty, everyone does."

They shook hands and exchanged pleasantries, enjoying a momentary respite from the rain. Neil, who looked suspiciously like an accountant, remained silent while Arty animatedly chatted with Kreyna and Frances about Flemington, the big race and how well they'd done in the betting. He interrupted Arty with a touch to the forearm.

"Perhaps the girls would like to join us for dinner?"

Arty grinned and said, "Great idea! Listen, we've reserved a large table at Harvey's Restaurant in South Yarra for seven tonight. It's top-notch nosh, please come."

"We're booked on a nine o'clock flight back to Canberra," Frances said.

Neil stepped forward. "I'll think you'll find there's a raft of cancellations this evening. If I were you, I'd check with the airline. It could prove optimistic to assume they're going to get off the ground in this weather."

"In that case, we'd best find out if the Grand Hyatt can accommodate us overnight." Frances spoke directly to Kreyna. "It's either there or we have to find an alternative. Is it okay if we just turn up? We may or may not make it."

"Not a problem," Arty said. "There'll be champagne—it's my birthday."

* * *

Frances sat across from Kreyna and Neil. Three other couples occupied the other end of the table where Arty was being a good host by mingling and gossiping.

Kreyna said, "We had to move to the Langham. You wouldn't believe how camp it is—marble bathrooms, cascading fountains, grand staircase—even chandeliers. The full catastrophe—I love it. And it's right on the Yarra with great views of the city and river."

They were coming to the end of their meal. The champagne was running low—everyone had eaten too much and felt the worse for it. Kreyna looked forward to a strong coffee. Without warning, the lights dimmed and the restaurant hushed. A waitress appeared bearing a towering pavlova that twinkled with lit sparklers. Arty clapped and roared with laughter, then covered his face with his hands and cringed with mild embarrassment. Obligingly, his friends chanted Happy Birthday until he turned beet red. Neil grabbed Arty and bent him back to plant a firm kiss on his compliant mouth. The surrounding diners wolf-whistled and cheered.

Kreyna sipped her coffee. Frances pushed a mound of pavlova around a dessert plate. She looked up to see Kreyna pointing, indicating a stray blob of cream at the corner of Frances's mouth. Simultaneously, they licked their lips until Frances dislodged the recalcitrant cream, running her tongue along her teeth. Kreyna grinned and Frances met her gaze, hypnotic black eyes glittering in the dimly lit restaurant.

Above Frances's right shoulder, a point of light expanded and burst like a tiny star. Smile fading, Kreyna's stomach did a somersault—Frances held her intense look. Seconds ticked by before Kreyna remembered to breathe.

"Have you two been together long?" Neil wanted to chat over the passion fruit-coated kiwifruit and meringue dessert.

Kreyna said, "I'm sorry?" Frances admired the decor.

Neil looked from one to the other. "Whoops, my mistake." Too briskly, he rubbed pale, elegant fingers on a napkin. "Did you enjoy the meal?"

Kreyna mustered coherent thought. "Yes, it's been a pleasure. You're both very generous to invite complete strangers to such a special occasion. Personally, it's made my day because it's my birthday, too."

"No! That's amazing—congratulations!"

Neil leaned over and gave her a peck on the cheek and a stiff hug across the shoulders. "I'm so pleased we invited you. How perfect!"

He called Arty over and told him. After some discussion, Arty and Kreyna surmised they were born on exactly the same day in the same year, albeit hundreds of miles apart.

Arty said, "We're practically astro-twins—too cosmic! When I first saw you, I knew we'd be friends. It's kismet, or something. We'll have to stay in touch."

Later, through the back window of the taxi, the two still immaculately dressed men waved wistfully, their figures fast receding. They might pursue the friendship. Or not. Sad and more than a little confused, Kreyna was about as comfortable as a sprat in the Simpson Desert.

"I wanted to thank you for coming down with me. Especially on your birthday, I mean." Frances's smile didn't extend to her eyes. "I hope you didn't feel obliged in any way."

Kreyna shook her head. "Not at all. I only do what I don't want to do under extreme duress. My parents are up in Cairns visiting my sister and her family, so it would have been a solitary day in Canberra. It's been different, particularly meeting my astro-twin and his trusty sidekick. Aren't they a riot?"

In silence, Frances surveyed the brightly lit buildings flashing past.

At the Langham Hotel, the women padded along a deeply carpeted corridor to their room. A queen bed and two singles were squeezed into the space, sumptuously decorated to within an inch of kitsch. Kreyna would have preferred to be alone to meditate. Or at least to have some privacy to sort the mess of thoughts and feelings storming around inside. She turned the television on low volume and opted for a scorching hot shower instead.

When Kreyna came back from the bathroom, Frances closed a paperback and took her turn. Since they were both ignoring the proverbial elephant in the room, polite, studied disinterest seemed an appropriate tactic. So be it.

* * *

The digital alarm clock showed 1:14 in the morning. Kreyna was still awake, tossing and turning fitfully. She had to be up at 5:30 a.m. to catch the red-eye flight home to Canberra. Some fool had screwed a smoke alarm on the ceiling directly overhead—its flashing red light distracted and annoyed incessantly. Six feet away in the queen bed, a sleeping figure was a gray blur in the gloom. Kreyna turned over, slowed her metabolism through sheer effort of will and began counting seeds in an imaginary sunflower. Sleep now.

* * *

"Christ!"

Kreyna woke up with a start and searched for the source of the anguished yell.

"Christ! Oh, Christ! Christ!"

Kreyna bolted out and scrambled across the queen bed, reaching for the rocking, curled-up body, now moaning and sobbing loudly.

"Are you okay? What's the matter? What's happening?"

Frances gasped, "Dear God, it was horrible. Turn a light on, will you?"

Kreyna fumbled for the bedside light switch and sat back. Frances struggled to her knees, still hunched over, clutching herself.

"Rape. I feel like I've been raped—assaulted—something like that. In my sleep."

She scanned the room, peering into the shadows, before setting a tearful gaze on Kreyna. "How is it possible? There's no one here. No one's been in here except us, have they? You would have seen or heard something, wouldn't you? Of course you would. This is balmy. Christ, it hurts!"

Kreyna's stomach lurched as a nasty suspicion grew into an ugly certainty. "Any idea what he looked like? Any impression, at all?"

Frances shook her head and rubbed her lower abdomen, tears beginning to dry on her cheeks. Briefly, she stopped and looked at Kreyna. "He smelled revolting, though—grass and too much aftershave."

Kreyna clenched her teeth and shut her eyes for a moment. "I'm sorry but I think I know who, or rather, what it was. And it's happened because I'm here. I'm very sorry, this is entirely my fault."

Frances took some tissues from a box on the bedside table and blew her nose. "I don't see how…"

Kreyna stumbled over her words. "You weren't actually raped, just psychically."

"Tell that to my nether regions. Feels like I've given birth again. He was big."

"I think it was Robert, my ex. He has a habit of seeking me out, wherever I might be, and—well, he must have mistaken you for me."

"What do you mean, seeking you out? In some way that's not physical?"

"Oh, it's physical all right. You feel everything, just can't grasp anything. Not unless you're very talented and highly trained like him."

Frances took a long look at Kreyna. "I think I need a stiff drink. Failing that, a cup of tea."

Kreyna flicked another light switch and plugged in a jug. She found the tea bags and put one in each cup. How could Robert have mistaken Frances for her? Had their energies become entwined because of their growing closeness? Perhaps he made no mistake at all.

Frances gulped tea and ran a hand through her hair, emerald and diamonds catching the light. "Is he always so brutal?"

"No," Kreyna whispered. "No, he takes—took pride in being a considerate lover. Outside the bedroom is another story."

"I see. Ouch, I'm rubbed raw. I haven't any painkillers, do you?"

"No, I'm sorry. I avoid drugs of any kind. Would you like me to call the night manager?"

Frances shook her head and rearranged herself, wincing. "What did you mean by highly trained?"

"Did I say that?" Kreyna put down her cup with a clatter. "I think he did a few New Age courses. Something about developing your psychic powers, going on a vision quest or deep male bonding—you know the sort of thing."

"Have you thought to develop your own gift?"

"Nup. So, may I help? I mean, what I can do is take pain away, using energy through my hands." When Frances looked doubtful, she continued, "This comes naturally to me, no training necessary."

"Do I do anything?"

"No, just try to relax while I focus."

Sitting on the edge of the bed, Kreyna carefully folded back the covers over Frances's pajama-clad abdomen. She closed her eyes and powered down her heart rate. Through her crown chakra, she drew a healing pink light that dropped to spin around her throat and heart chakras, and out through the hands. Energy surged through her palms and radiated like a furnace into Frances, a few inches below. Around her, the Filigrane gathered strength and channeled through healing energy. Humbly, she gave thanks for its assistance.

Frances reached up and pressed Kreyna's hands down to rest on her stomach. Shocks ricocheted back and forth as warm flesh pulsed with life, disrupting Kreyna's concentration. With a ridiculous amount of effort, she refocused, pouring through soothing energy.

Obviously relieved, Frances said, "You're right, it does help. Thank you."

* * *

Was it nearly three o'clock, already? Kreyna studied the sleeping woman. To the best of her ability, she'd enveloped Frances in a protective, pure white light. But she couldn't protect her from Robert, not if he was jealous. His rage could carry terrible force, beyond anything she believed herself able to muster as protection. Contrary to the romantic theory, she didn't believe for a second the saying, love conquers all. From experience, hate fueled by anger was the most powerful force, and Robert could be ruthless.

Had he psychically raped Frances? If so, she'd become a target only by association. Responsibility weighed heavily. It was time to guard the heart, especially its new occupant.

* * *

The aircraft approached Canberra airport on a flight path that curved low around Mount Ainslie. Heat rising from the searing land below created unpleasant turbulence, ensuring a white-knuckle ride to the tarmac. Kreyna had a meeting scheduled with Pankaj at ten a.m. For what reason, she chose not to ponder—the woman sitting next to her occupied her now.

She had tried to bury herself in an article about Angelina Jolie in *Who* magazine, but had been distracted by the animated conversation between Frances and the air steward who had served them beverages after breakfast. Earlier, Frances had commented on the steward's London accent, belying her Indian heritage. The woman had filled their coffee cups and continued down the aisle, promising to return. Now, they chatted about all things familiar only to them.

Kreyna appraised the steward, an unaffected young woman who seemed oblivious to her preternatural beauty. She stood in the aisle looking down on Frances, mouth flashing astonishing white teeth and eyes fluttering impossibly long, lustrous black lashes. Then she excused herself and hurried off down the aisle, not before she'd touched Frances's arm with lingering warmth. Frances smoothed the nape of her neck and gazed after the disappearing figure.

An ugly beast uncoiled from deep within Kreyna's belly and emerged through her throat. "Do you think she knows?"

"Excuse me?" Coloring, Frances cast a narrowed gaze at Kreyna. "Knows what?"

Kreyna flicked through the magazine's pages. "Oh, you know—that you just can't help yourself."

Frances swiveled in her seat, presenting folded arms and languidly crossed legs in Kreyna's direction. With the shadow of a smile, she examined Kreyna from under raised eyebrows.

"What?" It was Kreyna's turn. When no reply came, she looked up from the blurring pages. The green eyes seemed grayer today. With an audible exhalation, Frances reached out, clasped Kreyna's hand only briefly and straightened in her seat, expression impenetrable.

The sudden touch set Kreyna's heart racing and started an ache in her chest that she couldn't fathom. The beast coiled back into its lair, but remained alert. Watching.

* * *

It wasn't Kreyna's nature to skirt around problems. She preferred hazards out in the open where she could see them. Study and analysis gave insight. Coupled with formidable instinct, everything could be understood. Couldn't it?

All her adult life, she'd maintained her self-control, even when strongly attracted to someone. She had always appeared cool and calm. Since yesterday, she was anything but. Caught off guard by Frances's lingering smile, she would falter, lose her train of thought or need to take a steadying breath. The emotions that buffeted her were not gentle waves of pleasantness, no. They were king tides—giant rushing walls of compulsion that threatened to drown, overwhelm and shock. She was swept along, barely in control, unable to quell an attraction that resisted every attempt at reason.

Feelings were incomprehensible, illogical and could be baseless. They should be subordinate to reason, said the scientist within. And the intuitive smiled enigmatically. Like giant arrow-shaped neon signs, repeated incidents had pointed to Frances—enough hints to ensure even the most naive intuitive would notice. Kreyna was anything but naive. If her Sentinels were confident, adamant even, why was she so uneasy?

She knew zip about this woman—how on earth could she justify these feelings? Sure, Frances made her laugh with an irreverent, earthy humor. She was smart, quick-witted and astute. They shared similar tastes in beauty and pleasure, plus an easy sense of co-conspirator in the face of petty mindedness. She was a handsome, feisty yet elegant and charming woman. Aside from a shadowy sense of untold indiscretions, what was there not to like about Frances?

Kreyna had been innocently in love with Robert and thrilled when he wanted to be with her. She'd put him on a pedestal, certain he was everything she could ever want. She had been slow to notice when he wasn't exactly that. Even so, it wasn't his fault she hadn't wanted to see his nasty side. But she'd grown up since, surely?

What did Frances think and feel about her? Frances looked at a person properly, noticing expression, mouth, hands and bodily movement. She held one's gaze as few people do, as if she were seeing for the first time, every time. She seemed to really like Kreyna. Meaning what? Anything more than *liking* was pure conjecture.

But for Kreyna the urge to reach out and touch was increasingly hard to control. That burning compulsion defied every attempt to make sense of the insensible. If she were dead straight with herself, what she felt was more than a little frightening. She feared for her heart.

Don't be melodramatic because speculation is pointless. Frances would be gone in a matter of weeks. Make the most of the remaining time. Then build a bridge and get over it, as Morwenna would say.

CHAPTER NINE

Pankaj came around the desk and perched on its edge, ankles crossed and facing Kreyna. "What do you know about Project Stargate?"

"I heard it's being shut down by the CIA, at least that's what's on the grapevine. It's very similar to our own setup, isn't it?"

"Very good—you're correct. The project's apparent termination is political in origin, based on the extraordinary notion that remote surveillance is irreligious. The Republicans controlling House spending have taken exception and withdrawn funding."

"Apparent termination—do you mean it's going to continue?"

He strode back around the desk and sat, fingers steepled and tapping his mustache. With the file open in front of him, he leaned forward. "How would you like to spend some time in Fort Meade, Maryland?"

"But I thought my promotion was still pending?"

He gave a lopsided smile. "It's merely a formality. You're our star trainee, Kreyna. While you will be sorely missed, for ASIO it will be a source of considerable prestige and goodwill to have you further your training with the US military. Perhaps you can teach *them* a thing or two."

He sat back and laced his fingers behind his head. "Of course, your transfer will be highly confidential—only your closest relatives may know. You will receive an allowance for travel, accommodation, distance living, etcetera, adding up to a six-figure sum and very much worth your while. It will be a great start in life for your young self, and a feather in *all* our caps."

Kreyna tightened her lips, picked lint off her navy skirt and folded her arms, fists tightly closed. "This is news to me. When am I supposed to go?"

Pankaj rocked his head from side to side and rubbed his palms together. "You will commence operations with the Americans in the new year. Even more exciting, you will receive extensive training in non-local perturbation. Can you imagine how valuable you will be as a remote viewer with telekinetic ability? This is world-class, cutting-edge expertise." He slapped the desk. "Kreyna, I envy you this opportunity. If I were starting out—"

Kreyna interrupted, "How much time do I have to decide?"

He sat stock still and stared at her. "I don't think you understand. This is a posting. As a graduate ASIO operative, you are under orders. You are going, decision made."

"Who will be my direct superiors and what redress will I have if there are problems?"

"Problems? What nonsense is this? Obviously, while you're based in the States, the Americans will control your assignments. You'll be part of a unit highly trained in the remote viewing of key military targets. I'm sure your talent and skill will add tremendously to its success. Both Australia and the US stand to benefit from the intelligence you gather."

Someone knocked on the door. His gaze locked firmly on Kreyna, Pankaj snapped, "Enter."

The clerk kept his head down and handed over a sealed envelope. "Encrypted fax, Dr. Corea. Urgent, sir." The door closed with a soft click.

Eyes wide and darting, Pankaj smoothed his lush, graying mustache down the corners of his mouth.

"*Tatti!*" He swore in his native Hindi, his expression grim. "Oh no—this is very bad. Remember Piet Van Whalen in Rotterdam? He's been shot dead."

Kreyna jumped up and began to read over his shoulder. Pankaj traced lines of text with a finger. "A Walther P5 is the suspected weapon. I believe that particular gun is standard issue for Belgian police."

"Victor Deprez." She blurted the name, thoughts racing. It had been inevitable. Because her boss Adrian Frode had believed Robert instead of her, Deprez had not been charged—released under surveillance, yes, but a free agent—free to dispose of the nervous guy with the drug habit. Bile rose in her throat and she covered her mouth.

Pankaj scratched the back of his neck. "Possibly."

"Possibly? Almost certainly." Her voice rose. "Damn Adrian! And damn Robert! If they'd listened instead of trying to shoot me down in flames, that poor man would be still alive."

She paced and stopped to grip the back of a chair. "What's the point in me doing this job if they won't trust my judgment? Now someone's dead. And it's my fault for not making those two listen."

"The house is on fire, too late to dig a well. You've been proven correct, at least." Pankaj gave a slight shrug. "But the lasting lesson is you must learn to assert yourself with confidence and not get involved with fellow operatives. Perhaps Robert would have supported your conclusions if you had not had a failed relationship with him. This should never have happened."

Kreyna's face was in her hands. She shook her head and looked at him. "It's a good thing I won't be in the country much longer. That should avert further embarrassment for you."

* * *

Oma's gnarled fingers stroked the young woman's cheek. "Lovely meisje, it's not so tragic, not as bad as you think. I keep you safe. As does Frans who loves you, come to protect you in the flesh. Everything will come at the right time."

The phone rang. Any other day Kreyna would have bolted out of bed instantly. This Sunday morning, she let it go through to the answering machine, busy as she was with her grandmother on another plane of existence. Who the hell's Frans when he's at home, anyway?

Her heart was heavy. Dismay and a creeping dread had her bury herself under the coverlet trying, if not to sleep, at least to doze and rest. She had *not* signed up for working in the States, particularly as a political pawn of both governments.

The answering machine beeped and a distant voice left a short message—Morwenna, perhaps? Kreyna had been leaving urgent messages with her friend for days, entreaties that had met with thundering silence, thus far. At this rate, she'd walk the few blocks and pound on Morwenna's door. Too bad if she was in the throes with Helios.

She flung off the bedclothes and disappeared into the bathroom. Twenty minutes later, she was just putting in a load of washing when she remembered to check the answering machine.

"Hello Kreyna, it's Frances. Hope you don't mind, I gave Declan your number because he asked nicely. He'll call you soon, I should think. Cheers, bye."

She replayed the message, partly to give herself time to think, largely to hear the sound of Frances's voice. Still nothing from Morwenna. Her shoulders slumped and then straightened. She snatched up the handset and punched in numbers.

"Morwenna, I must talk to you. Get out of that bed and call me, okay? Now would be good." She slammed the handset into its cradle. The phone clicked, as if in protest. How odd. Gently, she lifted the handset and heard a double click, barely audible without exceptional hearing. She replaced the handset and stared at the phone, as if it might confess. If her focus had been vague before, now all her senses snapped to attention. Why was her phone being tapped? Were her calls being vetted?

Oma's clock cuckooed ten times. It was rudely early to descend on Morwenna who was not a morning person. But if she went via the Kingston bus depot markets, picked up some more incense and stopped for a coffee, by then her friend might be decent enough to receive visitors. Kreyna brushed her teeth and put on a lush, red lipstick in front of the bathroom mirror. She straightened the fitting white T-shirt and short black shorts that flattered her narrow hips and lean, bronzed legs. The outfit passed muster for a casual trip to the markets. Grabbing her handbag, she slipped on her favorite black leather sandals. The phone rang.

A deep voice boomed down the line. "Hi Kreyna, I hope I'm not disturbing you. Declan De Salles, here. How are you?"

Declan wanted to meet her for coffee sometime soon. She explained she was on her way out to the markets. Promptly, he asked if he might join her and hang out for a while. She hung up, checked the apartment was secure and left.

In the food court at the Old Bus Depot Markets, people were eating a wide variety of dishes purchased from the multicultural food stalls. Under the soaring, corrugated-iron roof of the defunct bus depot, the atmosphere was crowded and noisy, yet companionable and relaxed.

Declan nestled his cup back in its saucer and said, "Pardon my candor, but you're not involved with anyone at the moment, are you?" Head cocked, he examined her expression and waited.

Kreyna looked down at the remains of a croque monsieur. She'd managed nearly half of it. "My eyes are bigger than my stomach. Would you like some?"

Was she involved with anyone? She shied away from the bleeding obvious. "I was until a few months ago so I'm not sure I'm in the game, to be honest. You might say I'm a tad gun-shy."

Declan wiped melted cheese from his fingers and lips. "I know where you're coming from. Last August, my girlfriend of five years—Jenny's a general practitioner—she went to Africa to join Médécins Sans Frontières in the fight against HIV AIDS. She had wanted to go for a while and for me to go with her. But my work—my job and career—is here. I'm in no hurry to have another relationship, but I very much enjoy your company and would like to know you better. How does that sound?"

Did he have any idea the kind of person she was? As if he heard her, he said, "You've a great face for poker, love. I figure there's a whole lot more to you than meets the eye. I confess that's part of the attraction. Shall we go?"

He guided her through the crowd, a protective hand occasionally touching the small of her back—he was light on his feet, moving an imposing frame with balletic agility. They stopped at the essential oils stall where she bought lemon-scented incense sticks. Outside, they stood together awkwardly, like an ox and its whip.

He took her hand in farewell. Kreyna said, "Do you know John Donne's poem, *The Prohibition*?"

He looked up to his left and down to his right, and recited, "Take heed of loving me—at least remember I forbade it thee." With a hearty laugh, he kissed her on both cheeks and set off briskly, turning to smile and wave. She headed across the road toward Belmore Gardens in Barton. Toward that little minx, that strumpet, that harlot and lovesick lay-about, Morwenna.

* * *

"G'day sweetie!" Morwenna kissed Kreyna on the mouth and crushed her to her ample bosom. "It's been an age—how the hell are you?"

"A damn sight better for seeing you, you old tart. Why didn't you return my calls?"

"Whaddaya mean, not return your calls? I was in Darwin all week for work, rang in, got your messages, rang back and left a message every time. Can't do better than that, can I now?"

Kreyna stepped back and put her hands on her hips. "I called and left a message this morning. Did you get it?"

"After I got back. I'd been down to the servo buying milk for brekkie. Then I rang and left *you* a message. Don't tell me we've been playing phone tag all week?"

"Is Helios still here? Any chance of a cuppa?"

"He worked late last night and stayed at his mother's. And yes, I'll put the kettle on."

Kreyna sat at the old oak table in the tiny room that purported to be a kitchen. Morwenna ladled loose leaf tea into a pot shaped like a clucky chicken, ceramic eggs oozing from beneath fat, glazed white feathers—the boiling water gurgled and steamed on the way into its belly. Over a piping hot mug of orange pekoe, Kreyna reported that she had not actually received any messages—at least, none she could detect. She told Morwenna about the trip to Melbourne and the news that she was being posted to Fort Meade. When she had to explain someone died because of her, she dissolved into tears.

Morwenna looked solemn and cuddled her, tsking until Kreyna composed herself. Finally, she said she'd met Declan for coffee that morning. Morwenna puckered her mouth in an effort not to grin too widely, but her dancing eyes gave her away.

"Well, you have had a time of it, girlfriend. There're a few things that don't jell, particularly the disappearing messages—it's bizarre. I know your job is frightfully hush-hush, but could you be in over your head?"

Kreyna took a deep breath. "Paranoid Scorpio or not, I think I'm being watched."

The two women sat in silence, sipping tea—such a reassuringly normal activity.

"What I can't suss out is *why*. The organization is very frugal with its resources. This kind of surveillance costs money—time, money and staff. Why they're paying attention to someone like me, I can't imagine. I have limited access to top secret material and most of my training has been theoretical, so far. In a nutshell, I know zip."

Something rubbed against Kreyna's shins. She looked under the table and Merlin, a sleek black tomcat, said, "Mwah, per-prow?"

"I fed you breakfast an hour ago," Morwenna said, rising from her chair. "This cat's bulimic, I swear." She took a small plastic package of diced kangaroo meat from the fridge and spooned some into a bowl. Merlin stretched up, attempting to claw it off the bench. "Impatient puss. Keep your fur on—it's coming." She placed the bowl on a mat in the corner of the kitchen. Merlin purred and ate at the same time.

Kreyna sat back, relaxing a little. "What I do know is someone's been intercepting calls because yours never made it to my answering machine. They're monitoring what comes in, what goes out, letting through some, blocking others—it's all very labor intensive."

"Are you able to psych it out, so to speak?"

"Rules govern how we operate within the Filigrane. A strict moral code ensures that the way of the transgressor is hard. I'm forbidden to use it for self-interest and I mustn't invade people's minds without compelling reason. Occasionally, I slip up and go where I shouldn't, which results in reprimand. The Filigrane itself is constantly monitored and it's a case of obey the rules or be shut out. No ifs, no buts, it's intractable. At least, that's what Eadie told me."

"Eadie? Is she still running the Spiritualist Church? You haven't said how your reading went. Did she have any tips for wrangling Robert?"

Kreyna thought better of mentioning what Eadie had said about Frances, or the incident in Melbourne. Too confused and vulnerable to undergo any kind of interrogation, no matter how well-meaning, she shook her head. "Eadie's diabetes is taking its toll. She nagged me into doing psychometry at a church service sometime in the future, that's all."

"How do you feel about the posting to the States?"

Kreyna groaned and slumped across the table, hands combing through masses of dark curls. "No way, José. I do *not* want to leave Canberra and I don't trust the American brass to do the right thing by me. However, I have little choice."

"I'm going to miss you desperately. Let's pretend something will come up and you'll be off the hook. Deal?" Morwenna's eyebrows jiggled suggestively. "In the meantime, there's always Declan to distract you."

Kreyna couldn't help but smile.

* * *

To a ten-second count, Kreyna lifted the sixteen-pound barbell in her left hand. She concentrated on form and remembered to breathe steadily. At the fourth rep, the bicep was screaming, threatening to fail. She pushed through the pain, eyes narrowed with effort. Sweat drizzled into her eyes where its salt stung mercilessly. Despite the fingerless, leather lifting gloves, her moist grip began to slip. And down—eight, nine, ten seconds.

She dropped the lowered weight onto the sofa. Slow burn training was a killer but her body loved the aftereffects. Flat on her back, she launched into abdominal crunches, so excruciatingly slow she could barely manage six. Routine complete, she closed her eyes and relaxed, enjoying the warm ache of well-worked muscles. Against the background of her eyelids, full lips parted into a teasing smile.

What do two women do together in bed? Only this morning, she'd awoken and lain there wondering. Yesterday evening, Frances had rung and asked for help making chocolates as Christmas gifts. Pleased to be asked, Kreyna had promised to go over straight after work tomorrow night. Messing with chocolate and Frances sounded like fun. She was still grinning when her head had hit the pillow.

Who could she ask? Munching on scrambled egg and toast for breakfast, no one came to mind, at least no one she trusted to keep mum. And Morwenna wouldn't have a clue. Knowledge is power. If one doesn't know, find out.

At lunchtime, she drove into Civic and paid a visit to Smiths Alternative Bookshop. In front of the queer literature section, she sat on the floor with a pile of possibilities. The sex manual made her blink rapidly. Typically Scorpionic, she was not prone to blushing, but this volume broke the rule. Glancing around the shop, she flicked through the pages and put it back on the shelf. She read the last chapters of two short novels, finding one absorbing and educational until she ran out of time and had to drive back to the office.

Truthfully, had knowledge made the situation easier? Etched behind her eyelids were colorful images from the manual, even though she'd barely glanced at it. Transposed in front of them was Frances, expression enigmatic. The combination didn't mesh well. But the feelings and experiences she'd read about in the novel rang true, particularly emotionally. Yes and no—knowledge helped and it didn't. Now she had an understanding of the mechanics, yet no idea how to handle the intense, compulsive urge she had to simply be with Frances.

Kreyna sat up and put her face in her hands. An insistent, fluid longing welled deep inside her pelvis. Desire demanded release, commanded recognition, threatened domination of her every action and to engulf what trace remained of restraint, of reason.

This is madness. Tonight, even Robert could be welcome.

* * *

Frances's renovated kitchen boasted top quality stainless steel appliances and new marble benches, barely visible under equipment and chocolate products at various stages of completion. The room was too warm as the air conditioning struggled to maintain a bearable temperature against the heat outdoors.

Kreyna eyed the chocolate smear she'd made on the baking paper. "I think it's tempered properly. Take a look."

Frances wiped her hands on the white, Delia Smith apron she wore over a sleeveless, banana-yellow blouse and patterned harem pants. She took a stride away from the other kitchen bench. "Shiny and smooth. Looks a treat. Best to use a fork for dipping the truffles, I should think." She went back to wielding a cheese slicer to cut curls off a flat block of chocolate. Five yuletide logs were lined up, two already beautifully adorned with voluptuous, dark chocolate cylinders.

Kreyna dragged out a tray of truffles from the large refrigerator and carried it unsteadily across to the bench. She laid out more baking paper and began the delicate task of truffle dipping, keeping one eye on the thermometer in the double boiler monitoring the melted chocolate. The temperature had to hover somewhere between eighty-eight and ninety-one degrees Fahrenheit, with an occasional stir to keep it evenly warm. With a fork, she lifted each truffle, submerged it completely and lifted it out to roll gently onto the baking paper. Overtired from disturbed sleep, her hand trembled too much. This Wednesday evening, the two women had started work at five thirty p.m. It was now eight o'clock and nearly dark.

"You'll have to trim the bottoms off some of those." Frances stood behind Kreyna, lifting the edge of a truffle with a paring knife. For a moment, her woody citrus, chypre-style perfume unnerved Kreyna.

"See how they've got little wedges underneath?" Frances asked with a caressing smile, addressing Kreyna's mouth. Frances picked up a truffle and carved it into a neat globe. Kreyna tried to copy her, fumbling under her critical gaze.

"Best put them back in the fridge. Your hands are too hot. We'll have fingerprints all over them."

Kreyna picked up the tray and shuffled toward the refrigerator. "Good thing I love chocolate, though I think the smell is beginning to pall."

"Everyone enjoys chocolate." Frances licked a spatula. "It's the oxytocin level in the blood. Giving birth releases it, as does chocolate. And being in love."

The tray hit the tiled floor with a loud clatter and thirty roughly-round truffles careened off in all directions. Kreyna covered her mouth and squatted down, forlorn. Her shoulders shook and she sat back into the mess, giggles getting the better of her. Frances knelt and put out a reassuring hand.

"Don't! Go away!" Kreyna snatched up a few truffles and pelted Frances, who tried to duck. "You're way too nice to me and I don't trust you for it." Through welling tears, she glared when Frances crawled toward her through the sticky blobs and stopped only a short distance away.

Kreyna kissed her, tasted chocolate through the salt of her own tears and Frances's hot mouth. At the touch of a tongue tip, she pulled the woman to her, molten lava flowing through her hips. Frances clutched at Kreyna's ribs and pressed a hand behind her neck. Kreyna kissed down Frances's throat, finding the café-au-lait birthmark.

Suddenly aware, Kreyna clambered to her feet, ripped off her own apron and threw it on the bench. "I have to go."

Frances was on her knees. "Kreyna, wait!"

"No!" Kreyna turned and hissed, "I don't know *what* this is, but…"

She bolted to the front door, snatching up her handbag en route. Out on the street, she slammed the car door after her, fired the stroppy bema into action and took off. In the rear vision mirror, she glimpsed the fast receding figure of Frances under the porch light.

* * *

Thank God for hot showers. Kreyna shampooed out the congealed truffle and leaned against the shower wall, letting the water sluice over hot skin and wash away emotions that left her drained. She'd driven home at high speed, thrashing the M3 coupe through the backstreets to avoid being booked. Cleaning chocolate off the car seat would be a job.

Could she have made a bigger fool of herself if she'd tried? Now what was she going to do? Stepping out of the shower, she was surprised to see her usual self in the mirror—not whoever the stranger was who responded so fiercely to that woman's passionate kiss.

You kissed her, remember?

Toweled dry, she put on white shortie pajamas and a chenille robe. Should she call Morwenna? No point in leaving a cryptic message—she could jog over and tell her all about it. Tell Morwenna what, exactly? That she'd just swapped spit with Bryce Parrey's wife who objected not at all?

Stupid—so damn stupid. You impetuous fool. See where all your curiosity and your quest for knowledge has gotten you? If you get in any deeper, you'll drown. Oh God, no.

In midstride down the hall, Kreyna stopped and clutched herself.

This woman could be the death of you.

A horrid sense of impending doom descended. She fought it off with an angry shrug.

Nobody has to get hurt. You may not be able to control what happens, but you can control how you respond. It's entirely your choice. Don't give away your power to anyone, no matter what you feel. You made that mistake with Robert.

Sitting down to meditate, she reduced her heart rate and breathing until they diminished. At the shrine, Oma smiled back at her serenely. She missed Oma, longed to talk with her loving grandmother who always radiated an otherworldly peacefulness.

Oma, if you do nothing else for me this night, grant me sleep. Dreamless sleep.

The phone rang. Kreyna yanked the wire out of its wall socket.

* * *

By close of business Friday, Kreyna was back in control and resolute. Strolling home early from the office at DFAT, she looked forward to the weekend and visiting her parents who had returned from Cairns. As she walked, she caught herself smiling for no reason. During the day, bubbles of delight had risen through her chest, causing her to catch her breath in apprehension. An instant later, sadness and an aching sense of loss threatened to overwhelm her. Finally, the see-sawing feelings steadied and she felt better for it.

Freshly determined to regain her customary calm, she picked up a burger to have with the unwooded chardonnay chilling in the fridge. Immersed in a gory murder mystery on the ABC TV channel, she enjoyed a quiet evening indoors. The phone remained unplugged.

* * *

Originally settled by convicts until the village boomed with the discovery of alluvial gold in the surrounding hills, modern Braidwood was a heritage-listed haven for craftspeople and artisans. Parked on Wallace Street, the main thoroughfare, she met her mother and father at Café Altenburg for lunch. They scored a cool and comfortable table in the vine-covered courtyard. Wafting out from the kitchen, the aroma of grilled meats, vegetables and onions stoked the taste buds of a dozen customers.

Slim, with short blond hair, Kreyna's mother had a fix-it, nononsense manner that belied her maternal heart. Kreyna's sister, Lydia, was a close copy of their mother, while Kreyna took after their father. His thick, black curls were cut short and slicked back, the hairline only just beginning to recede. Here and there, a strand of silver detracted little from his youthful, tanned features.

Kreyna tucked into her grilled vegetable stack with a crisp and crunchy salad on the side. Busily sawing at a rare beef eye-fillet steak, her mother said, "Any potential boyfriends on the horizon, dear?"

"Don't nag the girl. She's only just gotten shot of Robert. That boy was mega bad news."

"It's all right, Dad. I met an interesting guy at a party recently. He runs the Centre for Consciousness at the ANU. We had a long discussion about string theory."

"As you do." Her mother had stopped eating to listen. "Seeing him again, are you?"

"We met for coffee last Sunday, which was pleasant. He's got a good heart and a sense of humor I like. We'll see."

Her father watched her over his beer glass. "You don't sound too keen."

"I think he's on the rebound, so I'll be careful. Anyway, I've a lot on my plate at the moment. Work is..." She was stuck for words. "Depressing. Can we skip it, please?"

Kreyna's parents cast glances at each other. The conversation drifted to agriculture and farming practices. On their small farm, they grazed goats and alpacas. Kreyna's mother was teaching herself to make cheese from the surplus milk and was considering selling it to delicatessens, such was the demand for high quality boutique cheeses. They rounded off their meal with coffee and miniature lamingtons. Her mother went to the bathroom.

Her father bent forward and took her hand, "I've never felt you this off-kilter. Who or what has gotten under your skin? Tell me, girlie. What's going on at work?"

Kreyna sighed, enjoying the warmth of his fingers that exuded the comforting scent of garlic. "My bosses want me to move to the States to work with their military. I've a bad feeling about it, but don't have a choice apparently."

"Not like you to have a bad feeling without good reason, you know." His eyes narrowed, peering at her. "How about you run it past me?"

"I'm only going on what I've heard from colleagues. It's common knowledge the Stargate program has a sinister reputation for burning out its remote viewers. They're trying to devise a method to train any soldier to remote view, on command."

"Any Average Joe? Admirably ambitious, but they must be dreaming."

"Turns out, they're wary of using natural intuitives during missions because they're too erratic and unpredictable, not to mention woefully unsuited to military life, let alone venturing as thought forms behind enemy lines. Can you imagine a bunch of sensitives put in the line of fire? It would be a circus."

"Serves them right—bloody silly idea," he said, a grin growing wide.

Kreyna gave a wry smile and sighed. "To an extent, I agree. The plan was to monitor the brain patterns of intuitives to establish how their minds and bodies functioned during remote viewing. Using that knowledge, they tried training ordinary personnel to mimic those functions, with mixed results."

"Yeah? No surprises there."

"Maybe not to anyone who knows, but they had great expectations. The bad news was, newly trained personnel struggled to master the technique, so they continue to use intuitives like me. And they especially want me because of my psych profile—an analytical intuitive is a rarity. But the most disturbing rumor that's filtered through is the intuitives develop mild mental health problems and the newly trained amateurs go stark staring mad."

"Crikey!"

"Exactly. I've heard they're hospitalized, medicated and discreetly discharged, their careers over, private lives wrecked and minds permanently damaged. I hate to admit it, Dad, but Robert has a point. ASIO wouldn't be able to ensure my safety, not at a distance. While I trust and respect Dr. Corea, I have no idea who I'll be answering to over there."

"Don't want my girl whistling a loony tune. If there's any way you can wriggle out of it, you could consider other options. There are always options. You just have to think things through until you strike the right one. You'll know when you do." He squeezed her fingers. "It's not like they're holding a gun to your head."

Her mother approached and they soon left the restaurant. Plenty of hugs and kisses later, she pointed the car in the direction of home.

Are you sure about that gun, Dad?

Driving toward Canberra, a summer storm cell coming in from the west began to darken an otherwise bright day.

CHAPTER TEN

Heavy rain woke her at 12:21 a.m. It was streaming down in torrents, interspersed with sheet lightning and shuddering thunder that reverberated through the whole apartment building. Kreyna arose, flicked on a light and padded down the hall, coming to a halt at the sliding glass door to the back patio. She watched the rain for a minute or two. When she turned away, she caught movement with her peripheral vision. A man launched himself at the glass door, hammering on it with his fists and shouting something at her. She hesitated, but he began to hammer more furiously. Heart racing, she hastily flipped the lock and flung back the door to let Robert in.

His blue sweatshirt was saturated—water dripped off his hair darkened by the rain. "Didn't you hear me pounding on your front door? What are you, deaf?"

"Who can hear anything in this storm? And what the hell are you doing here? You're wringing wet." She headed to the bathroom for towels and came back to find him waving the disconnected phone wire, staring at it pointedly.

"I've been trying to ring you for days—what's the story?"

"I'd prefer to be off the air for a while." She draped a towel around his shoulders and threw another over his head. He rubbed his hair absentmindedly and shoved the wire back in its socket.

"Now that we've exchanged pleasantries, what do you want?" She tugged on her white robe and retied the belt, emphatically. "As it is, I get the dubious benefit of your presence most nights. Why show up in the flesh?"

"I left a backpack in the wardrobe. You haven't tossed it, have you?"

"Should still be there..."

Robert was already halfway down the hall. Coming back, he tugged a tracksuit and well-worn runners from the backpack— the reek of rancid male sweat wafted past.

"It's the middle of the night. Couldn't it have waited?"

From a pocket in the track pants, he lifted a tiny plastic bag and held it up to the light. Inside, five minuscule white pills slid back and forth. He grinned maniacally.

"You bee-ooty! I'd forgotten about these."

She scowled at him. "You're a real prize. Stashing drugs in my house, I don't think so. Take your stuff and go!"

Robert was in the kitchen, busy washing down pills.

She stormed in and slammed his cup in the sink. "Down the rotten things somewhere else, will you? Just go!"

He sniggered. "Babe, the night's just begun. Take a load off and listen. I've got a job for you."

Firm hand on the back of her neck, he pushed her down onto a pine, colonial-style chair near the kitchen table. She looked daggers at him. Another chair creaked under his weight and he tugged the towel off his shoulders.

"Remember Piet Van Whalen and the Antwerp drug cartel? Of course you do. I'm sorry about Piet's death. True fact. Collateral damage, as they say."

Kreyna studied the knots in the table's surface. "Did you have anything to do with it?"

"Yes and no—sort of. Indirectly—best if you don't know. It's too bad. The good news is I'm turning a profitable trade providing information to that selfsame cartel." He sat back with hands laced behind his head and smirked at her. "Cool, huh?"

For an instant, she broke the rules—she scanned his thoughts. Or rather, she tried to. The drug, whatever it was, was kicking in nicely.

Blue eyes, stainless steel cold, grew wide. "Nice try, babe. I'm off the air for a while. Yee-haa!"

He leaned forward and coaxed, "You're going to take a trip to Antwerp for me and check out a rival gang's drug shipment. Date, time, boat name. Only take a few minutes, easy-peasy."

She examined the floor. "Do it yourself."

He rocked his chair back and forth. "Can't."

"What do you mean, you can't? You're a damn sight more experienced at remote viewing than I am."

He boxed and feinted at thin air, chewing imaginary gum and looking at her sideways. "Yeah, but I pick up company along the way. Very nasty, hang around for weeks. Difficult to shake."

"Entities?"

"Yeah. Whatever." He sounded bored. "Look, just do it and I'll be gone, no worries."

"And if I don't?"

"Poked some pommy chick down in Melbourne. Friend of yours, is she?"

Kreyna stiffened. "Leave her alone."

Robert studied her. Scrambling, she shored up her chakras, too late.

"What's this? Woo-hoo, Krey-nah! Did I know this about you? Should have told me sooner, we could've had some truly special nights. You, me, other love-lee lay-dees..." Perched on the edge of his seat, he was practically salivating. "A hottie like you? Bet she's gaggin' for it."

She groaned and rolled her eyes. "Robert, it's all in your head. She's married with children. Stop fantasizing."

"A husband? Wouldn't he like to know..."

"There's nothing *to* know. Now grab your gear and go home."

She rose and started for the door. With lightning speed, Robert seized an arm and shoved her back on the chair. "I'm not leaving and neither are you. I have to have the information by six a.m. and you're going to get it for me."

"Unlucky." Again, she darted toward the door. He slammed her back in the chair and slapped her hard. Holding her left ear that rang like a siren, she found herself on the floor. Fury making her strong, she leaped up and lashed at him—three bright red lines appeared across his left cheek. He gaped at her.

The back of his hand nearly broke her nose. Again on the floor. Blood streamed. She groped about and found one of the barbells. She swung the weight around and let go. The barbell caught him mid-shin with a sickening crunch and he sank to his knees.

With a howl, he rose like a nightmarish jack-in-the-box, hefted the barbell and slammed it, repeatedly, into the top of the table.

An anguished scream, "I don't want to hurt you! Just. Fucking. Do it!"

The timber cracked along the grain and collapsed inward. The barbell crashed through, bounced and rolled to a clanging halt.

Robert crumpled to the floor. He pushed his back up against a wall, teary and shivering, and punched his thighs, spasmodically. "I have to get them the information. Or they'll kill me, I swear. I need the coin. I need the ice to keep me going."

He turned bloodshot eyes to her. "Please, Kreyna. I'm begging. I won't ask again. I'll leave you alone. Dead cert."

Gingerly, she felt her nose—the blood was beginning to coagulate. This could go on all night with the monkey on his back, his addiction goading him relentlessly.

"Okay."

He looked at her hopefully.

"Okay, I'll do it. But you must keep your word and stay away from me. Forever."

He scrambled to his feet. "We don't have much time."

With no equipment, they set up her bedroom as a monitoring station. Robert pulled up a chair next to the double bed and they went over the sequence she had to follow.

"Rob, I'm scared. Without the Filigrane's sanction, I'm wide open to anything out there. How will I know what's safe and what's evil?"

"You'll know. The weight, color and sound of their energy are the best indicators. Anything murky, stay away from it."

"Before I go I just want to say how much it upsets me to see what you've done to yourself since we broke up. It's terribly dangerous, you know full well. Someone as sensitive as you cannot get away with dabbling in drugs of any kind. It's spiritual suicide."

He put on a crooked smile, eyes haunted. "Too late now, my pretty. I've done far worse than you want to know. That guy, Deprez? Adrian thought he'd be a walkover, but he proved too strong to control. Never meant anyone to die."

"Adrian? What's he got to do with any of this?"

"My babe in the woods. For a clairvoyant with mammoth talent, you sure miss a lot."

"Because I don't look where I shouldn't. The way of the transgressor is hard."

Robert scoffed, "No shit, Sherlock. Listen to me. It pays to think for yourself and be suspicious. Not everyone you trust has your best interests in mind. Now, I'm going to give you coordinates and an address. Start in the office, wherever it is. See if you can find anything written down. There's supposed to be a huge shipment leaving Antwerp within the next twenty-four hours. We need the name of the ship, its destination and estimated time of departure."

She focused on the red welts tracing his cheek. Not a bad shot. "Hearing" her, he gave a wry smile.

"Good luck. Get in, get out, come back safe, babe. Ready? Latitude fifty-one north twenty-six, longitude four east forty."

A familiar tearing and Kreyna shifted as fast as a laser, hovering over the city below. Robert's voice was faint above the rush of air that buffeted her. Other than smog and the soulful cries of seagulls, nothing hindered her.

"You're looking for Winkelstraat. It's northeast of the docks, back two blocks from Havenweg, a main road."

In thought form, she stood on a cobbled street bounded by terrace houses and shops. It was busy; people went about their daily work, shopping, talking and moving through her. Fragments of thoughts entered her awareness: *walk the hound—herrings for dinner—post greeting cards—buy coffee beans—invite Ton and Loes for Christmas.* She brushed them aside and focused her senses into a narrow point of intent.

"You must be on the street now. It's number fifteen. Find it and go inside."

Flagstone steps, iron gate, oak and glass door, musty and dark hall, staircase.

"There's an office. You must locate it, fast."

Peering through walls, floor, ceiling. No one—ah! Upstairs at the back, a movement.

Pokey room, tiny windows to the west, ancient leather-topped desk and worn captain's chair on rickety wheels. Folio-size shipping logs with leather spines, stacked high on low bookshelves. A man wearing a black mariner's cap, Gauloise burning in the deep ashtray at his elbow. Talking on the phone, rapid-fire.

"I tell you, there's no time. She leaves at first light tomorrow, with or without your consignment. Leopold dock." He drops the phone in its cradle. The name of the ship—need the name of the ship.

A sinister chuckle echoes and a singsong voice says, "We can see you."

Massive arms seize her. In an instant she's drowning, fifty feet beneath the North Sea. Two entities, once men, hold her struggling thought form. Panic rises as icy, salt water floods her lungs, pushing, wrenching, heart thudding. Moments blend into minutes, spirit weakening. Bearded forms, jagged teeth snarl and gnaw on her throat, her stomach, skin tearing, intestines exposed. Seconds remaining, she sends a klaxon call, pinging the Filigrane with vestigial strength.

Three fireballs roar up from the depths, ripping her loose in a vast energy burst that shoots a column of water high above the ocean's surface—they disappear straight up into dense cloud.

Held aloft, she coughs and heaves what seems like gallons of water from her burning lungs, draws breath and coughs, draws breath and fights tears of relief. Only then, she realizes she's being cradled like a baby in the arms of an enrobed woman—a seven-foot-tall woman who looks, for all the world, like a young version of her grandmother.

"*Oma, ben ik dood?*"

"*Nee kind*, not dead but close enough—you're in a bardo. We wanted to help, but you had to call."

Kreyna nods to a handsome, dark-haired young man, acknowledging her uncle Hans. With him is a shy girl of about twelve years old—her cousin Eva, long gone.

"You must go back now, mortal danger, no time to lose."

"But I have to find out the name of the ship leaving Antwerp."

"The *Empress*, a general cargo vessel bound for Hull. Go now. Godspeed!"

She slammed into the bed, breath driven from her lungs. And shot upright, vomit gushing over her legs. The bedclothes were saturated.

"Kreyna! You scared the crap out of me—I thought you were a goner."

Every breath proved agony, her lungs hurting as if they'd been scoured with barbed wire. She wheezed, not risking a cough.

"You thrashed about and coughed up buckets of what smells like salt water. Where the fuck were you? What happened?"

Mumbling incoherently, strength gone, she curled into a ball at the foot of the bed where it was dry. Robert shook her urgently, to no response. He prized open her fingers and squeezed a pen between them.

"C'mon babe, c'mon—write it down, won't take a second."

He slapped each cheek until she frowned and blinked. "On this pad. Ship's name, when it's leaving." Lying on her side, she put pen to paper, scribbled as best she could and lost consciousness.

* * *

Knocking, crashing and banging, breaking timber, yelling, grunting and swearing. Dark uniforms, shapes struggling on the floor, glint of handcuffs. Strong arms lifted her onto a gurney. Low voices, two familiar faces, flashing lights, engine starting, sirens. Blackness.

She wept. Wept for what might have been, what could have been if only she'd been stronger. Pain—sorrow—despair—no air.

"We do not choose who we love. Love, if it finds us worthy, chooses us."

"Maybe so, but I can choose what to do with it. Much as I can choose to live or die."

"Love knows no bounds."

"True for you, but here on earth?"

"Better to have loved and lost, than…"

"Arrant nonsense. Any more platitudes?"

"All apparent separation is routing and rerouting toward union and reunion."

"Cold comfort. I'm coming home now."

"Forbidden."

Plastic tubing inserted in one nostril made breathing difficult. She tried to swat it away. A man with buzz-cut hair, round red cheeks and smiley sapphire eyes caught her hand and replaced it under the white cotton blanket.

"Where am I?"

Fire in the chest. Her eyes stretched wide as she wheezed and wheezed.

"Don't try to talk, please. Duntroon Health Centre. You're in good hands."

She took in the antiseptic whiteness of it all, the pervading smell of disinfectant, the curtains surrounding the bed, the IV in her arm and slipped back into darkness.

* * *

Blistered, cracked and peeling, the door's sallow paint came away as a chalky mess on Robert's hand. He had given up knocking. Now, he slapped and pounded the west-facing front door of the Charnwood house. Bolts drawn, the latch turned and the door opened as far as the night chain would allow.

"Whaddaya want, mate?"

"Ice—got any ice?"

"No worries—two hundred, up front."

"How much? I've got sixty—what will that get me?"

"Fresh air."

The door slammed and bolts flew home. He punched the door until his knuckles bled. Nursing the hand, he hurried back to the car and thrashed the tired Hyundai Excel all the way home, holding his buttocks tight. His guts roiled and threatened to explode—diarrhea had plagued him in the week since he was released on bail.

His townhouse wasn't exactly pristine: unwashed cups and dishes, pizza boxes, plastic takeaway containers, papers and dirty clothes littered every surface. He trod over the debris in the lounge and went to the toilet. Everywhere he went, they went.

Shadows unseen by ordinary humans. A highly trained and innately talented intuitive, Robert was far from ordinary. Blurred figures jostled him, touching, pinching and jabbing with sharp fingers, their breath hot and fetid. Worst of all, they babbled constantly—the whole gang.

Steaming pile of rat cack—useless bit of shit—dick wad—loser— wanker—tosser—think you're someone don't ya—liar—cheat—brown nose—murderer.

He burst out of the bathroom and stomped through the house, hands clamped to ears, as if that worked. Where's the bong? Somewhere under the crap on the coffee table. Ransacking the kitchen drawers, bathroom cabinet, bedside table and every pair of pants. Found something promising. With trembling hands, the matchbox slid open. You bee-ooty.

The remnants from a head of cannabis barely filled the cone. A light—need a light. On the floor, searching down the side and under the couch. Used a blue lighter this morning—must be here somewhere. Where was it now? *Want heat? We can help.* Pain started in his lower back, like a welding torch to the spine.

He leaped up and ran to the bathroom. Running the cold tap in the shower, he stripped nude in seconds and jumped under the water, gasping in relief when it cooled his searing hot skin. *Want cold? Easy as.* He began to shiver—shiver uncontrollably. And slid slowly down the shower wall, mewling helplessly, stomach throwing bile up the throat. *Want sick? Coming right up!* A stream of yellow slime hurtled out. Continued retching, skull ringing, throbbing from thumping the wall. He pulled a towel down from a rail and crawled out of the shower recess, patting his body ineffectually.

"Kreyna, help me. For pity's sake, help me. Where are you, babe? Can't find you anywhere. God, I hope you're safe. I'm sorry, so sorry I fucked up. Big-time. Need you. Please. Get me outta here."

The girl laughed—the vicious, sadistic bitch liked twisting his donger, scratching and clawing until it was raw. She was nastier than the three guys. They enjoyed slicing him with flick knives when he wasn't paying attention. In horror, he'd look down and see fingers missing or blood streaming from slashed flesh. They'd all laugh raucously, deafening hysterical screams and howls, mouths pressed to his ears, nauseating, rank breath.

Die, ya worthless arse wipe—better off gone—float off to heaven— join the grateful dead.

He tugged on his jeans, struggling to follow one leg with the other. Fallen, he crawled to the lounge room and dragged himself onto the couch. Exhaustion sank him into fitful sleep.

The night is deathly dark at three a.m. Why was it light, flickering red light? Alarm turned to panic. Eyes open, thick smoke and swirling flames crackled and hissed. Adrenaline coursing through his veins, he flung himself at the front door, wrenched it open and ran straight out into the middle of the road.

Blinding headlights—a carload of hoods swerved and screeched to a stop. "Get off the friggin' road! Yous fucked in the head, or what?"

Cackles and yells. A longneck beer bottle, half full, bounced off his right ear and he crumpled like a speared kangaroo. The driver revved the engine into a scream and dropped the clutch. Exhaust roaring, tires squealing, the souped-up bomb disappeared in an acrid cloud of black smoke.

Blood streaming, head threatening to explode, he crawled to the curb and stared at his townhouse—dead black and quiet as a morgue. He got to his feet and started walking.

Enjoy the show? We did. Sneering giggles.

"Get away from me, you parasites! The only power you have is what I give you."

So you say. As long as you live we're here. By your side. We're in for life. Lifers with you. Together forever. Get used to it.

"Get the fuck out of my head!"

No.

He walked and argued with them. Sometimes they would argue back; sometimes they stabbed or scratched or pulled or pushed him. He flailed his arms about, threw punches and screamed at them to go away. Hour followed hour of aimless tramping through the suburb by streetlight, shrinking into shadows when a solitary car passed by.

A hint of dawn. Halted, he took his bearings and walked home. Everything would look better in the light of day.

The first toke on the bong was bliss. Breath held for an age, absorbing as much as possible from the drug in his lungs. Exhaled in a rush, coughing and wheezing.

Die now. Get dead now. Easy as. Why wait? No pain. No us.

Creeping disbelief became fear. The dope usually blocked them out. Usually.

Oblivion. No worries. Carefree. Bullet in the brain. Piece a cake.

He lit the cone again, sucking for all its worth, air pressure drawing a perfect white ring around his mouth. Holding—holding—coughing out the smoke, wheezing badly, tears oozing from reddening eyes, fanning smoke away.

Smart guy. Smart moves. Chunk a cord. Hanging. Super smart. Where?

It had merit. Career and reputation up shit-creek in a barbed wire canoe without a paddle. Pending prosecution for services rendered to the Antwerp mob, plus confiscation of all assets as proceeds of crime. With conviction a certainty, guaranteed to do time in Pentridge Prison. Full of tough guys looking for new bitches. Not a weakling, but still too pretty to stand a chance.

Pack rape. All day every day. Piercing pain. Bleeding. Like it now. Love it later. Hanging on a cord. Super smart move.

The perfect answer. But where? The drug helped him get creative. A smirk, a chuckle, and he's laughing out loud. He slapped his thighs in triumph. Oh yeah, way cool—let's go!

Grinning until his face ached, he dressed for work. Gone out to the car—hang on a minute—raced back through the kitchen, grabbed a knife and into the laundry. With two swift hacks, the clothesline cord came loose. Carefully rolled into a tight ball, it fitted in a suit jacket pocket. With the rest of Canberra's commuting public servants, he drove to work.

Once inside the building and with a map of Parliament House in one hand, Robert steered the electric cart along yet another featureless corridor. Stopped at an intersection, he checked the map again—three more turns to find the stairwell down to the Cathedral, a little known, yet immense void under the new federal Parliament House building. Until now, he'd believed it only a rumor—time to see for himself.

The staircase stank of musty concrete. At the bottom stood a steel exit door. With undue caution, he turned the handle and stepped through.

Black as a pit bull's rectum. He groped around the doorjamb, found a switch and flicked it on. Below, lit by huge tripods carrying klieg lights, a thirty-foot deep hole plunged into the rock of what once was Capital Hill. Cool, dark, deep and powerful, the Cathedral was beautiful, magnificent and inspiring. It even had a natural platform in the layers of rock that resembled an altar. Perfect. The tripod towering nearest to it looked even more perfect.

"Whaddaya reckon?" The words soared to the concrete ceiling and bounced back operatically.

Super smart move, smart guy. Too easy.

* * *

Kreyna woke to the same nurse injecting liquid into a shunt fitted into the back of her hand. Finished, he noticed her watching.

"How are you feeling?"

She blinked, not risking speech.

"You're a minor celebrity—bods are lined up to talk with you. Are you good enough?"

When she nodded, he continued, "You can take your pick of cops, secret service suits, or intelligence spooks. Any preference?"

Pankaj poked his distinguished head through the curtains. "Me first, I'm afraid."

Discreetly, the nurse closed the curtains when he left.

"I understand talking is very painful, right now. So. I will tell you what has transpired. If you wish to ask or tell me anything, I have pen and paper. Clear?"

His black eyes shifted. "The Secret Service wants to ask you certain things. Therefore, what I am allowed to tell you is necessarily brief. This is in your best interest as well as mine. I do not want to be seen as priming you in any way, understood?"

She studied the bruising on her arms. It was beginning to yellow—she'd been here at least a week.

Pankaj was not a happy man. "Kreyna, you've had pulmonary edema, a life threatening condition caused, in your case, by near drowning. We've been very worried, not least because we don't know what happened. We can discuss it when you're better. For now, we know you remote viewed a site in Belgium and gathered information. A monitoring intuitive picked up your cry for help via the Filigrane and notified me immediately. The Secret Service broke down your door and arrested Robert. You may be facing charges."

She beckoned for the pad and pen. The shunt made writing awkward when she scrawled WHY?

He read it and rubbed the back of his neck. "Drug money, possible blood money, the extent of your involvement in Robert's activities. You are under deep suspicion, I'm afraid."

He stood and looked down at her, his concern palpable. "I'll do my best to keep the wolves at bay. All that matters is you get well." He was gone.

CHAPTER ELEVEN

There were two of them—Secret Service agents in sober suits and ties. One had piggy little eyes behind tinted lenses; the other had shaved his head until it shone. Mr. and Mr. Smith, perhaps? Pointless to ask. They were the epitome of politeness when escorting her into the room, bare except for six plastic chairs, a beige manila folder and a microphone front and center on the table. Who would listen in, she would never know. Just the three of them, allegedly, were privy to their conversation. She knew she had no recourse, no chance to redress any slipup she might make—everything would be held against her. Robert was in way over his head. Was she to join him?

The bespectacled agent took off his jacket and hung it on the back of a chair. He hoisted up his belted gray trousers, but his pot still overflowed. Addressing the contents of the manila folder, he said, "As an ASIO operative, Ms. Katz, you will be aware of the gravity of our investigation. There are a number of incidents precipitated by your colleague, Robert Varazslo, for which we seek clarification from you. In these situations, we find it effective to have you describe what happened in your own words. We will ask questions as we see fit. You are reminded this interview is being recorded. In your own words, please begin."

Dispassionately, she related the events of that night: Robert's unexpected arrival, their fight, her compliance and the remote viewing.

"Before then, when was the most recent meeting with Mr. Varazslo?"

She hesitated since she "saw" him most nights. "He accosted me a few weeks ago at forty-one Blackall Street, the Remote Viewing Centre."

The shiny knob-head looked up from his note taking. "Why did you comply with his demand to remote view the target?"

"I told you, he threatened me. Hit me twice, in fact."

"Only twice? How do you account for the bite marks on your neck and abdomen?" They had been thorough, had done their homework and read all the medical reports.

"It happened when I was remote viewing. I was attacked." Kreyna stared at the microphone. "By non-physical beings."

"Non-physical beings? Curious, in light of the manifestly physical evidence. The medical report states you inhaled a large amount of salt water that washed away the surfactant in your lungs, proving nearly fatal. We believe the likely scenario is that you and Mr. Varazslo indulged in drug-enhanced sadomasochistic sex, including asphyxiation by drowning, when it all went inconveniently wrong."

Kreyna clapped her hand over her mouth in an effort to suppress the overwhelming desire to laugh. The two suits were bereft of humor. "That is a ridiculous fabrication."

"Fabrication? Be warned—for someone asserting she was attacked by non-physical beings, your credibility is tenuous, at best. Were it not for Dr. Corea's current position of authority, we would be recommending you certifiable. Now, what were the drugs?"

With a pulse far faster than was comfortable, Kreyna said, "I'm sure the medical report shows I was drug free at the time."

"Drug tests can be inconclusive. We know you were sexual partners until recently and you allowed him into your apartment.

The degree of your collusion with Mr. Varazslo is under close scrutiny. You must be aware our assessment of what you just told us will inform our conclusions. Is there any further evidence that might substantiate your version of events?"

She shook her head and quietly said, "Only Dr. Corea can vouch for my integrity."

The men glanced at each other and stood in unison. She took the hint and headed for the door. A hand on the lever, she checked herself. "By the way, did you intercept the shipment?"

Malice obvious, the piggy-eyed agent said, "As you will appreciate, Ms. Katz, such information is passed only to those who need to know."

So they had. It might save her in the end. If the drug shipment had gotten through, her neck would have been on the block for sure. Still, the risk of prosecution threatened and her career hung in the balance. Whatever happened, her reputation would, in all likelihood, remain questionable because of her association with Robert. Nothing she could do about it—she was at their mercy.

Sufficiently recovered from her injuries, she had bigger fish to fry. A barracuda, perhaps? Not expected, she would have the advantage. With a frozen heart and steely resolve, she took a taxi home to Macquarie Street.

* * *

At nine a.m. it was already eighty degrees Fahrenheit and guaranteed to reach blood temperature by midday. On Rusden Street, Kreyna parked the car under a tree and spread the foldout reflective shield inside the windscreen to protect the dashboard. A towel over the steering wheel would prevent the leather getting too hot to handle. The better to maintain her cool, she'd dressed in a crimson sleeveless cotton blouse and fitting black capri pants.

Pulse quickening, she knocked softly on the front door, gave it thirty seconds and knocked a little louder. Her mouth was dry—this wasn't going to be fun. She knocked again, slow and loud. Footsteps and the turning of the latch.

Kreyna slipped past a startled Frances into the cool of the foyer.

"Good morning. Not expecting me, I see."

"Kreyna, how are you? I heard you weren't well."

"You heard correctly. But I'm fine now, thanks for asking, although I thought you might have called."

Frances's pine-green eyes slid away, fingers flicking through her hair. "I've been very busy. In fact, you caught me in the middle of packing. We fly home tomorrow morning, first thing."

Kreyna's stomach sank to her knees. Oh no, oh no—she was ready yet she wasn't for this piece of news.

"Would you like a coffee? Bryce is out, finishing paperwork at the consulate."

Kreyna gritted her teeth—she *had* to do this. "Love one."

They sank into a strained silence while Frances put the kettle on to boil and spooned instant coffee into two mugs. Kreyna feigned a calmness she was nowhere near feeling. By the minute, she wavered between being utterly gutted to soporifically numb and back again.

Frances handed her a steaming mug.

"I saw you." Kreyna's voice broke. "I saw you that night when the medics wheeled me out."

Anguish flitted across Frances's face and vanished. "Sorry, you must have imagined it. Morwenna told me you had trouble with Robert. Said you were recovering well."

Kreyna put down the cup and took a step toward her. "Don't bother lying to me. I know you're very good at it, but I have an unerring bullshit detector. Why were you there?"

Frances shook her head, the back of one hand pressed to her mouth. She stared through the window at the brilliant summer sky.

"Don't mess with me, Frances, as I suspect you have. You owe me the truth. Any minute now, you're gone out of my life, never to be seen again. Here's your one chance to redeem yourself."

Frances turned on her heel. "Come with me."

After a moment's hesitation, Kreyna followed her down the hall to the master bedroom. Inside were two single beds, side by side, and a clutter of suitcases strewn around the floor. Frances perched on a small stool in front of the dressing table. It was covered in photo frames featuring a boy and a girl at varying ages. They had been photographed riding ponies, playing hockey, posing on ski slopes, dressed for outings or lined up for family portraits. Frances picked up one featuring her squeezing them close, delight written over all their faces—happy times.

"This is Megan and this is Craig. They are everything that matters. All that matters to me. I love them more than life. They were my only joy."

Kreyna sat on the nearest bed, ready for flight. Frances spoke, resignation in her voice. "Bryce and I have had an understanding, you might say, for a few years now. He has certain peccadilloes to which I'm willing to turn a blind eye. Provided he returns the favor. We value each other's discretion to ensure the children are well looked after, it's agreed."

"Indoor sports in Abu Dhabi."

Frances dropped her chin. "Indeed. About two years ago, he proposed I work, in secret, for our government and others, as directed."

"Doing what, exactly?"

Face drawn, Frances wet her full lips. For the first time this morning she looked directly at Kreyna. "To become intimate with suspect operatives and find out their involvement in illegal activities."

With honesty came a grief that dredged Kreyna's insides, emptying her of any remaining hope or trust.

"Female operatives? And I was suspect?"

"By association with Robert, yes. We knew about his activities, just short of proof. Your psychological profile suggested you might be open to being approached by a woman. It's why they employed me."

Kreyna's stomach threatened to relinquish her breakfast. At least it explained the persistent interest in Robert. But her original question remained unanswered.

"So, why were you there that night?"

"Your phone had been fitted with a microphone for surveillance. We were trying to establish what you and Robert were doing for the Belgian drug cartels. There are huge sums of money involved. Much of it very dirty from not just drugs. Arms dealing as well."

"What, you mean money from selling weapons?"

"Yes, arms for the Taliban. Bryce is still investigating and keeps Interpol informed."

"I thought Bryce was a cultural attaché." Kreyna met Frances's blank stare. "Silly me."

Frances said, "Only recently, we've found solid proof to back up Piet Van Whalen's allegation that he was passing cash to Victor Deprez for protection. Four months ago, Deprez paid a thirty-five thousand guilder bribe to Walter De Vries, a Belgian liaison officer at the embassy in The Hague. The bribe ensured De Vries conveniently misplaced an international warrant for the arrest of Piet Van Whalen. All this happened before Van Whalen turned informant on Deprez. Since then, investigators in both Belgium and Holland have dug up so much evidence against Deprez, Piet's allegations can no longer be ignored. He was scheduled to give a statement to the Belgian magistrate investigating Deprez."

"And got himself murdered the day before. I heard," Kreyna said.

"De Vries is under further investigation. Only last week a Rotterdam CID officer was arrested, caught selling Van Whalen's confidential dossiers to criminals at ten thousand guilders each. The Dutch and Belgian police had thought Van Whalen's allegations too incredible. But now?"

"In death, Piet's vindicated—better late than never. I'm positive Deprez shot him. Poor man—if only he hadn't had that drug habit."

"Deprez is back in custody. He'll be tried for murder and his conviction is inevitable. Case closed." Frances said. "But I want to know what happened to your phone."

"I unplugged it," Kreyna said with a shrug.

Frances looked at the ceiling and made a tsk sound. "If you only knew how worried I was. The surveillance team couldn't hear anything for days. Someone must have plugged it back in that night. We heard Robert talking and a rash of shouting and crashing, that's all. I was afraid he might hurt you, badgered Bryce to do something. Fortunately, Dr. Corea sounded the alarm and the whole crew descended on your apartment. I had to be there, to see you were unhurt."

In a flash, Kreyna understood. It was all painfully clear beneath the stark spotlight of truth. Time to go. She stood to leave. "I'm sure you've told me way more than you should. Thanks for that, I really appreciate you taking the time. I'll let myself out."

"Kreyna!" The force behind Frances's voice startled her. "You should be furious with me."

"I was. But now? What's the point? I know how the intelligence field works. Nothing personal, it's all about national interests. You were just doing a job."

She walked out. Frances caught up with her in three strides. Side by side, they walked the length of the hall. "But it is personal. It got personal, much to my surprise. I...I don't know how to say any of this."

"Say what." Kreyna halted. "That your previous assignments were easier to manipulate?"

"Ouch. Okay, I've had one previous assignment—another Australian girl. Other methods proved her to be in violation of the Crimes Act long before I got to know her well enough to be deployed."

Kreyna leaned against the wall, hands in pockets. "Do you *really* think you're predatory dyke material?"

"If I'm brutally honest, it would depend on the prey. If they were all like you? You're more than a little unusual. I've never met anyone even remotely like you. Very much doubt I ever shall again. Believe me, I thought our association would be mutually pleasurable."

Kreyna bristled. "I'm not one for soulless sex."

"No, of course you're not—I underestimated you. Not surprising, since the character profile they gave me was perfunctory at best. It didn't occur to me that I might hurt you. Or get emotionally involved. Remember Arty's birthday dinner? It was then I realized I care for you a whole lot more than I've ever done for anyone."

"You flatter me, Mrs. Parrey."

"I'm stating the facts, Ms. Katz. I know flattery will get me nowhere. It's too late for that. It's too late for anything other than plain language. Let's sit in the family room, shall we?"

To Kreyna's bemusement, Frances took her hand and Kreyna trailed along behind her, like a toddler.

In the family room stood a low-slung, chintz-covered Parker suite gathered around a handsome cherry oak coffee table, with matching side tables. Apparently little used, a television and stereo crouched in one corner. Frances sat Kreyna on the sofa next to her. Kreyna looked down at their hands together, not knowing whether to smile or cry or stay or run.

Frances lifted Kreyna's hand and looked into her eyes, brushing knuckles with her lips. "Do you care for me?"

"Need you ask?" Kreyna was entranced. "Please, I can't—this is unbearable—let me go."

"When I was showing you photos of the children, I said they were my only joy, with emphasis on the 'were.' Next to them, now there's you. Exactly when you took up residence in my heart is beyond me. It feels like you've always been there, veiled, waiting to step into view. Now, I need only think of you to feel joy."

Kreyna withdrew her hand and surveyed her. "What difference does it make if I believe you? You'll fly out tomorrow anyway, won't you?"

"Of course. My babies. Please. Wherever you go, whatever you do, remember you are loved. I will think of you."

Kreyna said, dryly, "Even thinking has its price."

"Excuse me?"

"How shall I put this? Let's say we all have a unique psychic signature that works like a code for locating individuals via alternate dimensions. Once others recognize your signature, they may interfere in your life without your knowledge. It can be highly disruptive, if not outright dangerous, permanently. One way to gain access to your psychic signature is through orgasm. If you thought sexually transmitted diseases were bad news, remember what happened in Melbourne—Robert looking for me and finding you for his gratification. There are some very disturbed individuals in the world."

"Are you telling me I must not to think of you? Especially not that way?"

"It would be safer for both of us and I must do the same."

"Christ! This is hard enough as it is."

"You have to forget about me for your own good and mine."

Frances looked stricken. "I don't know if I can."

"You have to. God knows, you owe me."

Kreyna rose and left the room. Frances followed a short length behind her. In the lobby, Kreyna turned to say goodbye but it was Frances who spoke first.

"I never meant this to happen. What I mean is, I didn't imagine for a moment it could. I hope you'll forgive me, one day. A mite sooner than I forgive myself, in all likelihood."

"Let's not drag this out. Please?"

"May I hold you? Just once—we never have."

Better not.

Kreyna steps into Frances's waiting arms. Love changes the improbable into the possible. A sliver of existence encapsulates pure happiness. Frances bends, mouths crush and arms enclose. Kreyna is undone. From beneath her navel rises a wondrous beast, reveling in long awaited freedom. She soars to the surface, brandishing passion like a conquering sword.

Frances holds her, mouth at the throat leaving livid evidence. Palms crush breasts, stretch elastic and fingers slide in. Kreyna can fly no higher—she shudders, cries out and glides to earth. Frances catches her, comforts her under the stained glass gum leaves, crimson rosellas and sprays of golden wattle.

"Now you will always be able to find me. But I mustn't do the same for you. If I did, he'd find you too—I can't protect you from him. Promise me you won't think of me—then you'll stay safe."

"I promise I'll try."

* * *

Kreyna caved. Grief and an overwhelming sense of inadequacy threw her into a dismal spiral down into despair. Engulfed by hopelessness, within twenty-four hours she developed a bout of the flu that had her shaking with fever and weak as water. When the phone rang, she staggered out of bed and picked up just as the machine clicked on. Pankaj's executive assistant said he wanted to see her immediately, regardless of her current condition, no excuse accepted.

She tugged on black jeans and a loose white shirt, roughly tucked in. Pale and nauseous, she rang for a taxi rather than risk the short drive to Russell Offices.

Like deck chairs on the Titanic, the crowded building's occupants and their belongings were shuffled regularly in an attempt to accommodate transfers and attrition brought on by resignations. Pankaj had been moved to the southwest corner where his new office was cool and gloomy, with any view obscured by mature evergreens.

He barely looked up when she slumped into one of the two visitor's chairs in front of his desk. With the light behind him, she didn't immediately notice he was staring almost sightlessly at a document between his palms flat on the desk in front of him.

Pankaj licked his lips. "Now, I don't want you to be upset."

And Kreyna knew. Cold surged through her viscera like an Arctic tsunami.

"Robert. What happened to him? Where's he now?" As fast as she asked, she answered herself. "Oh. Oh. It's horrible." Through trembling fingers at her temples, she gaped at Pankaj. "Tell me," she quavered, heart hammering under clammy skin.

"He was found hanging from a bank of lights in the bowels of Parliament House. The body had been there for some weeks—only the stench alerted the guards. They identified him from his security pass."

Kreyna slid off the chair, onto her knees and howled. Her keening brought a rush of people into the room. Urgent hands lifted her back onto the chair, stroked her arms and smoothed her hair. Someone well-meaning murmured, "It's okay, everything will be okay." Kreyna registered little beyond the gruesome visions of Robert's lifeless, bloated body. Nausea engulfed her.

An age later, Morwenna appeared, took Kreyna's face in her hands and said, "Come on, sweetie, let's go home to my place."

*　*　*

After two days in a fetal position, more or less, she managed to sit up so that Morwenna could feed her meager spoonfuls of chicken soup heavily laced with ginger, garlic and chilies. Morwenna's eyes widened at the fading love-bites on Kreyna's neck but she chose not to comment. Nearly a week later, Kreyna went back to her own apartment, with Morwenna promising to visit and bring food, if she had the need.

She was alone. In silence.

Weeping. She got a rash around the nose from constant blowing. What had possessed Robert to take his own life? The question provided the answer and again she wept for him, imagination working overtime. She knew how vile entities could be. They drove people insane, given half a chance.

Because of Robert's activities, Frances would have been told Kreyna was a potentially drug-addicted security hazard. Could Frances be blamed for doing her job? As far as Frances knew, it was a fact requiring confirmation, nothing else. Frances was the hunter, Kreyna was the target and she had no more expected to get emotionally involved than had Kreyna.

Kreyna grieved for what might have been under different circumstances, all beyond her control. Worst of all, she missed Frances. In the short time she'd known her, Kreyna experienced a mutual recognition, a meeting and exchange at the soul and heart of them both. She'd been moved as never before, by anyone. Simply, she missed that easy, comfortable, timeless presence. The memory left her hollow, refilled only with a deep and abiding sorrow.

Morwenna arrived with a stack of individual serves of moussaka and cup-size containers of zucchini soup for the freezer. More importantly, she cuddled and rocked Kreyna who apologized for being unbelievably tragic and pathetic. Morwenna kissed her on both cheeks and departed.

Declan phoned and made sympathetic noises.

Her father called to express his shock and dismay, with sympathy.

She was alone again.

Wondering what she could have done differently or better. Could she have loved more or done anything toward a better outcome? What? Frances was married to her husband and children; Robert was "married" to drugs and dreams of untold riches. And neither was of a mind to give up any of that for her. The truth was, they both had other priorities and she came a distant second.

* * *

For the first time in weeks, Kreyna dressed in gray shorts and a black T-shirt, and tied the laces on a new pair of white running shoes. She bundled up her hair and pushed it out the hole in the back of a baseball cap. Sunglasses on, she jogged down to the edge of Lake Burley Griffin, aiming to complete the three-mile circuit between the lake's two bridges before the sun climbed too high.

She had been used, abused, humiliated, trifled with, cheated, rejected and lied to, and had come off second best. Falling into an easy rhythm, she admired numerous black swans with their broods, swimming serenely, purposefully. Every few hundred yards, she ran full tilt before dropping back to a jog. Full speed, she was wild-eyed, frothing, blood-boiling, fire-breathing and murderously, violently, ragingly angry. Definitely getting better. Someone was going to wear it.

* * *

Kreyna paced the floor in Pankaj's office. "Did you know I was under surveillance?"

"I was briefed about Robert. It occurred to me they might include you, but I thought it unlikely. What does it matter now?"

"It matters to me. ASIO's policy of information being distributed on a need-to-know basis is laudable. Except when it's some incompetent moron making a decision about what I should know. I'd like to say a few harsh words to that imbecilic bureaucrat, whoever he or she may be. Perhaps you can pass on the message."

Pankaj glowered at her. "Your dramatics serve no purpose. Let's get back to business. In a few weeks, we'll be flying you out to Fort Meade. I have papers here for signature."

"Really?" She smiled tightly and slid an envelope across the desk. "I have some paperwork for you also, Dr. Corea—my resignation. I refuse to work with the US military. They cannot be trusted."

He picked up the envelope and glanced at it, unopened. Stretching every word, he said, "You must realize that release from the organization is a far more complex process than this single sheet of paper."

"I'm sure the termination form's as thick as an airport paperback. Post it."

She turned at his door. "I'm curious—was Adrian disciplined, or did he get a ritual rap over the knuckles? Thought so. Goodbye and thank you for all you've taught me. Nothing personal."

She had another appointment with a far more formidable energy.

* * *

It wasn't going to be easy, but she was determined. After five unsuccessful attempts over an equal number of weeks, even she had to concede temporary defeat. In her current state of grief and anger, she couldn't lift her energetic vibration high enough to access the Filigrane.

She hungered to vent her fury at not being protected. Her Sentinels had let her down, seemingly deserted her, and left her exposed and vulnerable. A psychic grave stomp was what she had in mind. Daily, she would rant out loud to those who might be listening.

You didn't warn me, you didn't tell me. And how could you let this happen? How did I transgress? What have I done to deserve this? Answers!

If she was out and about, silently she'd berate herself for loving and trusting too much. Places and hours passed unnoticed. Friends and family would address her and she'd find herself apologizing for not hearing. Discreetly, they left her alone.

A government courier knocked on the apartment's front door and handed her a yellow envelope. She took it out to the courtyard table and left it there while she pruned the photinias, the click of the clippers satisfying a burning need to methodically destroy something, or bring it under her control at least. She swept the paving, emptied the ashtray of Morwenna's bidi butts and opened the envelope.

The letter was from Pankaj. He wrote that, in view of the emotional circumstances in which she had tendered her resignation, in particular the loss of a close colleague, her resignation was not accepted. Her actions, allegedly under duress, did not preclude her from police prosecution should she step outside of ASIO's jurisdiction. He reminded her of the terms and conditions of her employment and reiterated that, while she may have grounds for a temporary suspension of duties, only permanent, debilitating ill health was sufficient for release from the organization. She was required to make an appointment with the Commonwealth Medical Officer for an exhaustive assessment, immediately.

Kreyna sighed heavily. If she wasn't already a head case, the hoops she would have to jump through to get out would make it so. And there was a strong likelihood ASIO would never let her go at all.

* * *

This evening's meditation went deeper than she'd experienced for months. Despite agonizingly slow progress, she'd been forcing herself to go through the motions, the ritual providing a degree of comfort, if little else. Now, calmness descended and her thoughts stilled to a peaceful, aimless hum. Before her, Quan Yin held up an open palm and smiled knowingly. The votive candle flared and spluttered, casting mobile shadows on the walls. Into the full white state Kreyna flowed.

The hair on the back of her neck went up and tingles went down her spine, along her arms and into her hands. She sensed the Sentinels spatially, as beings of radiant light shifting their energies within the room—behind, a little above and shoulder to shoulder with her. Out of the corner of her eye, she caught movement. Bright and six others—six! She was deeply honored and bowed her head, humble in their presence. Compassion rippled and intense love swirled within grasp.

Come with us, Kreyna. We request.

She rose from her body and hovered on her back with forearms crossed across her chest, fingertips on the opposing shoulder, body and legs rigid. Thus, she began to accelerate up, as if drawn by the shaft of light in which she traveled. Not a breath of wind, but she moved fast and closed her eyes against the sense of vertigo. At last she halted, only to begin rotating continuously until she lost all sense of either gravity or direction. Movement ceased and she opened her eyes.

Along a road, Kreyna jogged with a big black dog. *He's yours.*

Across a paddock skipped a girl with masses of blond curls. *She's yours.*

On a beach, Kreyna walked hand in hand with a woman. *She's yours.*

Kreyna closed her eyes.

All is as it should be.

Before you incarnated you asked for every experience, every challenge.

Some you nominated to handle without us. This was one of them.

A world of possibilities awaits you when you integrate logic with the illogical.

Realize you can trust your own judgment.

Through realization, anger transmutes into forgiveness.

Forgive yourself and others for hurting you.

No one and nothing is hurt without transformation.

Release them all with love. Detachment draws love near.

You are becoming. Allow it.

Silence.

There is great good yet for you to do.

Your training will ensure resolution for those injured of old.

You are never alone, always loved.

With effort, her eyes opened. Light at the end of the tunnel. For a change, it wasn't an approaching train. Gratitude.

PART FOUR

Fourteen years later – 2009

CHAPTER TWELVE

The mobile chimed as she took the steps two at a time. Frances swore and raked through her handbag.

"Hello Mummy. Is it convenient to have Tom to tea tonight? We'd like a chat with you and Daddy."

"Only if Tom finds a good Australian wine to bring along. Sorry, darling, I'm late for an appointment—have to go. See you tonight." Chat about what?

She read the few doorbell options and pressed the name matching the card in her pocket. It was a brisk, autumn afternoon in the London suburb of Acton Vale. Plane tree leaves swirled around her brown-booted ankles. Impatiently, she waited for a reply. Pulling the camel hair coat snug around her ears, she cursed Bruno, her hairdresser, for cutting her thick, graying hair a mite too short. Through the intercom a muffled voice told her to take the stairs to the third floor, room 309.

Upstairs, she knocked and entered through the black, gloss enamel door. A heavily built man stepped from behind a desk, hand held out in greeting. She took his warm, comforting paw in her too cool fingers.

"Pleased to meet you, Mrs. Parrey. Have a seat." He indicated a Marcel Breuer-style chair. The room was overly warm—she took off her coat and sat on the rigid, wide black leather strap.

Listening to answers to a series of routine questions, he typed her personal details into the laptop perched on the desk. Housekeeping complete, he consulted a letter from a paper file.

He spoke with the remnants of an Australian accent. "Your general practitioner, Doctor Johnson, writes you're suffering from night terrors. And he prescribed diazepam three months ago from which you've had little relief. Is that correct?"

"Yes, although I should say I don't much like taking them. I tend to forget the evening dose. My doctor suggested psychotherapy as an adjunct to the medication. Recommended you. Have you dealt with this condition before?"

"Yours is one of a raft of possible responses to disturbing stimuli. I have treated any number of patients with similar conditions using a combination of psychotherapy and hypnotherapy. I propose a minimum of three appointments in quick succession. In that time, we should see some relief. Fees will total four to five hundred pounds, depending on the time spent."

He removed his reading glasses and regarded her. "If at any time you're unwilling to proceed, rest assured you may discontinue treatment. I prefer my patients to be cured. If I am unable to help, another professional may suit you better, okay? Please accompany me to the treatment room where you can relax."

In a room filled with tall, overflowing bookcases, Frances settled back into a well-worn, black leather recliner. Seated separately, he wrote on a leather-bound pad while she related the details of her problem: the crying out in fright, usually between midnight and two a.m., the difficulty her husband had waking her up and the disorientation when he succeeded.

"Do you remember having fearful dreams? If so, what are they about?"

"I remember perfectly because it's always the same. I'm in a totally dark room. Slowly, the scene in front of me begins to lighten, from what light source, I can't tell. The shape of something very large, and I mean huge, becomes terrifyingly apparent."

"Do you recognize what it is?"

"A black widow spider. He has his back to me, filling the whole room with his enormous body and legs. And I think, if I don't move or breathe, he won't notice me and I'll survive. Otherwise he will turn, sink in venomous fangs and devour me." Frances shivered and grimaced. "When I was a child, we lived in the outer suburbs. Occasionally, we'd see such spiders. I never knew I could be this frightened of them."

He stopped writing to twirl his pen. "Do you share a bed with your husband?"

"Up until fairly recently when I moved into one of the spare bedrooms. My son has moved to Nottingham, my daughter is engaged. We don't see much of either of them these days, more's the pity."

"Have the night terrors reduced with your changing rooms?"

Frances took her time. "Yes, but it coincided with me beginning the diazepam. I think it's had some effect."

"One last question: do you drink more alcohol than might be considered strictly healthy?"

"Perhaps."

"There are two things I'd like you to do: keep a sleep diary and record what you did before going to bed and at what time, plus anything you might think of when you wake up—a monitoring exercise, if you like. Second, see if you can moderate your alcohol intake. It combines poorly with diazepam, I'm afraid."

He returned to the office and she slipped off the recliner.

She read the back of his business card showing details of her next appointment. "Thanks very much, Dr. Hansen. I feel a mite better for having hope, if nothing else."

* * *

"This haddock's pukka, Mrs. Parrey. You're the uber cook of the family, I reckon."

Sipping from her glass, Frances appreciated the endearing, red-haired young man her daughter had managed to snare. Tom

Jetta was ridiculously tall at six foot four, with broad shoulders and narrow hips. Freckles blended under the ginger hair on the backs of his hands. The hands and wrists extended well beyond the cuffs of his mint-green shirt, too short in the arm for his rangy limbs. Brilliant blue eyes darted between her and Bryce who sat at the head of the table, divesting the fish of its sauce.

Tom peered down at the fair young woman beside him. "Megan and I've been having second thoughts about the wedding, haven't we?" Studiously, Megan shoveled minted peas into her mouth and nodded.

"Rather than burden you two with the whole palaver, we thought we'd ask my parents to play hosts. Earlier rather than later. Before Christmas, actually."

"*Your* parents? Before Christmas?" Frances couldn't believe her ears. "But it's less than three months away. Besides, don't they live in Australia?"

"That's the whole point, Mummy." Her daughter's pale green eyes pleaded. "We could get married sooner. And in lovely warm weather—it'll be marvelous!"

It must be fourteen years. In the dark recesses of long suppressed memory, yearning stirred.

"You're sure about this? It's a tremendous imposition on your parents, Tom. As parents of the bride, it's our duty to organize the wedding here. Isn't that so, Bryce?"

The silver-haired man dabbed his mouth with a napkin and placed it next to his dinner plate. He stood up and straightened his cufflinks.

"If it's held in Australia, I won't be able to attend. Prior commitments. And now I must see to paperwork. Good night, Tom." To a stunned silence, he left the room.

"There, Megan. Your father won't be available to give you away. Is that what you want?"

"Oh, Mum, like I care if he's not there. Hasn't been around for anything else of consequence—why change now? Welcome to the twenty-first century, Buck Rogers. I can give myself away, if necessary. *You* could, for that matter."

"You think I *want* to give you away in bloody Australia? Sorry Tom, but she's a mite rude."

Tom's freckles darkened. "It has its pluses, I reckon. You could enjoy a holiday away from London's gloomy winter. My Mum and Dad will organize the whole shebang. I've okayed it with them already." He gazed from under thick, ginger eyelashes. "You wouldn't have to do anything except turn up with a smile."

As if.

As if she could land in Australia with anything other than a heavy heart.

Reluctantly, she conceded. "Brisbane will be hot. We could crack on down to the Gold Coast. Do the touristy thing."

"Didn't I mention? They've moved back to Canberra."

* * *

As per every Wednesday morning, Frances and Sally met for coffee and a bite to eat in a café in Knightsbridge. This time, it was Caffe Espresso on the ground floor of Harrods on Brompton Road, south of Hyde Park.

The Italian-style café produced premium quality espressos and pastries for its loyal clientele. The women positioned themselves behind a white marble table in one of a row of circular booths. Behind them, the walls were tiled to the ceiling in a gloss white glaze. Every few yards, a large gold and blue urn full of flowers featured in the tiled wall. The recessed ceiling boasted ornate, richly painted ceiling roses. In keeping with Harrods' penchant for tasteless ostentation, the café's crowning glory was a multicolored, glass chandelier.

Frances considered Sally to be her oldest and dearest friend. They'd married budding diplomats at about the same time and endured the posting in Abu Dhabi together. The less said about who got up to what with whomever, the better. They'd remained confidantes ever since.

"To be blunt, Sal, part of me is relieved the wedding's going to be held in Australia. Another part is wounded at being usurped. Yet another part is apprehensive because I'll have little control over the arrangements. I want it to be perfect for Megan."

"Your hair's frightfully short."

"Excuse me? Oh, Bruno was having a moment. And I'm forty-four. Who cares what I look like? Any minute now, I'll be a nana."

Sally slathered the last scone with jam and clotted cream. "Nana or not, I wish you'd come to our dinner party on Saturday. There'll be at least two single chaps with potential. Since you're thinking about divorce, it could be time to start looking. A little of *l'amour* could do you the world of good. Plus Bertie's cooking."

Frances measured the depth of her friend's twinkling gray eyes. "Oh well, since Bertie's cooking. Look, I'm not willing to *faire l'amour sans l'amour*, any more. I'd rather go without. And you know full well I've felt this way for some time. Why are you chewing this old bone?"

"Fran, you're too sad and it worries me." Sally leaned so her head nearly touched her friend's. "You haven't been at all happy since the Australian posting. Maybe a hearty romp would take you out of yourself."

Frances regarded the gaudy chandelier which didn't improve with looking. "I appreciate your concern, but nothing could be further from my mind. First, I want to see Megan married. Then I have to dismantle what remains of my marriage. The next few months will be very confronting and I'm dreading it—just have to get through."

Sally put down her cup. "Maybe when you're free you'll feel differently. Have you decided when you're going to file for divorce?"

"I had thought I'd wait until after the wedding next spring. Now, given the happy couple want a December wedding Down Under, I'll be on my tod by Christmas, I should think. Wouldn't *that* rock Bryce's boat?"

"I don't know how you've stayed the distance."

Frances grunted. "With difficulty. His latest mangles the English language. And looks too young to vote."

"You've seen her?"

"Only photos she's emailed. Of the soft-porn variety—perfectly ghastly. And I've had her on the phone, bold as brass. I don't know where he finds them."

"Money. They understand money, the universal language. Apropos of money, what did your solicitor say about settlement?"

"Complicated by Bryce's hidden assets. He won't cooperate, it's certain. It could take months to finalize. Or maybe a year."

"It will pass quicker than you think. Then you'll be free of all that angst. I've been meaning to ask, how are you going with that shrink? Is he any good?"

Frances downed the last of her coffee and twisted her watch. "I've only seen him once. Actually, I'm due there shortly. It's queer. There's something vaguely familiar about him. I could have met him before. Can't think where. Anyway, I'd best be off." She pressed her cheek to Sally's and waved goodbye.

On the street, she waited under a green awning until one of London's ubiquitous black cabs swerved into the kerb and picked her up.

* * *

Notebook and pen in hand, Dr. Hansen pulled up a chair while Frances settled herself on the recliner. She showed him her sleep diary and he scanned it briefly.

"I was less than diligent, I'm sorry. But nothing has changed since we last met."

Gentle eyes narrowed, he asked, "Are you depressed about your life, either as it is now, or because of past events? I'm after an estimate of your mental health and positivity. Or lack of it. Your philosophy of life, if you will."

He sensed her hesitation and continued, "Everything said within these walls stays within these walls. You have my word as a professional. While caution is appropriate, we'll get further faster when you talk to me."

She sat back, arms crossed. "My philosophy, as you say, is realistic and practical. Any youthful belief in the ability to control my own life has evaporated over time. I try to change what I can and not worry about what I can't. In the past I've made quick decisions I've come to regret. Doesn't everyone?"

He scribbled notes, watching and listening intently.

"Am I depressed?" Frances said. "Sometimes I feel dead inside. When you've felt a certain way for many years, it's difficult to judge. But very soon, I expect my life to become more positive and pleasant. I'm leaving my husband of twenty-four years. Before it can happen, I intend to see my daughter married to her Australian boyfriend. They're very much in love—"

He interrupted, "You've been waiting for your children to leave?"

"For most of my adult life, my goals have been to raise my children and support my husband's career. By 2010, I believe my obligations to him will be fulfilled and I can get on with life. I intend to return to university. It's something I've put on hold for too long. My time is come. Nearly. A few hurdles to clear first."

"Thanks for putting me in the picture." He closed the pad on his lap. "Phobias, be they of heights, confined spaces, or spiders, respond particularly well to hypnotherapy when the patient is a good subject. I would like to proceed with eliminating your spider phobia quickly. That should produce an instant result in regard to your recurring dream. Have you been hypnotized before?"

She hadn't. Patiently, he described what she could expect to experience during the process. His client reassured, he began to talk her into a deeply relaxed state through a series of trance-inducing scripts. After nearly twenty minutes, he gave her subconscious mind instructions that reiterated the harmlessness of the arachnid and her lack of interest in its presence, ever after. Returned to conscious awareness, she said she found it surprisingly pleasant and relaxing. He booked her in for the following week.

* * *

"What are you doing?" Megan stood at the door of her mother's bedroom. Assorted clothes were piled high on the bed.

"I'm sorting out what I want to keep and give away." Frances straightened up. "I've an awful lot of clothing from when we used to entertain. I shan't wear any of it again. Time it went." She pushed a pile out of the way and sat on the bed. "Come in, darling. Is there something I can help you with?"

Megan sat down and her mother put an arm around her waist, squeezing her close. "Mum, are you proper vexed about the change in wedding plans? I'd far rather you were happy about it."

"It'll be fine, I should think. A few less relatives from our side of the family may make the trek across the globe. But Tom's family will make it grand. Have you found a venue yet?"

"Google to the rescue. We've managed to book a spot Tom's fond of. It's the National Carillon on Aspen Island—a tiny island close to shore in Lake Burley Griffin, I believe. We can't have gone there—I don't remember it at all."

"You were too young, but I know it. It'll be splendid, perfectly splendid."

They sat in silence for a few moments. Megan's cheek rested on Frances's shoulder.

"You're going to leave him, aren't you." Not a question. "What took you so long?"

Frances's chest trembled. Megan looked up to see her mother smiling tremulously, tears sliding down her cheeks.

"It's a question of timing. I have to wait for the right time. I've not always chosen the right moment for things, you see. I want to get it right."

Megan hugged her mother, who responded with a kiss between the eyes and atop her head.

"You're the best mum in the world and I *so* want you to find someone who'll care for you properly. You deserve to be loved and appreciated. Cherished."

"Dear girl, there's slim chance at my age. But I appreciate the sentiment. Don't worry about me. The next few months will be very exciting for you. I'm thrilled you're marrying Tom. He'll make you happy, I feel it."

Megan stared at the nearest pile of clothes. She reached and pulled out a wad of folded fabric. On her feet, she shook out a tailored shantung suit with a mandarin collar.

"You can't throw this out! You look gorgeous in this. Here— try it on. I bet it still fits."

"I'd rather not at the moment. Besides, it's awfully dated. Someone else will have fun with it, playing dress-ups."

"Nonsense! This style's a classic. Do keep it—you never know."

* * *

Megan had gone. Frances squeezed the last outfit into a black garbage bag destined for Oxfam. Until now, she hadn't allowed herself to think about revisiting Australia. Neither had she dared think about a certain young woman she'd struggled to forget.

Kreyna Katz. What could Kreyna have been capable of, given the chance? If they'd had more time, could they have found a way where there was no way?

The reality of circumstances had brought home its hopelessness. Out of time, too much had been at stake. An illusion of choice contrasted the children's security and future against a tenuous love—no choice at all. Kreyna had not, and could not fit into her life.

Since then, it had taken numerous affairs to bury the longing. She'd layered rigid crusts of indifferent sexual experience over the wound in her heart.

If you pick hard enough and lift that old scab, you'll start oozing all over again. Keep picking and you'll never heal. What's the point? You know you'll never see her again. Leave it alone.

* * *

With a deep frown, Dr. Hansen read her sleep diary. Frances stretched out on the recliner, laced her fingers and waited. He slapped the booklet shut and smacked himself on the forehead with it.

"No change at all? I think we need to shift tactics. I want to regress you back to childhood and locate the first occurrence of the fear of spiders. If necessary, I'll take you back into a previous life, or lives, to locate its origin. Then you can be rid of it."

Hair rose at the nape of her neck. "Excuse me, but is it safe?"

"Safe? Of course. I will be guiding you with my voice and can bring you into the present with the snap of my fingers, just like that." He snapped his fingers, as if that proved how safe it was.

He began with his standard sequence of deepening relaxation and two trance-inducing scripts. Frances slipped into a deeply relaxed state, drowsy and close to sleep.

"I want you to imagine standing on a broad white line. In front of you stretches your future, much as your past stretches behind you. Now, go back in time to when you last saw a real black widow spider and tell me where you are."

"In a room at school. The science lab."

"How old are you?"

"Nine years and five months. It's nearly Christmas—there's snow outside the window."

"What can you see and what are you doing?"

"Other kids. And glass terrariums. All sorts of creepy crawlies—stick insects, cockroaches and beetles." Frances squirmed and spoke in a voice as if she were there, at exactly that age. "And spiders—ugh! Oh, how horrible! It's eating a bug! We're supposed to watch."

"Do you see it's inside the terrarium and you're on the outside, safe?"

After a short silence came a tentative, "Yes."

"Is this the original source of your fear of spiders?"

She shook her head emphatically.

"Did the fear originate in this incarnation?"

"No."

Dr. Hansen paused. His patient had been unduly apprehensive about past life regression—he must proceed with caution.

"Frances, I want you to go back to the time when you first became frightened of a black spider."

What an odd tearing sound, much like a baguette being ripped apart. Or skin from flesh.

* * *

It was getting dark too soon. Frans ran low toward the Arnhem Bridge over the Rhine. He tugged the young woman behind him—she stumbled and scrambled to keep up. Ahead, he spotted the sentry's wooden shack and they scurried around the back. Kryna turned an ankle and drew breath sharply, a tiny whine escaping her throat. He clamped his hand over her mouth, her frightened eyes growing wider until her breathing steadied. He took his hand away. And put a finger to his lips in warning.

Snatching off his beret, he edged up to the window and looked in. Satisfied, he tugged the beret over his dark blond curls and pulled four slim packets of cigarettes from his jacket. With a nod to the girl, he stepped around to the door.

"Good evening, *Unteroffiziere Spinnenschwarze*. I have gifts for you in exchange for safe passage across the bridge for me and my girlfriend, as agreed."

The door closed. Kryna heard three, maybe four different voices, but couldn't make out what was said. Praying silently, she waited and grew more frightened by the second.

The door opened. A mouse-haired Nazi soldier peered around the corner and ran a metallic glance over her slight form. He leered at her and disappeared. Frans dashed behind the shack and snatched up her hand.

"Run!" he whispered urgently. "Run before the bastard changes his mind."

They ran up the approach road to the bridge, negotiating shell holes, rubble and wooden barriers. Kryna's heart thudded dangerously in her chest. She knew she was horribly weak from hunger, but desperate not to slow him down. Adrenaline surging, she found untapped speed. They were at the other side. Frans glanced over his shoulder and skidded to a stop. He stepped behind her. A rifle shot rang out. He swung her around and hurled her down the embankment, rolling over and over in her wake. Stunned, they lay sprawled together, a tangle of arms and legs in the field below.

"Get up. We must keep moving." He hauled her to her feet and they set off across open ground, falling into a large shell hole to shelter and catch breath. They clambered out and headed for a distant track and some trees that showed promise. Interminably, they half-jogged, half-ran, keeping low until they crossed the track and reached the trees. Slowing to a walk, they picked their way through the trees. It became harder and harder to see where they were going.

With a bloodcurdling growl, a huge black beast launched itself at Frans's chest—he was knocked to the ground. Kryna squealed in terror and jumped on its back, beating it frantically with her fists.

"Stop! No, Kryna! Leave him alone. It's my dog, Wodan."

She fell off and lay in the dirt, panting. "Your what? He's as big as a pony." The Bouvier licked his master's face and began sniffing under his jacket. Frans pushed him away and sat up slowly.

"We must find shelter before it's totally dark. There's an old barn behind this wood—we can sleep there. In the morning, Wodan will escort us into Arnhem and a safe house. There, we can meet up with my resistance comrades and set about finding your family."

The threesome threaded their way through the trees, the large black dog padding ahead noiselessly, cropped ears pricked like rifle sights. The barn loomed, a door slightly ajar. They squeezed inside—nothing but musty straw and decaying feed troughs.

Together, they raked the meager straw into a makeshift bed and settled to rest. Hesitant, Kryna reached out and stroked the wiry coat covering the dog's flank—he was all ribs. Silently, she apologized for the beating. He licked her hand and dropped his massive, weary head.

Lying next to Frans, the metallic odor of blood overshadowed his stale male scent. Sick with fear, she reached and touched his chest. He winced and pulled away, but the stickiness remained on her fingers.

"You've been shot. Where exactly? How bad is it?"

"Just below the left collarbone. The bullet could have nicked the top of the lung, I can't tell. Hurts to breathe. Still bleeding."

"We should get you to a doctor."

He laughed feebly. "We should do many things before we die. Like learn to run faster from Nazis. Ah, ha—too late now."

"He was aiming at me, wasn't he?"

"Of course—murder the Jew, then the Jew-lover." His breath rattled faintly. "When I looked, he was aiming at your back. The bastard waited until we were almost home. For greater sport—a more challenging distance for his eye, plus the glee in killing us with hope in our hearts. The perfect revenge."

"Revenge for what? My people did nothing to the Nazis."

"Revenge for being different, smarter, working harder, and being wealthier and more powerful because of it. Your people are the perfect scapegoats—a whole race to victimize and punish with lethal, jealous rage. They can't stand you and your kind."

"What about you—can you stand me?"

He searched for her eyes in the gloom. "I'm here, aren't I?"

"Yes, and dying for your trouble, crazy gentile."

"I believe in freedom and equality. Mere ideals unless I stake my life on them."

She lay beside him, taking in his words, listening to the night drawing in. The dog snuffled and twitched in his sleep, chasing dream rabbits. Frans's chest bubbled when he exhaled. She rose to kneel beside him. Inexpertly, she undid the button fly of his wool serge trousers and touched him.

Alarmed, he said, "What are you doing?"

She caressed his warm body, pleased to gain a rapid response. "Thanking you."

"You know nothing about me."

"I know your heart. That's all that matters. Today, you saved me from being shot. And tomorrow, I could still be shot—it's all a big risk."

She bent and took him in her mouth, heard his sharp inhalation and a feeble chuckle. "You're killing me."

"Might as well meet your maker with a smile."

She lifted her skirt and sat astride him, sliding back onto his penis. Increasingly, she bounced, noting his erratic breathing with pleasure.

"Oh. Christ."

* * *

A clicking sound, over and over—click, click, click. Dr. Hansen was snapping his fingers, frantically. "Frances! Return to the present. Now!"

Had someone hit her with a brick? She opened her eyes, blinded by the glare from the banker's lamp emitting a dim, greenish glow. With both hands, Dr. Hansen rubbed his cropped hair in agitation and picked up a tumbler, guzzling water thirstily.

"You've been unresponsive for seven minutes. Sorry about that. I was panicking a bit. I'm thrilled you're back."

Hoarsely, she asked, "May I have some water, too?"

"Of course—of course!"

He bounded from the room and returned with a carafe and another tumbler. "Where were you?" He filled the tumbler and handed it over. "What happened?"

"I died."

"Yes, well—we all die, dear. Could you be more specific?"

She rubbed her forehead. "I was shot by my husband. Only he wasn't my husband then because I was a man—too confusing."

"Try starting from the beginning. Name, where, when?"

"Frans, the bridge at Arnhem in Holland, 1944. I was escorting a Jewish girl out of Germany. Kreyna? Can't be. It's too long ago. This doesn't make any sense."

He froze. "Shit. Now I know where we've met. You were with Kreyna. Melbourne Cup, 1995."

"Arty? Now I remember—how come you're in London? Is Neil here too?"

"He's working a computer systems contract up in Edinburgh for three months and is due back for Christmas."

"Have you been practicing in London long?"

Arty rubbed his jaw, a smile growing. "Nearly ten years, I'd say. What a surprise. After all this time, it's a small world. But enough of old home week, I'm supposed to be helping you professionally. We can talk personal stuff later, if you'd like."

"To be blunt, I'm exhausted. But I need your help to make sense of it all."

From the beginning, she recounted what she'd experienced during the regression. He took notes, occasionally interrupting her to clarify a point.

"What was the German's name again?"

"Spinnenschwarze. But as I said, he felt like my present-day husband."

He bolted into the next room and came back with his laptop. "Google's wonderful. Let's put it into the Babelfish translator. Ah. Perfect."

"Care to share?"

"Black spider."

She shivered and took a deep breath. "Fine—tell me what you think it all means."

He closed the laptop and scanned his notes. Worrying a thumbnail between his teeth, he said, "It looks like in a previous incarnation, you were a male member of the Dutch resistance operating out of Arnhem in World War Two. Seems you were smuggling allies and Jews across the Arnhem bridge and out of Germany. One day in 1944, you bribed a Nazi border guard to let you pass with a Jewess. He used you as target practice and you were seriously wounded. The Jewess jumped your bones as a parting gift. She must have made it to Arnhem proper somehow— maybe thanks to the dog. The next question is who was she?"

"I think Kreyna told me that's how her grandmother escaped during the war. But my memory is hazy. Could be."

"Let's suspend incredulity for a moment and say it's correct. If so, that's how her grandmother conceived who? Her mother or father?"

"Father, I should think." She took gulps of water and rested back into the recliner, eyes closed. "Never met the man. Though I do remember her saying she resembled him."

"If there's any truth here, then you and Kreyna are intimately connected."

"Excuse me?" Frowning, Frances stared at him. "Pardon my ignorance, but are you saying she and I have a past life connection?"

Arty's eyes lost focus and he was quiet for a long moment. "My personal opinion is you're both part of the same soul group—we all belong to a soul group. Each group has experienced past lives together, possibly over thousands of years. And you will again, changing role, gender, sexuality and purpose each incarnation. We take only our relationships with us when we die—everything material turns to dust. Sometimes souls can turn up in your life as apparent enemies, but they're here to help you learn. Even the Nazi sentry, who must have been killed later. He reincarnated as your current husband. You're married to a man once named 'black spider' who shot you, albeit in a previous life."

He looked over his reading glasses. "No wonder you're terrified of black spiders. Why are you leaving your husband, again?"

"Because my daughter is getting married. Both my children will have left home safely. I shan't stay in the house with him alone. Not a chance." Frances rubbed her cheeks, fingertips lingering on her lips. "She was lovely. No—yes—really lovely. Kreyna's grandmother, I mean. A brave and beautiful soul."

"So is her granddaughter."

How much did Arty know? "When did you see her last?"

"Just before Neil and I left for England. We met Sofiya. She was only two and utterly gorgeous."

"Sofiya?"

"Her daughter. She married Declan, late ninety-six."

Frances couldn't stop it happening. She tried but couldn't. She pulled up her knees, buried her face in folded arms and sobbed. Arty sat on the edge of the recliner, one arm around her, patting a shoulder.

"You've got a lot of processing to do, not to mention some soul searching. I'm always available at the end of the phone, so call me if you feel the need."

* * *

Stone-cold sober, Frances stepped out of the bath. In the mirror, she contemplated her dripping reflection. That well kept, middle-aged woman—was it really her?

Just below the left collarbone, the café-au-lait birthmark stained the skin milky brown. Since childhood, it had embarrassed her and made her self-conscious. Now, it stood as testament to a previous life, the site of a deadly wound that took that life. A badge of honor. From what she'd learned of Frans, he had been a man of character who stood up for his beliefs, no matter what. That part of her could stand a revival.

Wearing warm pajamas, she snuggled under the duvet and switched off the electric blanket. The events of the day were bizarre. New and still fresh in memory was the odd sensation of stretching limbs, changing shape to fit a purely masculine physique. Even odder, Kryna's essence; her touch remained vividly etched, seemingly real and yet, surreal.

What of Kreyna, a mother and happily married to the old boss, Declan De Salles? Hardly surprising. If so, why be upset to hear it? She was overwrought and a mite hysterical which was justifiable, given the day's experiences. Once she divorced Bryce, she could do whatever she liked. What did she like?

Umpteen years alone stretched ahead, the time occupied primarily with being a baby-sitting nana until death. She loved babies, but what else? A return to study?

Quantum physics has always excited, and would continue to do so. She was fortunate to have good friends. And one or two prospective lovers, just watching and waiting for her to leave her marriage. None that appealed, but passable. Companionable at a pinch.

What more did she want? A full-blown, torrid romance replete with wild nights of transcendent passion?

With a self-mocking smile she drifted toward sleep. When she wondered why she always deferred to other people's desires and expectations, anger swelled and subsided. The cold, hard facts of her life with Bryce were that he had money, power and influence that she had used to create a bearable life and a future for their children. For them, she could and did tolerate most anything. She hadn't dared to dream of leaving Bryce until they were grown up. Not like she'd been left when she was a child—not possible. Her love for them was absolute. If she loved at all, it was always absolute.

Bryce had controlled the money and used it to control Frances. Her only currency was sex, judiciously used for barter. After five years of marriage and two babies, sex had lost its value during the posting to the embassy in Manila. Bryce discovered the pleasures of young Philippinas. She had endured an endless parade of simpering, exploited girls ever since. At least he had stopped pestering her.

She had lived on his terms. Any illusion of freedom was just that—illusion. And she had bought into his venomous view of the world.

Once upon a time, she believed in the universe and its power to shape reality through positive intention. Exactly when cynicism overwhelmed faith, and self-doubt outweighed trust in her judgment, she couldn't pinpoint. What had made her discount the superior wisdom of her own heart?

Even Kreyna had told her to forget her—not think about her ever again. Wuss, wimp. Would Frans have complied? Don't be silly. He would have scooped up Kreyna and the children and ridden off into the sunset. Alone in the dark bedroom, Frances allowed herself a chuckle.

And then there's the real world. Well, the world and its arbitrary rules could go to hell in a handcart. As for Kreyna Katz, what right had she to impose a bloody intolerable rule based on some incomprehensible, esoteric theory? For the first time in fourteen years, Frances gave herself permission to think whatever she liked and not stress about the repercussions over ten thousand miles away.

At last, her little smile faded and she slipped into sleep.

* * *

She undressed her. Rich chocolate, flashing eyes set deep beneath an intelligent forehead under shiny black curls. Straight jaw with a letterbox mouth. The mouth, she knew well—sweet, moist, soft lips growing rigid with desire. Warm artist's hands, strong bronzed legs with pretty feet. Slim hips curving back to a muscular backside. Honey skin blending to milk coffee beneath a crimson shirt. Unbutton to the waist, hands stroking smooth skin, reaching around to her back, bending her to fit, mouth wet at her throat. Unzipping, sliding searing searching fingers into white-hot, black curls. Oh. Christ.

Frances cried out and swung bolt upright in bed, breath ragged. Release had been fast and furious. No, not a night terror, not a spider in sight—she would never suffer from that again. With a gleeful laugh, she threw herself back on the pillow and smothered her mouth to muffle throaty guffaws.

She knew she was being willfully wicked and, like as not, had lobbed a large boulder into a small pond, thereby creating a bloody great tidal wave that might ricochet all the way to

Canberra. Even worse, she failed to muster any sense of guilt—in fact, she rather relished the idea.

Buried deep in the past, all the old bets were off. It was time to put an end to self-censorship and to unleash the hunger.

For Kreyna.

CHAPTER THIRTEEN

Wodan's toenails tip-tipped across the polished jarrah floorboards in the living room. Heading down the hall, he found the study and its owner, and nuzzled a bare arm attached to a hand that tapped at the keyboard. Absentmindedly, Kreyna stroked one cheek and fondled his ears. Disgusted at the lack of attention, the Bouvier padded to his slung canvas bed next to the desk and flopped down, stretching his large frame from end to end.

Kreyna's gaze darted between the computer screen and the photo propped up on the document holder. Deep in concentration and intent on recording everything she could about the subject, she continued typing erratically and at speed. A homely young woman, aged about eighteen, smiled shyly back at Kreyna—she'd been missing since 2002.

* * *

Late night, party, pizza, Stolichnaya, end of school louts gunning for the Miss Goody Two-shoes, get her pissed, touch her up, pass her around, tabs of Ecstasy, her and two guys alone in a room, intercourse, her too drunk to notice who did what, more Ecstasy, intercourse, more booze, strangulation. Nobody cared. Hours later, stone cold on the floor. Get rid of her. In the state forest near the beach at Broulee. Shallow grave, red gums, tire tracks rained away. Nobody cared.

* * *

Outside the house on Weeroona Drive in Wamboin, a white Holden Commodore pulled off the road onto the long, gravel driveway. The doorbell rang. Silence. It rang again, twice.

"Sofiya! Would you get the door, please?" Silence. Another ring.

Hastily, Kreyna saved the document and strode down the hall to the front door.

"Detective Murdoch? I wasn't expecting you this early. Sorry to keep you waiting. I seem to have misplaced my daughter."

The plainclothes policewoman stepped past the screen door, held open. "Is she hard to keep under control or do you usually let her wander about as she pleases?"

Kreyna looked blank. "Sorry? Oh. Not usually. She must be down at the pony club. Or over at her best friend's place. May I get you a drink, hot or cold?"

Leading the way to the kitchen, she picked up mail off the hall table and rifled through it. At the kitchen bench, she checked the water in the kettle and put it on to boil. "I was about to make myself a pot of tea—would you like a cup?"

"If you can spare it, white with one, please. Have you made any progress with the cases you've been working on? My boss says you're our last resort, pretty much. Oh, I hope I haven't insulted you."

Kreyna spooned leaf tea into a chrome teapot. "Hardly. In regard to the boy, I've got a couple of promising leads. As to the young woman, I'm getting the gist of the situation now—could stand to have more time, if you don't mind. It takes some doing to tune in and sort substance from background noise." Boiling water sloshed through the tea in the pot.

"We appreciate anything you can tell us, Mrs. De Salles."

"Please. Call me Kreyna."

"Quite the flash house you have here, Kreyna, in what seems the middle of nowhere. When I drove in, I couldn't believe there were all these houses hiding away. They're so far apart from each other that they must be on huge blocks of land. I wouldn't want to live in such an isolated place. I'm a city girl, through and through—can't imagine starting a day without a large latte. How do you cope with the silence? It must be a real problem sleeping with no traffic noise. Have you many neighbors and do you have much to do with them?"

With an appraising glance, Kreyna passed a mug of strong tea to the detective. The woman's white-blond hair was combed into a severe ponytail. And the black suit did her no favors, either. With such pale skin, she needed to wear a warm brown color.

Kreyna said, "About two thousand people live in the Wamboin area. It's a tight-knit community and everyone knows everyone. We all watch out for each other which makes it a very safe place for families with children. I know most of the neighbors by sight and some quite well. My daughter has grown up with the local kids—we've got scouts, brownies and guides. The pony club is a favorite with Sofiya and the other young girls."

"You wouldn't want to have any secrets, by the sound of it." The detective looked doubtful.

"Privacy is not an option in Wamboin. But it's a great place to raise kids and very reasonable for commuting into Canberra—it's the best of both worlds. If you follow me down to the study, we can talk there."

On guard in the study doorway, Wodan unleashed a slow, deep growl directed at the detective and looked to Kreyna. Upon her small nod and a gesture, he backtracked to his bed and sat alert.

The detective sat in Kreyna's visitor's chair and opened a black briefcase. She placed a small recording device on the desk and a slim, paper file onto her lap. Kreyna picked up a photo of a young boy wearing football gear and waited. A barely discernible eyebrow lifted in her direction.

"Ready?" Kreyna asked. A buzzing noise started up somewhere on the desk. She scrounged under papers and found a mobile phone, tapped a key and read the screen.

"Excuse me—it's just my daughter telling me she's three houses away. Shall we continue?"

The detective turned on the recorder and poised a pen over a notepad. Kreyna began with background to the disappearance of the nine-year-old boy in the photo. "It seems the perpetrator was employed as a caretaker or cleaner at the primary school. I see him emptying bins of food and rubbish, perhaps in the kitchen. How anyone allowed this guy within cooee of any children, I can't imagine."

"Do you think he was a pedophile?"

"Or a serial sex offender. He has priors and should be on the register. It feels like he hails from Adelaide, originally."

"Is it possible for you to give a physical description?"

"Late forties, a small, boyish guy who could be taken for gay which he isn't. Mid-brown wavy hair, hazel eyes, looks inoffensive, acts charming and friendly, although he's a bit slow mentally. I see an earring with a tiny cross in one ear—the right ear. Otherwise, he was clean-shaven and presentable. He lived in a caravan park and bused to work and back. The victim caught his eye, although he would have preferred another boy he was watching. But he wasn't as easy to con, so he made do with the victim who happened to be in the wrong place at the wrong time. I think it was after school football practice. I get the impression of a backpack and boots with studs. The crime itself, I get anal penetration and suffocation. He didn't suffer long, relatively. Questions?"

"Well, that's a load of specific information that we may or may not be able to use to pinpoint possible suspects. If I were to ask you where the perp is now, would you be able to describe the region?"

For a few moments, Kreyna was silent. "Orange blossoms? Yes, he's in the Riverland area, picking citrus—somewhere around

Berri or Renmark in South Australia. He's possibly traveling between the two, depending on itinerant work."

"I see. That's very helpful. I'm sure it's unlikely but can you tell us his name?"

"Beginning with a P. Pip—Phil—Philip is what I'm getting. But I could be confusing him with the victim—names can be tricky."

"That's better than we hoped for. It is difficult, isn't it?" Detective Murdoch said. "Let's move on to the other three cases we gave you."

Kreyna related the information she'd gathered earlier on the eighteen-year-old. "Please give me a little longer on that one and I've yet to start the other two. May I phone you? Or email?"

The detective found a card in her suit pocket and tossed it on the desk.

"Briony?"

"I prefer Bree, it's so much friendlier. They say dripping honey catches more friends than spitting vinegar." The detective laughed, trying to make eye contact. Failing, she cleared her throat. "Phoning is best—I'd prefer to be anywhere else than sitting at my desk. Oh, and my mobile number is on there, too."

Kreyna propped the card up against the monitor.

The detective was packing up. "Does all of this stuff that you do come easily? Or do you have to really work hard at conjuring up a story?"

"Depends what you call easy. Boiling an egg or climbing K2? These cases can be harrowing."

Bree looked around the tidy yet lived-in room. "Oh, I don't know. To be honest, I have to say, with respect, I don't believe whatever it is you think you're doing."

"Really? With respect, please don't mistake me for someone who cares what you think." The detective blinked rapidly and stared at Kreyna.

"I do what I do for the sake of the victims of crime, so they are heard and acknowledged," Kreyna said. "And to assist your superiors to obtain a conviction, where possible. Rarely, I receive feedback as to the usefulness or accuracy of my information.

While I fully understand the police are reluctant to publicize the input of intuitives because such evidence won't stand up in court, I think you could be more transparent about the source of your new leads. Not for the publicity but for the sake of my own credibility and that of my peers. I don't need applause from an audience of thousands—none at all suits me perfectly."

Bree dropped her gaze. "Oops, that was a bit clumsy of me. You say it's harrowing—what do you mean by that? Aren't you just making up pictures in your head?"

"Do you *really* want to know? I'm not a circus act for you to gawk at. Don't waste my time."

Doggedly, Bree said, "Sorry. I didn't mean to be rude. I mean, I know a little bit about you. I've read your file and studied your background. The chief says you're very low profile for what you do and both highly regarded and qualified through your connections to ASIO."

Kreyna was mollified, somewhat. "Okay, it's harrowing because, to know what happened, I have to get inside the victim's body and feel all their feelings during the attack. As if that wasn't bad enough, I go into the attacker's mind to find out what he or she was thinking and feeling. It can be a very dark place that I can't get away from fast enough. The combination of victim and perpetrator energy can haunt me for weeks. Can you imagine experiencing full-on viciousness, absolute horror, murderous rage and mind-numbing terror, all at once? I get sensations and vivid, often gruesome and disturbing images that linger on for weeks in my mind. There's nothing even vaguely pleasant about the whole procedure."

"I think I understand better now." Bree wrestled with the recorder and jammed it into the black briefcase. "I guess you get some satisfaction out of knowing you've come up with information we may not have. It could make a big difference to victims and their families."

"When I can give your people concrete leads, yes, that makes it all worthwhile."

Bree put the suitcase on the floor and sat back. "The chief inspector told me you first helped us solve a home invasion out at Penrith. It struck me as incredible that you could possibly have come up with new leads in such a cold case."

"The old Lebanese couple?" Kreyna said. "Yes, I remember. When I concentrate on the evidence—names, places and dates— it's like I relocate my consciousness to that time and place and observe what happened. What I see is like a jumble of scenes from a movie in fast forward. For instance, that couple had been to a family funeral—the man's brother, I believe. They went home and had just sat down to supper." Kreyna closed her eyes to recall what she'd seen.

* * *

It had been early evening. Sitting at the kitchen table, Ahmed nibbled on a lamb kibbeh from a plate of mezza and his wife, Hanen, poured arak mixed with water over ice cubes in two small glasses. The elderly woman sat down heavily and took a sip of the milky, aniseed flavored liquid. With a sigh, she slipped off her headscarf, picked up one of the stuffed vine leaves and ate it without relish. Grief had robbed both of their appetites. Ahmed reached out and squeezed her fingers. They sat in an extended silence shattered only by the front doorbell.

Ahmed disappeared down the dimly lit hall. Still fit and strong from years of hard work in the restaurant business, he was anxious to stop the repeated chiming—whoever their visitor was, he had no patience.

From the kitchen, Hanen heard the night latch spring open, the front door creaked and voices grew louder. Suddenly, Ahmed shouted, "Jamil! In Allah's name, no!"

A sickening crash brought Hanen to her feet and she started toward the hall. Two figures came toward her, one carrying a machete, the other a contorted piece of metal. She looked past them and saw Ahmed lying slumped against a wall, the floor beneath his gaping neck awash with blood. Backing up, one hand over her mouth, she wailed, "Jamil? Rafiq? What have you done? Murderers! Oh, my poor husband—what do you two want?"

"Revenge, old whore. Waqas has destroyed our business, stolen our family's pride, and thousands of dollars. It should be ours, that money. You tell your son to close down or we'll be back to kill you too."

"Allah have mercy on you boys. You want money? I have money, jewels—whatever you want." Hanen lurched into the kitchen and dragged a coffee can from a shelf. Knotted hands shaking violently, she wrenched off the lid and wads of banknotes hurtled out, strewing across the benchtop. "I beg of you, leave my son alone. Haven't you done enough?"

"Shut up or we'll kill you now." Rafiq was stuffing money in his pockets. Wailing, Hanen fell to her knees and clutched at his jacket. Contemptuous, Rafiq swung the wheel brace and knocked her to the floor. With their weapons, the two men swept family photos and treasured knickknacks off shelves and ransacked kitchen cupboards until they stumbled over their own mess. With most of the remaining banknotes stashed in pockets, they sprinted out.

From her vantage point near the ceiling, Hanen's spirit watched them leave and marveled at how prettily the blood crept across the linoleum, away from her shattered skull.

* * *

Detective Bree Murdoch said, "What I don't understand is how they were positively identified from anything you could tell us—it would have to be very specific."

"Your inspector said the killers tried to make it look like a random home invasion gone wrong, not at all convincingly," Kreyna said. "But she—Hanen's spirit—told me it was revenge against their son, Waqas. He owned a restaurant in Brighton-Le-Sands that was doing too well and outselling his competitors, his own countrymen. The restaurant was plagued with drive-by shooting sprees and smashed windows, all meant to intimidate and get him to close down."

"So what, where's your proof?"

"Initially, Hanen gave me their first names—at least, what they sounded like, because I'm not familiar with her language. She showed me a security camera—I get an impression, a picture in my head, you understand. She insisted there was security footage of the exact same guys, wielding wrecking bars and a block-buster, in the process of destroying the restaurant's glass frontage. Also, the Road Traffic Authority had speed camera photos of the cars they'd used for the shooting episodes. It was just the kind of concrete evidence required to arrest them. I passed on everything Hanen told me and your people did the rest."

"Thanks to a dead woman and your vision, we had all we need to get them convicted," the detective said. "Good work."

They both heard a door close and a distant shout. "Mum, I'm home."

Kreyna swung her chair toward the open study door. "I've lost count of the cases I've been involved with since. More often than not, I receive further information. It may not always be critical, but that's for you to judge. Please understand I don't *do* anything, it comes through me."

"Well, thank you for talking to me and explaining the whole psychic thing so I can get to know you better and work with you. I know my boss believes in you and that's the highest recommendation I know of so that's good enough for me." The detective rose and held out a hand, her glance appraising Kreyna's physique.

At the front door, Kreyna thanked her for coming. They both saw her daughter as a vague figure in the relative gloom of the distant kitchen.

Detective Bree Murdoch took the steps with ease down to her car, pausing to wave as she opened the powerful Holden's door. She performed a three-point turn and sped away. The policewoman's appraisal had been something more than strictly professional. It would be a safe bet that the detective's work colleagues knew nothing of her personal life. Kreyna shut the door and sauntered into the kitchen.

"Has the pig gone?"

Kreyna came to a halt. "Where did you get that charming expression from?"

"A fully sick girl at school hates cops. She says they're all pigs."

"Fully sick, huh?" Kreyna watched her daughter's painted black thumbnails moving like a machine over the mobile phone keys; she was texting someone about something. "Top of the class, is she? Thought not. Here's a scenario: you come home from school, there's no one home, except it's obvious someone has broken in, stolen all the electronics and trashed the place. Who you gunna call?"

Sofiya shrugged. "The cops. Whatever."

"I rest my case." Kreyna headed back down the hall.

"Still don't like her."

Why did she always have to have the last word? At the computer, Kreyna checked her emails and news.com.au for the headlines.

"What's for dinner?" Sofiya read over her shoulder.

"Atlantic salmon and a Greek salad. I'll dice feta if you'll slice red onions."

"Yukko. Swap you for the feta." She wrapped both skinny arms around Kreyna's neck. "Remember Laura's older brother, Tom?"

Laura was Sofiya's childhood friend who lived three houses away and where Kreyna knew she had been earlier. An image of a gangly, red-haired youth popped into Kreyna's mind. "Yup."

"He's coming back from England with his girlfriend. They're going to get married at the Carillon on the fifth of December."

"Is he old enough to marry? How exciting for Laura's mum— she must be thrilled." And panic-stricken.

Sofiya flung herself into the visitor's chair and screwed up her nose. "Dunno. Because the bride's from over there, she's not got any bridesmaids here. Laura's going to be one and her mum thought I could be one too. Can I, Mum?"

"What, you in a frock? Seriously?" Kreyna examined her twelve-year-old. "If you really want to, I don't see why not. But do you want to get involved in the whole dresses and shoes and hair and makeup debacle?"

Sofiya critiqued her nail polish and nodded. Kreyna kept a straight face.

"Okay, I'll talk to Laura's mum and find out what's expected of you. There's some responsibility involved so you'd best be prepared." Sofiya continued to study her nail polish. Kreyna went back to reading the news, smiling to herself. Her daughter was growing up.

"I had a weird dream last night."

Kreyna snapped to attention. "How weird?"

"It was Oma again, with a message for you. Frans is on his way."

Frans? Never did find out who he was. "Okay. Thank you."

"Dad's late tonight. I'll go dice feta." Sofiya unwound her long legs, shook strawberry blond curls into a semblance of style and headed down the hall.

Kreyna checked the time on the computer. Declan *was* running later than usual, with no phone call as explanation. The unease she'd been feeling off and on all day, escalated.

* * *

Weight on her, breast to breast, juicy mouth attending to each nipple, throat, a tongue caressing her left ear, lips sucking the lobe. Want you. Fingertips stroking her belly, teasing her inner thigh, drifting higher, too slow. She whimpered, muscles contracting in anticipation. Her name whispered, deliberate as the touch, become a dripping tongue. Parting, flicking, sucking. Arching her spine, striating her breath. Love you. Feather kisses on her eyelids.

Two magpies warbled outside the bedroom window. Kreyna peered at the clock reading just before seven a.m. On her right, his back looming, Declan snored peacefully. She slipped out from beneath the sheet and stepped into the bathroom. Under the shower, pounding hot water brought her fully awake. With visceral shock, it struck her. That was no ordinary dream.

Quelling a rising sense of panic, she dried herself. Oh no, this can't be happening. She promised. Liar. Unfair. Damn it, Frances, you promised!

* * *

On this, her thirty-ninth birthday, Declan had taken her to dinner at The Chairman and Yip restaurant in Civic, the city's main business center, where they had savored a delicious and delectable menu over two indulgent hours. He came in from parking the BMW X5 safely in the garage.

Kreyna was making plunger coffee even though it was after ten p.m. Sofiya had gone to bed when they all got home. "Do you fancy a Cointreau as well?"

He threw car keys onto the island bench, pulled out a chair and sat rubbing his face in both hands. "Just coffee will do nicely." She carried over two mugs and settled them on coasters protecting the oiled, red gum table.

"There's never a good time to say what I have to say, but on your birthday it's very ordinary. I cannot apologize enough for it. However, urgency dictates."

She sipped coffee and stared up at him. "Please make sense soon."

"I've been in touch with Jenny. I went looking and found her email address on the Médécins Sans Frontières website and sent her a polite hello."

Heart beginning to hammer against her ribs, she said, "Jenny the ex? How long ago was this?"

He folded his arms and leaned back, stretching neck muscles with a grimace. "Mid-September. We've been emailing back and forth since about then. I've rung her from work a few times and we had a long talk last night, which is why I was late."

She managed a whisper. "And the upshot is?"

"I want to go to Uganda. No. I mean, I'm going to Uganda in two weeks' time."

"Two weeks!" Her cup hit the table. "Are you serious? What the hell are you going to do in Uganda—you're not a doctor."

He glanced at her, discomfort making him squirm. "They need people with other skills as well. I could work in administration or drive a mobile clinic. Or manage their HIV drug treatment supplies. They desperately need help."

"But you're going because she's there."

"Look, I'm not stupid." He bowed his head, rubbing the back of his neck roughly. "After all this time it may not be a goer, so I've decided to give it a shot for six months. I'm taking a sabbatical from the faculty—they've given me leave."

"And you want me to agree to you having what? A trial affair? Have you lost your mind? What about Sofiya?"

He cringed. "You'll take good care of her."

"She's only twelve, Declan, a very vulnerable age. She needs her father."

"Shit! I *know* how selfish it sounds, but I have to *try*—I have to *find out*. Don't you get it?"

"At what price?"

"I'm forty-seven and not getting any younger. If I don't follow my gut now, I never will. And I wouldn't forgive myself. It doesn't mean I don't love Sofiya and you—I do. But what I feel for Jenny is different altogether. I can't explain."

Kreyna slumped over her cup. "What a coincidence. Just when I'm feeling old and ugly, here's irrefutable proof."

"Old, maybe one day. Ugly, never." He stood, pulled her to her feet and gently wrapped her up in his arms, letting her tears dry on his best shirt. "What I want is for us both to be happy. Truth be told, I think I won you on the rebound."

She looked up at him.

"You were so sad around the time Robert died that I figured you still carried a flame for him. I hope I've given you some happiness since."

She hugged his comforting body. "Absolutely." His instinct was good, except the target was wrong.

"You'll have to tell Sofi. I won't do it for you."

"She probably knows."

* * *

In a large, loud McMansion built on an elevated block overlooking the Canberra suburb of Isaacs, Morwenna and Helios were bringing up their four children. Working long hours as a tiler in the construction industry, he'd kept her barefoot and pregnant for years. Morwenna helped his mother keep the books for her three suburban restaurants, when she could spare the time from motherhood. The family had plenty of money and were stalwart members of Canberra's close-knit Greek community.

Kreyna accelerated up the steep, pale brick drive and parked outside the double garage built under the house. She stepped down from the X5 just as her mobile played a tune. Tumbling it out of her handbag, she slid open the case and looked at the caller's number: unknown.

"Kreyna De Salles."

"Hi Kreyna, how are you?"

"Well, thanks—who's this?"

"Sorry. It's Bree Murdoch. Listen, I want to apologize for the other day. When I think about it, I must have been terribly rude which was totally inappropriate and I'd like to make it up to you."

"Nothing I haven't heard before. I'm a big girl now, thanks Bree—not a problem."

A sensuous chuckle. "I'm so relieved to hear it, it's been worrying me ever since. The best news is it seems I'm to liaise with you until the chief inspector says otherwise. It's important, therefore, that I remain as open-minded as possible."

"Not too open, I hope—your brains might fall out."

On cue, the detective cracked up. "I can tell we're going to get along famously. When you're ready with the other case, give me a call and I'll come down. Maybe I could make it later in the afternoon and after, we could share a meal in town, my shout?"

Kreyna did a double take. "My daughter's too young to be left, but thanks for the invite. I'll be in touch, bye for now." She slid the phone shut. Pass.

Guarded by two white marble, rampant lions, wide stairs led up to the front door. Morwenna waited with a wriggling, three-year-old Stavros on her hip. The two women kissed and hugged.

"Come down to the kitchen. I'll park this barrel of mischief in front of Angelina Ballerina—that'll keep him occupied while we talk."

The kitchen led off a large family room dominated by black leather furniture and a giant plasma television. Toys littered the floor around a square, charcoal-colored coffee table centered on a maroon Persian rug. Morwenna settled the starry-eyed boy with the bounteous black mop onto a child's size beanbag. She picked up two remotes that controlled the television and video player, and pushed buttons until a mouse-headed girl in a pink tutu danced into view. Stav squealed and clapped, gaze riveted to the screen.

"Half an hour of Angelina and he'll be ready for his afternoon nap."

On the bench next to the double-door stainless steel fridge was a large coffee machine. Morwenna held a jug of milk under a spout, moving it up and down to create froth. She pushed a button and brewed coffee dribbled into two wide cups. Cups on saucers, she added the hot milk and finished with scoops of froth and a sprinkle of cocoa.

Kreyna took a sip. "To die for."

Morwenna twinkled at her. "Here, sweetie, I've made *biskota amigdalou* just for you—any excuse." She sat across from Kreyna, lifted the lid from a plastic container and held it out. Kreyna bit into an almond biscuit and licked powdered sugar from her fingertips.

Morwenna said, "I haven't seen you for a while, sweet cheeks. What's up?"

"I've been busy with a couple of cold cases for the Sydney police. Very time consuming but I'm nearly done for this year, fingers crossed." Kreyna replaced her cup onto the saucer with undue care, hands trembling. "In other news, Sofiya's going to be a bridesmaid and Declan's going to Africa."

Morwenna chewed rapidly, watching her. "What's in Africa?"

"Uganda, to be precise. And it's not what, but who—his old girlfriend, Jenny."

"You're kidding me." Morwenna's mouth opened and shut and opened. "If anyone else had told me, I wouldn't have believed it. He adores you."

"Once upon a time, maybe. Not anymore."

Morwenna contemplated the pink creature cavorting across the television screen. "Any warning signs?"

"We haven't been intimate for many months. And he's been coming home late from work—emailing and chatting to her from the office, apparently."

Morwenna put her head in her hands. "Oh, sweetie, I'm so sorry. You must feel like shit. I know I would." She looked up. "Are you okay?"

"No. Not really. I'm numb—don't know what I feel."

Morwenna got up and came around the table. She put her arms around Kreyna who leaned into her, silence disturbed only by a little boy's muted giggles.

"I don't understand. Why's he doing this?" Morwenna asked. "I mean, it must be years and years since they were an item. You'd think he'd be over it."

"Some things you never get over. He says he has to find out. The ANU has given him six months—until the end of first semester, I gather."

"Yeah? Not very mature. When's he going?"

"In about ten days."

"What, before Christmas? That's rough. Does Sofi know yet?"

"He's telling her tonight." Kreyna inhaled through her navel, trying to lift some of the weight off her heart. "Strange as it may seem, I do understand where he's coming from. When I met him, he did tell me how much she meant to him. As the psychs would say, he needs closure—to either get over her, or be with her. He's been patient with me. The least I can do is return the favor."

"What favor? I'm not following."

"He said he always feared he'd caught me on the rebound from Robert, which is true, after a fashion. Seems like we were the proverbial booby prize for each other."

"I know the world's gone mad when Declan and Kreyna De Salles break up. This is awful!" Morwenna released her hold and hurried into the lounge. She scooped up the boy with his thumb in his mouth, fast asleep, and carried him down the hall out of sight.

Kreyna kept breathing. It gave her options.

Morwenna resumed her seat at the table. "Stav should be out to it for about an hour. You probably don't want to hear this right now, but when word gets around, you'll be beating them off with a club."

"Really?" Kreyna snorted. "Many moons ago, I recall a certain dear friend saying to me, 'If I'm so fabulous, how come I'm so alone?' But that's enough whinging—I'm sick of listening to myself. Your kids will be home from school soon. I should go."

"Hang about. What's this about Sofiya being a bridesmaid? Tell all."

"You know Laura, her best friend? Laura's older brother Tom is bringing his English fiancée here to get married. It's a considerable distance and expense for most of her girlfriends, so Laura and Sofiya are stepping into the breach. Imagine, if you will, Sofi done up in a frock with makeup. Can you believe my tomboy is volunteering? Mind you, I'm not sure she realizes she may have to lose the black nail polish."

They strolled down the hallway to the front door.

"Where and when's the wedding?"

"The Carillon on the fifth of December. The weather should be perfect by then."

Morwenna hugged her close. "After Declan's gone?"

Kreyna stepped away, nodding. Undecided, she studied her longtime friend. What the hell. Out with it.

"I want to tell you something I haven't told anyone. And I should have told you long ago, but the time never felt right. And then I thought it didn't matter anymore. Do you remember Frances Parrey, who worked for Declan?"

Morwenna's eyebrows nearly disappeared into her hairline. "The Englishwoman who threw the party where I met Helios? Certainly—what about her?"

"I fell in love with her."

Morwenna sagged to sit on the top step, her back against the cream brick wall of the house. She whistled, long and slow. "Wow. Spectacular."

Kreyna joined her on the top step, leaning a shoulder against the white, metal banister supports.

"Did she know?"

Kreyna nodded.

"Jesus, Mary and Joseph. Did she feel the same way?"

"So she said."

"Did you do anything—y'know?"

"A lip-lock or two."

"And you're telling me this now, because?"

Kreyna's face resembled sagging cement. "In all fairness to Declan, I can empathize. I understand why he's doing what he's doing, despite how hard it is on me and Sofi. Part of me is as mad as a cut cat, another part admires his courage." She shoved stiff fingers through her hair.

"What sign was she?"

"Sorry? Oh. Same as Declan, I think—he's a Cancerian."

"Hmm, one of those sooky-lah-lahs. Until they make up their minds and then they're relentless."

"Whatever else, he'll find out where he stands. When he does, he'll either stay there or come home. I get the feeling he won't be back in a hurry." Kreyna stood up, resolute. Morwenna reached up and dragged Kreyna back down to sit beside her.

"I don't get it. You and Frances."

After a moment, Kreyna whispered, "What makes you think you should?"

"It would be the first time I don't get what's with you." Morwenna massaged her eyebrows. "We've been through so much together. It makes me nervous to discover there's a part of you I don't understand."

"No need to be either nervous or understand." Kreyna held Morwenna's hand in both of hers. "What's important is that it doesn't change our friendship. No one can be everything to anyone. Each relationship has a place in your life that cannot be filled by someone else. I can't be what Helios is to you and he can't be what I am to you. Neither could Frances be what you are to me—you're irreplaceable. I have no doubt you and I have been friends for centuries and will continue to be so. I love you and you know that won't—can't change."

A teary Morwenna murmured, "Love you too."

"Besides, it happened so long ago, it's academic. Now I must get going, having unburdened myself after all this time." Kreyna stood up again. "Dearly beloved, thank you for listening and I trust we'll talk soon. If you have any brilliant ideas about Declan, you know where I am."

She scampered down the stairs to the car. Morwenna waved until the black four wheel drive was out of sight.

CHAPTER FOURTEEN

The email message looked ordinary enough. Short and simple, it requested that she contact the office at the earliest opportunity. The initials PC were the only signature. She held her breath, stared at the screen for too long and exhaled heavily. What did he want this time? Only when he had exhausted every possible tactic did Dr. Pankaj Corea draw down the last card up his sleeve. It had been February 2008, nearly two years ago, when ASIO had last made contact and reeled her in for a remote viewing assignment.

* * *

"What's so urgent that has your staff pounding on my door first thing on a Monday morning?" Kreyna adjusted the recliner beneath her.

Pankaj said, "The Timorese president, Ricardo Cabral, was shot this morning. We have a dead suspect and no clear motive. I want you to view the scene and find out what you can. The matter is critical to Australia's national security and its political relationship with East Timor. You must go immediately." He completed attaching electrodes to her wrists.

"Is he dead, the president?" asked Kreyna. She fidgeted with the wires and tried to relax.

"No, but seriously wounded. The suspect was Major Alfredo Alves. You're going to the presidential compound in Dili. The coordinates are zero eight point five five south, one two five point five eight east. Hurry up!"

Kreyna closed her eyes and hunkered down, slowing her breathing and crashing her pulse to a deathly pace. The Filigrane echoed a ping of recognition and she shifted into the full white state. Down and up, up at the speed of thought, another intuitive close by. Monitoring her.

* * *

Khaki uniforms slung with automatic weapons and ammunition. Black-booted men in berets and sunglasses stood in clusters as a gurney carrying a patient was loaded into an ambulance. The vehicle flicked up gravel when it left. Kreyna cruised the parking lot until she found the dead guy. Major Alfredo Alves was squatting next to a body, his head in his hands.

Kreyna concentrated on him and he looked at her with one soft, brown eye. Kreyna glanced at the corpse dressed in camouflage greens—the left eye had been blown away with his mortal life. Blood had caked his military haircut and splattered across the even features and neat, black mustache.

Alfredo stood and tried to touch her. "Are you dead or alive?"

"Alive, but from another place. Hello, Major Alves. Would you tell me what happened? Did you shoot the president?"

"Shoot Ricardo?" Alfredo said. "Is that what everyone thinks? No, I did not. I came here with my fellow petitioner, Ivo Pires. Two years ago, I led a mutiny within the Timorese army. Those from the west were treated unfairly by powerful eastern officers. The army split in two and we've been hiding in the hills. Today we were to meet with the president to discuss the terms of an amnesty—just to talk. He was due back from his morning walk along the beach. We decided to wait and we were ambushed. Executed. Shot at point-blank range. Poor Ivo in the back of the neck."

"Who stands to profit from your death—yours and the president's?" Kreyna asked.

Alfredo was lost in thought. He shrugged and said, "When I died, I guessed Ricardo arranged to have us murdered. Then I saw him taken away wounded. Someone has set us up—all of us. Whoever it was did not want this amnesty. I have to go."

Alfredo's essence was dissolving as he walked. Kreyna followed him. "Did you see who shot you?"

"Two masked soldiers with high-powered rifles. I was no longer useful to the prime minister's coalition—he was afraid of an amnesty. I'm going."

Silently, Kreyna wished him peace. And wished herself back to Canberra.

* * *

She blew air through her cheeks, shaking her head at Pankaj. "Those who want to know may not like what I have to report."

"Your job is to gather information. What they do with it is their problem. Well done."

* * *

Whatever Pankaj wanted this time, it mustn't be too critical. The cold cases for the Sydney Police would take at least another week—ASIO could wait. Kreyna turned her attention to a more pressing issue—the fate of an innocent young woman, gone too soon. The eighteen-year-old shone out from her photo on the document holder, all youth and hope.

Let's find out who did this to you, shall we?

At the computer, Kreyna brought down her breathing and heart rate until she vibrated at a level of serene detachment. She assumed the full white state and pinged the Filigrane, a low hum crooning in reply. All her senses heightened to extreme, gaze locked onto the young woman's eyes, she began to type.

Oow, he's nice! Oh, he's looking at me. Coming to talk to me—can't believe it! A drink of something blurky—better swallow fast so as not to taste it. And the blue pill. On the bed, rough hands squeezing and going everywhere.

Sweetheart, what's he look like? Got a name?

Taller than me, just. Real slim, too—hunky. Straight brown hair pushed up into a Mohawk. Brownish eyes, two eyebrow rings close together. Little bit of beard under his bottom lip. Homemade tattoo of a star on another star inside one wrist, can't remember which.

Name sounds like?

Jas. Short for Jason. And that douche bag, Anthony. We all call him Ant. He's got beady black eyes and skinny hairy legs. Stares at my girls. Can't stand him. Jas's mate, but.

Do you know them from school? Where's Jas now?

Ant's from school. Jas—they put me in the back of his ute, y'know. Went north, cutting cane. Tully. His mate's up there.

How are you feeling?

Better for the telling. Tired. Can I go home now?

When you look, you'll see. They're waiting for you. Go on.

A star on another star—a pentacle, perhaps? Kreyna read her jottings and wondered if any of it was of use to the police. All she could do was to pass it on. Further thought and editing added little, she'd found in the past. But she cleaned up her typos and printed a copy for the file.

Shouldn't they be back from the reception by now? Kreyna checked the computer's clock. She'd dropped Sofiya at the end of the driveway outside Laura's parents' house at nine thirty a.m. in plenty of time for them to get ready for the one o'clock ceremony at the Carillon on Aspen Island. The reception at Olims Hotel had been scheduled to start at four thirty p.m.—it was now after eight. Her daughter would be exhausted.

Mobile secure in a back pocket, she wandered down to the kitchen, closely shadowed by Wodan. Her home felt very odd. Declan had been gone a fortnight, yet she could still feel his personality, if not his presence. Everything in the house held memories of the three of them living and doing things together. It would have felt perfectly normal to hear a key in the lock and to see him walk in. She was switching the kettle on when her pants buzzed.

Wan2 stay. U cum 2 plz @ lauras xxx

Bugger. All she wanted to do was drive up, throw the kid in and come home. She wasn't feeling at all social and certainly wasn't dressed to meet a bunch of well-heeled strangers. Like it or not, she trudged down to the bedroom and changed into something considerably more presentable than her comfortable cargoes and T-shirt. At the front door, she reminded Wodan he was in charge and had permission to eat any burglars. His wagging rear end threatened to topple the hall table.

In Wamboin, three houses down the road translated to over a mile—too far to walk on a dark night with no streetlights. Kreyna motored slowly down the neighbors' driveway and parked with five other cars on the lawns. She walked up to the sprawling, ranch-style house.

"G'day, Sofi's mum—come on in." Laura's mother, Shirley Jetta, had piercing blue eyes, dark auburn hair and a face full of freckles holding hands. A distinct gap between her two upper front teeth made an easy smile eye-catching. Shirley and Kreyna had been young mothers when their daughters met as seven-year-olds in First Year at Queanbeyan East Primary School. A little too conservative for Kreyna's taste, Shirley was a warmhearted and conscientious member of the Wamboin community, especially as she was responsible for organizing the Brownies and Girl Guide troops.

Shirley led Kreyna through the house, in the direction of the back patio where over a dozen people stood talking and drinking. Through the sound system, Andy Gibb lamented love lost and found again.

"Mum!" Sofiya galloped over like a filly. "You missed a great party. It was wild rad, super fully sick. Look at all the photos I took." She had her phone out and was scrolling through dozens of blurry close-ups. "That's me and Laura—don't we look bee-ootiful? Megan's mum took this one."

Kreyna studied the only clear photo, barely recognizing her daughter. "You do, you look absolutely gorgeous, no doubt about it." She felt a hand on her shoulder.

"May I talk to your mother, Sofiya? Just for a minute—we'll be back."

Shirley beckoned Kreyna into the study and all but shut the door. "Thank you for letting us borrow Sofi. She was a joy to have around, perfectly behaved and did you proud. I just wanted to say how sorry Geoff and I are to hear about Declan."

Kreyna considered this. "You make it sound like he's died. He's gone overseas on a sabbatical, that's all."

"Oh, I'm sorry." Shirley covered her embarrassment. "We got the impression he'd left you for another woman. Oh dear, I'm so sorry—kids say the craziest things. Let's go back and join the others, shall we?" She opened the door and gestured for Kreyna to walk through. Kreyna was ready to murder a certain Sofiya De Salles.

"Mum, you *got* to meet Megan. And Tom. They're both fabbo. And *so* nice to me. Megan helped me with makeup and her mum, she's just the best, got me dressed really good—real nice. She said I looked lovely." With a giggle, Sofiya said, "Can you believe it?"

Kreyna squeezed her daughter tight. "Yes, because you are. Except when you tell people stuff about your dad and me. Keep it zipped, please."

Sofiya squirmed loose and dashed over to a tall, red-haired man with a very pretty girl on his arm. Sofiya grabbed his shirt sleeve and dragged him toward Kreyna. He, in turn, led the young woman.

He held out his hand; his new bride smiled. "Hi, Mrs. De Salles, good to see you again. I'd like you to meet my wife, Megan."

Kreyna shook hands. "How do you do, Megan, and g'day, Tom. You were considerably shorter last time we met. Where are you off to for the honeymoon?"

"We're flying to Phuket tomorrow evening." He looked to Megan for confirmation. "Several friends and Megan's mother are staying here overnight. We're putting on a barbecue breakfast first thing tomorrow, say eight o'clock. Would you like to bring Sofi? Then we can have a decent catch-up. Must be getting close to her bedtime." He winked at Sofiya who blushed.

"Sounds unmissable, but it's time to go, kid. Sorry—lovely girl. Your mother needs her beauty sleep."

Kreyna steered Sofiya in front of her toward the hall and Megan tugged Tom away. They joined a woman in an oddly familiar gold shantung suit with a mandarin collar. Her short, thick, dark blond hair was shot with silver. Smiling, she turned and waved at Sofi.

Kreyna's heart stopped—then tumbled on.

"Mum, what's wrong? Mum!"

Her legs wouldn't move, struggling as they were to merely hold her upright; she leaned on Sofiya's shoulders. The girl paused to look from one woman to the other. She reached back and grabbed her mother's hands, pulling her into the hall and all the way to the front door.

Out in the cool night air, Kreyna regained her senses. In silence, she drove home and sent Sofiya to unlock the house while she put away the car. For a few minutes, she stayed in the dark garage, trying to make some semblance of sanity out of what she'd seen.

Inside, she met Sofiya in the kitchen. "Some vibe, Mum."

"*Tell* me about it."

"She's Frans."

"What? Who the hell is Frans, anyway? I never did find out."

"Now you know she's Frans. Oma said he was coming."

"Whatever *that* means."

"Dunno, just passing on the message."

Kreyna massaged her scalp under the mass of black curls. "My head hurts. What a mess."

"No mess. All is exactly as it should be."

Kreyna stared at her. "Who are you channeling now?"

"Dunno. I'm going to bed. Can I have Wodan back in my room?"

"No! For now, he sleeps with me, keeps me company."

"Barbecue breakfast at eight, remember?"

Kreyna grunted. Sofiya loped off.

* * *

Even though the moon had reached full over two days ago, it cast considerable light through the curtains into Kreyna's bedroom. Despite all her discipline, she struggled to gain any sleep, so much had seeing Frances again rattled her. She tossed and turned, slid out of bed, wandered down to the kitchen for a glass of water and badgered Wodan into stretching out beside her on the bed. His presence provided scant relief from her missing Declan. Right now, she needed all the reassuring comfort she could get.

She dozed fitfully, the visual sequence of Frances turning to face her playing over and over like a jagging silent movie. Delete. Think of nothing. Think of pink elephants. Counting seeds in a sunflower works. Unlucky. Again, she slid out of bed. The dog opened one eye to watch her leave and went back to sleep.

In utter desperation, she turned on the television in the living room and watched the Shopping Network. It was either that or a z-grade, black-and-white melodrama made in 1934, broadcast on the ABC. Who in their right mind bought marquisette jewelry, these days? She fell asleep on the sofa.

Oma said, "In the end there will be joy, wherever you may be."

* * *

A fist-thumping evangelist made her open her eyes. She found the remote and shut him down. Back in the bedroom, she squirmed into a rugby knit tracksuit and slipped on battered runners. The dog raised his massive head in surprise for it was five thirty a.m.

"Yup, I know it's only sparrow-fart, big guy—how about a run?"

Together, they tiptoed to the front door. Out on the road, she let him run to the full length of the fifteen foot retractable leash. Usually, she ran toward Shirley and Geoff's place. Today, she set off in the opposite direction. Coward.

The narrow, undulating country road wore asphalt to its grass verge, leaving no room for a driver to pull over in a hurry. Behind wire fences and scrubby hedges, cattle, horses and mobs of kangaroos grazed the dusty brown paddocks. At regular intervals, yellow, diamond-shaped traffic signs warned of horseback riders.

Every residential five-acre block had erected a rural delivery letterbox by the roadside. Metal gates protected driveways that disappeared through native trees and shrubs to the residences. Very few were visible from the road—those that were offered barely a glimpse.

Kreyna jogged steadily with her contented beast. Occasionally, he jerked her to a halt and insisted on sniffing a particularly transporting, exotic aroma.

After all these years, seeing Frances again brought back feelings she'd fought to forget. It was too disturbing to dwell on, yet she could barely concentrate on anything else. As an action woman, what was she supposed to do in this situation? A bubble of excitement rose in her chest and she stopped to catch her breath. Wodan ground to a halt and cocked his head at her.

There was the oddest sensation of time slowing as the veil between this world and the other thinned. She began to walk, only too aware of a sense of watching herself, of déjà vu. Refocusing, she sprinted hard over the next thirty feet and settled back into her earlier rhythm. Twenty minutes later, they reached Mac's Reef Road, crossed to the other side and doubled back.

She should have recognized the dream visit as a warning—seeing Frances again was not a total surprise. Even so, her own reaction suggested that she still had feelings for Frances—how crazy would that be? Forget it. It's all ancient history—don't give it another thought.

They arrived home, sweaty, panting and marginally less stressed.

"You stink, you beast. Matter of fact, I do too."

She led Wodan into the laundry and made up a bucket of diluted dog shampoo. In the backyard, with him securely tethered to a post holding up the pergola, she brushed him down thoroughly. Coarse black curls released the soft undercoat and she collected piles of hair destined for the compost bin. The Bouvier stood thirty inches tall at the shoulder and tipped the scales at over a hundred pounds. She loved his powerful shoulders and muscular hindquarters that belied his calm and gentle personality.

A sponge worked the shampoo into his coat and she stepped back to check she'd not missed any part of him. Grinning, he shook violently and sprayed foam all around. With a shriek, she ran back into the laundry, filled buckets with tepid water, stood back and threw them over him. He barked a resonant woof and shook until she was sodden.

"Bit early in the day, isn't it?" Sofiya finished a banana, looking glam in her favorite Twilight-themed nightie. "You're making a helluva racket, you two."

Kreyna poured water over his head and smoothed the hair back from his eyes. "Would you fetch the dog towels for me, please? What time is it?"

Sofiya dropped the towels on the outdoor table and began to dry Wodan. "Just after seven—better get a wriggle on." Gently, Kreyna wiped inside his ears and around his eyes—the most important parts. The rest of him would dry off as the day progressed and she'd give him another brushing later.

"Take him inside before he rolls in something disgusting. Come on, princess, shower time."

What to wear? Kreyna critiqued her freshly washed body in the bathroom mirror. Dissatisfied, she strode back into the bedroom. Truth be known, nothing had changed substantially since she last saw Frances.

What's the difference? Fourteen years have passed, so what? Big deal. She was fatigued from lack of sleep and emotionally overwrought. Get a grip.

Still, she dressed to please, whoever the audience.

* * *

Sofiya led the way around to the patio and outdoor barbecue area. She spied Laura and the two girls launched into a wedding post-mortem. Kreyna found Tom bent over a trestle table, busily separating sausages with a chef's knife.

He glanced up and waved. "Good morning. Let me rescue you from the decibel duo. Come and meet Meg's mum. She's making tea, I believe, and she's dying to meet you."

Kreyna found that a stretch. She swallowed hard and followed him through the sliding doorway.

"Hi, Kreyna, how are you?" Shirley smiled broadly and said, "I hope you're hungry, we've got stacks. Geoff thought we were catering for a horde of starving Ethiopians, didn't you, dear?"

Geoff Jetta was a strikingly handsome man of Aboriginal descent. An army reservist, he and Declan had regularly volunteered together for the village's fire brigade. Geoff flashed pearly whites and winked at Kreyna. "Similar—just Sofiya. 'Struth, those girls can eat, can't they?"

A clearly English voice said, "Wait until they're older. Then they worry you silly by eating like sparrows." Pouring water from a steaming kettle, Frances filled a row of mugs sporting fluttering tea bag labels. "Would you like a cup, Kreyna?"

Kreyna didn't trust herself to speak.

Tom gestured at Kreyna. "Sorry, how rude of me." Even more flustered, he said, "Mrs. De Salles, this is—Mrs. Parrey?"

"Frances is fine, thank you, Tom."

Kreyna took the outstretched hand and gazed into pine-green eyes glittering with interest, veiling what? A flicker of fondness? For an instant, she felt unspeakably sad—she'd forgotten how good-looking Frances was.

"Sofiya told me you made her look grown-up for the wedding. She was thrilled."

"She's yet young. But blessed with superb genetics, I see." Frances's smile was positively beatific. She slid over a mug. "Tea?"

Kreyna clenched her teeth. This could be death by a thousand cuts. Murmuring thanks, she took the mug and followed Tom back to the barbecue.

"If you can find a spare apron, I'll help with the cooking."

Tom opened a cupboard in the massive conglomeration of stainless steel that housed a six-burner barbecue, wok ring, small fridge and a sink. He handed her a wad of folded, clear plastic. She passed a cord over her head, flicked her hair loose and tied on the apron. Tom swung switches and fired up four burners, while she fetched the prepared sausages. At least she could keep busy.

An hour later, the group lounged around the long table, finishing their coffee. Among the condiment bottles and used plates lay strewn the remains of beef patties, sausages, bacon and bread rolls. Kreyna had managed to sandwich herself between Tom and another couple, the best man and his girlfriend—well away from Frances who sat down the other end with the two young girls and Megan. Kreyna's gaze drifted to Frances and lingered. With an effort, she made herself listen to the couple chatting about their fabulous new home in the Canberra suburb of Harrison. Inevitably, her attention shifted back to Frances who smiled too sweetly.

She knows you're watching her.

Kreyna pushed back her chair, whisked up four plates and made for the kitchen. Sofiya jumped up and followed her.

"Mum, have you seen the vineyard? Laura says it was planted three years ago and has grown like mad. Would you like a look?"

Once the plates were safely on the draining board in the kitchen, Kreyna went back outside and fell into step with Sofiya. They followed a track through a smattering of gum trees. Overhead, high branches were laden with screeching, white sulphur-crested cockatoos. Beyond, they crossed an open field and headed toward a fenced block of young grapevines. Footsteps thudded behind them and Laura bounced off Sofiya's shoulders. "Wait for us!"

Frances followed a few strides behind.

At the vineyard, Laura opened the gate and explained that the fence was to keep the wildlife—kangaroos and wallabies in particular—from munching the vines to oblivion. She led them down a distinct trail into the center.

"Isn't this lovely?" Sofiya dragged her mother to a metal park bench wedged under a mature crab apple tree. A couple of dozen standard, hybrid tea and floribunda roses flowered abundantly in two concentric circles surrounding the seat. At the entrance to the rose garden, a pale pink Cecile Brunner climbing rose smothered an ornate archway.

"Laura's mum loves roses, doesn't she, Laura?" Laura nodded, obligingly.

Frances lowered herself onto the bench, next to Sofiya. "This is glorious. From the outside you wouldn't know it's here. What a marvelous idea."

"Most vineyards grow roses at the end of each row." Kreyna sat back to admire the display. "I think it's because if there's mildew or aphids about, they're attacked first—an early warning system. Clever."

Sofiya stole a look to her left at her mother and one to her right at Frances. "Stay here, Mum. Laura and me will be back in a minute." The two girls dashed through the archway and disappeared.

Kreyna pointed and said, "Is that Peace or Just Joey?"

"Just Joey, I should think. Peace is out of fashion."

Silence stretched between them. Kreyna's throat was dry.

"You broke a promise."

Frances turned to look at her. "No credit for all the years it was kept? Besides, I heard talk that Robert committed suicide. Is it true?"

"I'm afraid so. It was weeks before they found him and cut him down." Kreyna rubbed her lips.

"What a waste. I'm sorry to hear it." Frances spoke with deliberate slowness. "And I'm sorry about the circumstances in which we met. And parted ways. Deeply sorry for it."

"You forget you saved my life."

"Did I? Thought it was Dr. Corea."

"You had an equal hand in it," Kreyna said. "About that promise—have you any particular reason to break it now?"

"I'm filing for divorce when I get home. Now that my son Craig has moved to Nottingham and Megan's married, my obligations to Bryce are over. Come the new year, I shall find somewhere else to live. I may go back to university. Not sure yet."

"What has any of this to do with me?" Kreyna asked.

"Rules. I'm discarding obsolete rules that have run my life for far too long. And what you made me to agree to, over what seems like a million years ago, is one of them."

"It's disruptive…"

"Disruptive? You say that like it's a bad thing. And from what I hear, it should be said in the past tense."

Kreyna winced and Frances took pity. "Excuse me. I didn't mean to wound. The state of your marriage is not my business. If you're heartbroken, you have my sympathy."

"He's pursuing an old flame."

Frances stared at her, at length. Slowly, she chuckled until bursting into laughter. "That's priceless. Well, bully for him. I remember he lived with a Jenny for a while. Is it her?"

Kreyna nodded, her smile growing, relieved to see the ironic side of it for a change.

"I liked him a lot. He's a fine man. I wish him every success. Oh, dear me, it's too much." Chuckles faded to subdued giggles. They enjoyed a mellow silence, the roses providing plenty to contemplate.

"What about you, how do you feel?"

"I miss him." Tears prickled, but Kreyna swallowed them. "He's been good to me and deserves the chance of happiness. We all deserve a chance."

A flock of silvereyes descended onto the rose bushes. They chatted amongst themselves, squeaky tweets exclaiming over the plumpest aphids. Flitting at speed, they were gone.

Frances said, "Rumor has it, Sofi's flying to Surfers Paradise on Friday. For five days away with Laura's family."

"Yup. She wants to go to Sea World and the other amusement parks—very exciting."

Frances took her time. Then she took Kreyna's hand. They could hear the girls talking animatedly, not far away.

"Tomorrow and Tuesday I have people I want to catch up with in Canberra. I've hired a car to crack on down to the coast on Wednesday. There's a cottage at Gerroa overlooking Seven Mile Beach I've rented. It's just north of Nowra, accessed via Kangaroo Valley." She looked around for the girls and turned to search Kreyna's expression. "I'll be there until the following Tuesday when I fly back to the UK. I'd love you to come and spend some time with me. Walk along the beach, read a book— that sort of thing."

Laura and Sofiya approached the archway. Frances dropped Kreyna's hand. "I'll give you the details so you can find the cottage. Think about it, please."

Kreyna's hand throbbed with warmth. Light-headed, she stood up just as Sofiya wrapped arms around her and clung like a limpet.

* * *

She slept as she hadn't done for many a year—deep, dreamless, intoxicating sleep. When she awoke, every cell sighed with relief and seemed to be cruising, buzzing and humming in harmony. The phone rang. From down the hall, she heard Sofiya's voice growing louder.

"Aunty Morwenna for you."

Kreyna took the handset and sat up, shoving pillows behind her for support.

"Morning sleepyhead—it's after nine, you lard-arse. Had a late night?"

"For the record, I went to bed at eight thirty fall down tired. How's every little thing?"

"Snugly tucked away, last time I looked." Morwenna's voice held a smile. "I have good news of the rocks-flying-through-space variety. After you left, I checked your progressions and the current transits. You do realize it's fourteen years since you and Frances met? That's a half cycle of Saturn and very significant. The planetary movement indicates things coming to a head—a culmination, if you will."

"Really? As a matter of fact, I saw her yesterday. Turns out, she's Laura's brother Tom's new mother-in-law and in town for the wedding." Kreyna heard a protracted whistle.

"That fits. Sweet cheeks, you're in deep trouble."

Kreyna wrung the handset. "Why? What's coming down?"

"I doubt you remember, but I told you ages ago when your Venus progresses to conjunct your natal Sun, you'll get happy, which is right about now."

"Morwenna! Don't scare me like that—rat-bag."

Guffaws echoed down the line. "Gotcha. My advice is whatever's on offer, take it and run with it. Fortune favors the brave, as they say. Go with the flow, follow your instincts and all those other cheesy expressions meaning be brave and take a risk. This situation is a test of your faith in which fear must play no part. Am I making myself clear?"

"Crystal, thank you. I'm marginally less terrified. She's rented a house at the coast and invited me to visit this coming weekend."

"Has she, indeed?" Morwenna drawled. "What a good little girl scout, being prepared and all that. And are you going? What about Sofi?"

"Sofi's going to Surfers Paradise with Laura's parents on Friday. I'll be home alone with Wodan."

Throaty chuckles. "I think you'd better ring round for a kennel to board him for the weekend, hmm?"

* * *

Blasting through the car's powerful array of speakers, Celine Dion belted out "It's All Coming Back to Me Now." Kreyna joined in with a husky contralto, intermittently. It was after eight p.m. and the road ahead was so dark that she battled the alarming illusion she was driving into the sea. Although the Sat Nav in the X5 was top quality, she doubted it now. Nerves jangling from fatigue and anxious anticipation, she followed the directions.

Turn off Crooked River Road onto Headland Drive and into Stafford. Stop looking—found it. Deep breath, grab backpack, lock car, here goes.

"I'd given up on you. Almost." A silhouette in the doorway, Frances stood with her arms akimbo. She reached out and took the backpack. Their hands touched and Frances drew a ragged breath. "Have you eaten?"

Could she be just as nervous? Kreyna followed Frances who wore a blue and white striped, boat-neck sloppy-joe over figure hugging jeans.

"Not recently," Kreyna said. "Their flight out was delayed nearly two hours, so I was pushing it, trying to get here before nightfall. I didn't want to be looking for you in the dark but it ended up that way. It's pitch-black out there."

They walked down a short hall and into a bedroom. Frances rested the backpack on a luggage stand. "We're on a promontory with sea both sides."

"So I noticed. The sea air smells wonderfully clean and fresh." Kreyna took in her surroundings. "What a lovely cottage. Has it two bedrooms?"

"Plus a couple of bathrooms and a kitchen. And a lounge that opens onto a deck overlooking the bay. That's about it. Let's have a look in the fridge, shall we?"

In the kitchen, Frances filled two oversized goblets. "Evans and Tate classic white—will it pass?"

Kreyna took a sip of the icy, pale greenish wine. "Hits the spot, thank you."

Frances's gaze darted from Kreyna to the fridge contents. "Let's see, now. You can have rock oysters, a green salad and Italian bread." She lifted out a salad bowl and a plate covered in cling film. Kreyna carried them over to the dining table.

On a wooden board, Frances sawed slices from an elongated, crusty loaf wrapped in luncheon paper. "This is excellent. They bake it in Gerringong. The oysters are harvested locally, too. Can't get any fresher."

She brought over the bread board and a tub of butter. "Please go ahead. I ate around seven, though I might have a piece of bread. Are you comfortable enough with Sofiya interstate while you're here? I used to worry terribly about Craig and Megan."

"She has her own phone, so she can call or text me." Kreyna ladled out salad and fished through the bowl for remnants of avocado. "And she'll be safe with Shirley and Geoff—they're good people. Sofi and Laura have been best friends since First Year at school."

Frances buttered a slice of bread and ate between sips of wine. "Are there any signs she's inherited your psychic abilities?"

"Sure. It's difficult to assess to what extent because I'm too close to her. Time will tell. When she was born, I thought she might be my grandmother, Kryna, come again. Declan and I— we did wait for over a month before we decided otherwise and named her." Kreyna slid down another oyster. The tang and bite of the sea permeated her mouth, bringing a smile. "These are gorgeous."

Frances watched her, eyes dancing. "I hope you know I'm delighted you've come down. Just to spend some time together again is a pleasure I haven't dared to dream of over the years. It matters a good deal to me. At the same time, I want you to know I have no expectations. What happened between us was all a very long time ago..."

"Not so very long," Kreyna said quietly, and she met Frances's gaze. "You wear it well."

With a relieved grin, Frances said, "Why, thank you! I haven't had a chance to tell you before but I found Arty in London. Not that I recognized him immediately. He was a great help."

"Really?" Kreyna stacked up empty oyster shells. "I remember he and Neil were thinking of migrating. They came up to Canberra a few times. Neil was keen to further his IT career over there. I gather there's plenty of demand for qualified Aussies and Kiwis. I'm afraid we lost track of each other over the years. I haven't even an address to send them a Christmas card. Are they well?"

"Neil hadn't returned to London before I left, but Arty is in fine form. Did you know he's a psychotherapist?"

"Yes, of course. And highly qualified, I believe." Kreyna picked up a fork and pushed lettuce around her plate.

"Did you tell Arty about us? He seemed to know."

Kreyna savored the salad, well dressed with extra virgin olive oil and lemon juice. "He didn't hear it from me, but neither of those two misses much. How come you found him?"

Frances told her everything—from the night terrors to the past life regression and all its implications, as summarized by Arty. Occasionally, Kreyna interrupted for clarification. Mostly she listened, watching from behind her glass, the analyst in her working overtime.

"Your grandmother was quite a character. Passionate, yet compassionate. And courageous." Frances smiled at the memory. "Maybe too bold. She had an infectious, wild quality."

"Sofiya talks to her all the time. She's been banging on about Frans since you and I met. It's only from what you've told me that I finally understand why. It seems you saved her life."

"I can't take any credit for that." Frances shifted in the chair. "To assume it's all true—well, it could be my imagination."

"Are you prone to making things up? Besides, you were under hypnosis. I understand your instinct to take it with a grain of salt but the sequence of events fits well with what little we know. What about the psychotherapy process you went through with Arty—did it help?"

Frances mulled over her thoughts before answering. "With no exaggeration, I'd say immeasurably. Initially, the hypnosis changed nothing and Arty said it was because the cause hadn't been found and addressed. After the past life regression, the night terrors vanished along with the fear of black spiders. Forever, I should think. And I stopped taking medication with no ill effects. But going back to a time when I was Frans was life changing."

"Life changing? Wow!" Kreyna left the table and went looking for the wine bottle in the fridge. "May I ask in what way?"

"I think you understand all this better than most people." Frances nodded when Kreyna poised the tilted bottle over her glass. "Frans believed in himself and trusted his own judgment. He was willing to risk everything for his beliefs and his convictions. In the end, it cost him his life. But he had integrity."

Frances's eyes glistened and she took a quick swallow of wine. "After the fact, I'm trying to be more like him. Self-esteem before self-interest is how I think of it. Yes, he was male and lived in a different time. And under radically different circumstances that made him the person he was. Much as I'm a product of my own unique circumstances. I can't change the past and what I've done, some of which makes me cringe. What I can change is my intention, out of which I hope to create a new reality. You know what I mean, don't you?"

Kreyna arranged her cutlery to one side of the plate. "Sure. We're all here learning about personal integrity."

"I'm doing my best to believe in myself more, to risk more. Challenging. A new experience. And I hope to make fewer mistakes than I've done in the past. But it's early days."

"Fair enough. And thank you for revealing a whole lot more of yourself than you ever have. I appreciate the show of trust. Speaking of which, are you aware that I've never been completely released by ASIO?"

"Ah." Frances paused and chewed a lip. "That is news to me. I'm privy to little that is confidential now. Bryce should have mentioned it. Does it bother you?"

"Some. I do what I have to and make the best of it. I'm due to go into the office on Tuesday, about when you'll be boarding a plane."

Frances said, "In that case, come and look at the view." She walked through the lounge and opened wide French doors onto a wooden deck. Outside, a fresh sea breeze buffeted the two women standing behind a low railing. In the distance, phosphorescence highlighted the waves breaking against a sandy beach. Lights sparkled from towns stretching along the seaboard.

"Ever seen a sky this dark and stars so bright?"

Kreyna touched Frances's wrist and gazed up at the dazzling, bejeweled canopy that soared above from black horizon to horizon. Frances turned and Kreyna reached up to rest a hand lightly on each shoulder. Frances seemed so solemn that Kreyna's throat closed over and began to ache. Had she misjudged the situation? Her heart clamored and she began to withdraw her hands. But they were caught, midair, and fingers laced through hers.

Plush lips enveloped hers. Hungrily, she kissed Frances back, telling a tale of pent-up longing, echoed by a luscious mouth and her own surging response.

"You taste delicious. Oysters and fine wine," Frances said.

Kreyna stepped into Frances's arms and held her, heart aligned with heart. "I'm glad I dared to come, but I'm horribly nervous and scared stiff."

Frances tightened her hold and whispered against Kreyna's left ear. "Shh—don't be. It's only you and me. Just us, alone together. No hurry, no fires to put out."

"Speak for yourself."

Frances drew away—a flash of white teeth, black pools for eyes. She took Kreyna's hand and they reentered the cottage. The bread got put away and the dishes made it into the sink, only just.

Her touch on Kreyna's skin took her breath. Frances had unbuttoned her shirt and slid hot hands around to her spine, their kiss deepening perilously close to mutual annihilation. Kreyna unzipped her own jeans, allowing Frances's palms to capture her backside.

Kreyna came up for air. "I'm losing my knees."

"Promise?"

"Mercy."

"Not a chance. Take it off."

"You first."

Frances chuckled softly and stepped away. Kreyna stood disheveled while Frances undressed with deliberate sloth, maintaining eye contact, lips twitching with amusement. Frances drew back the bed coverings and Kreyna swallowed hard.

"Let me look at you. Imagination alone has served too long," Frances said.

"The real thing could be a disappointment. What's more, I have only the vaguest…"

"I want you for you, not what you might do for me." Frances held Kreyna's face, stroking her cheeks with her thumbs. "I don't need a performance. Whatever happens, we'll both start out awkward." She kissed Kreyna's forehead. "I don't know what you like. And I'm way out of practice. So bloody rusty, I should be in a museum."

Kreyna laughed and Frances wrapped her naked self around her. Kreyna closed her eyes, distracted by the delicious scent of her beloved that sent waves of sheer want through her chest and belly. Beneath her astonished palms, satin skin over a strong back almost destroyed any remaining thought. With an effort, she said, "You'd be a very popular exhibit."

"You're too kind." Frances leaned back to search her face. "I'll help, you know. We'll muddle through. Now kiss me. We're worth the risk."

Kreyna obliged, divesting herself of clothing, in between kisses. She pushed Frances back on the bed, face gaunt with desire, and spread herself over the length of her. Reveling in the sensation of skin to heated skin, she lost all sense of separateness through touching, kissing and caressing whatever she could reach of Frances. She found wetness and stroked, her teeth grazing Frances's pulsing throat, just above the birthmark.

"Oh. Christ."

She threaded her fingers through Frances's hair, both hands holding her head, kissing lips, cheeks and eyelids.

"That was quick."

Frances's groan turned into a feeble chuckle. "After fourteen years of foreplay? You're wicked, you are." She lifted a thigh between Kreyna's legs and turned her over. "This'll be so slow you'll be begging me to hurry."

* * *

Dull daylight crept through the pale blue curtains that swayed, back and forth. An open window let in a stiff breeze and seagulls called in the distance. The hand cupping Kreyna's right breast was attached to an arm under her neck. She touched the tender skin that gave off the scent of salt, lemons and lovemaking. A nameless ache emerged in her chest, troubling her until recognized. Oh. It was almost as strong as the moment she'd held newborn Sofiya, when she first knew pure happiness.

It was different. She had previous experience of her lips being still slightly swollen, a satiated hum in her hips, and sinew and skin feeling vibrantly alive. But the lightness in her heart? Nothing like it, ever. As if she'd never made love before. And she hadn't—not like that. Nor had she ever been kissed like that.

Frances had held a cheek, fingers buried in Kreyna's hair and cradling her head while she explored Kreyna's mouth. At first slow, soft and lingering, the kisses became deeper and more demanding, until utterly merciless. The deep kissing stoked a smoldering fire to furnace heat, wrapped around and inside wet, skin melting and flesh melding, a whispered "come to me, darling," breathing in unison, gazes locked, even in release. No, not like that.

Even weirder, they wouldn't shut up. Constant banter, all night long—most of it sweet or funny—some of it raw. *Dear heart. Awesome kisser. Shag you senseless. Make me. In a heartbeat. Beloved.*

There were attacks of the giggles, smothered snorts, mock wrestling, and gentle teasing. Bouts of abject silliness had Kreyna giggling, almost in tears. And Frances doubled up, ribs sore from laughing. If last night was anything to go by, laughter was going to figure prominently in this relationship. Assuming they had a relationship.

In another instant, she was afraid. What chance did they have, living in separate countries? Dread of loss crept through her. Just when they'd found each other again, it would all come to naught. She'd risked her heart, only to have it destroyed by separation. What a fool for love, she was—Eadie had told her so. But Morwenna had said fear must play no part. There had to be a way to turn this opportunity into a possibility.

Frances stirred. Deftly, Kreyna lifted the embracing arm and slipped out of bed. In the next bedroom, she found her backpack and searched for a bathroom. Under a hot shower, she washed and brushed her teeth, brain motoring in overdrive, intent on devising ways to make everything work out for them.

Out of the shower, she dried off in front of the vanity unit. Kreyna glanced at her reflection, stopped and wiped away steam. A livid mark sat low on the left side of her throat and when she lifted her hair, there was another just above her shoulder.

And then there was a presence.

It is what it is. She loves you, and has for lifetimes.

To her reflection, Kreyna said, "And you love her warmth, the soft strength of all she is."

Silently, she thanked her Sentinels, found her red and black kimono-style dressing gown to put on and padded down to the kitchen. With the kettle on to boil, she hunted in the lower cupboard for tea bags, smiling. Options—there were options.

"Good morning, I hope." Frances lined up two mugs on the bench. "Top left, above the stove."

"No question. How about you go back to bed and I'll bring it down?"

Frances backed out and disappeared into the bathroom.

Kreyna carried the brimming cups to the bedroom. She pulled back the curtains and discovered the room had its own private deck beyond a set of French doors. One door opened a few inches served to refresh the room. Beyond the windows, closely mown grass curved down to the bay and around to the right toward the beach that stretched off into the distance. The metal-gray sea carried wild horses—choppy crested waves— toward the shore. Wheeling seagulls played in the air currents, keening and whistling.

She slipped into bed, leaned back on plumped pillows and sipped tea while a jumble of thoughts jostled for attention. Frances returned under cover of a leaf-green bathrobe. As if they'd done so for years, they drank tea and talked.

Unable to stop smiling and barely believing reality, Kreyna examined her lover in the harsh light of day. She raised her fingertips to a cheek. "You've a lovely mouth. And hardly a line on you—it's sickening."

Frances kissed her palm. "England's summer has its pluses. Don't look too close, will you?"

Kreyna chose to be brave. "Have you considered applying to study at the ANU? I still work with staff at the Centre for Consciousness, occasionally. I could find out, if you're interested."

"Must say I hadn't thought of it. Has potential. I know the university encourages mature age students. I'd have to see if I can get a study visa. I'm sure I know enough people in the Foreign Office to ask. A few judicious phone calls would get some answers."

Frances put down her cup and lowered herself to the horizontal. "What are you thinking?"

Kreyna wriggled down into the bed until their eyes drew level. "I'm thinking I don't want to lose you. If it's at all possible for us to have quality time together, I'd like that to happen. What about you?"

"Divorcing Bryce could be protracted and messy. He won't make it easy. This is why I've engaged a good lawyer. It could take as long as a year. I really should be there, I'm afraid. I'd have to take advice on the best strategy. In the interim, I could commute using tourist visas. It's only twenty-three hours on an A380."

Searching Kreyna's expression, she added, "I'm willing if you are."

Kreyna's smile grew into a beaming grin. She leaned over and kissed Frances, repeatedly, until dressing gowns flopped to the floor.

Kreyna turned and wrangled her spirited bare woman, stripped her free of finesse and ran her ragged. *Love, do you?* Frances tussled with her, in sweet revenge. *You and me both.*

And then there were tears. Tears for fourteen years lost, deprived of each other—cold wet mouths, dripping cheeks and whispered words of residual sorrow and apology. Limbs strung tight, they wrapped each other as close as humanly possible, murmuring words of comfort. Moment by moment, clutching mellowed into hands held lightly, listening to the other breathe.

* * *

"We should get up and eat," Kreyna said. She sat astride Frances's hips, sensuous hands caressing every part within reach.

"Mere food couldn't entice me away from this view. Thoroughly nourishing and deeply satisfying as it is."

Kreyna chuckled and draped herself alongside Frances. "The thought of letting you go back to England is unbearable. Just when we're getting to know each other again." She traced the uneven birthmark with a fingertip.

"Again?" Frances smoothed Kreyna's mass of curls back off her cheek, the better to see her.

"No idea which incarnation, but we've been together before."

"I feel it, too." Frances's eyes grew limpid, bottomless. "Do you think we'll get it right this time?"

"What's right or wrong? From here on in, it'll be an adventure. I know I want to stay with you. Eternity's a long time. With love and optimism, we'll manage what remains of this life." Kreyna nestled a cheek into Frances's throat.

"Can't bear the thought of not seeing you, now. For bloody months at a stretch, I should think. You'll have trouble keeping me away. You know that, don't you?"

"Email, text, Skype with a webcam. If you're desperate, pick up the landline phone. I adore technology. We can see and hear each other, but not touch, except through imagination—you're allowed to imagine."

Frances snorted. "Just try to stop me. Expect to be ravished nightly. Think you'll cope?"

"I'll enjoy the struggle." The pulse under her ear was sweet, resonant and strong, keeping in time with her own. "By the way, my mother's father was English."

"Excuse me?" Frances swung Kreyna into the air and onto her back. With a delighted grin and green eyes shining, she said, "You can get a UK ancestry visa. Live in England."

"If I wanted to—I hear it's cold and miserable." Kreyna said, smiling back. "But it's an option, once Sofiya's finished school. She'll go on to university, probably."

Frances kissed the knuckles of each of Kreyna's hands and moved them to behind her neck. With a sigh, she lowered her mouth to Kreyna's and lingered. "It keeps getting better. But my stomach insists on toast and marmalade."

* * *

Kreyna opened one of the French doors and stepped down to the deck. Frances stood just behind on the step and put her arms around Kreyna's waist, her chin nestled in the black curls atop her head.

"I've often wondered about our meeting on the plane—how was it set up?"

Frances extricated herself and crossed the room to her handbag. She flicked through a purse and came back, once again putting her arms around Kreyna and her chin on her head. She showed Kreyna a dog-eared passport photo.

"Wow, this is an old one—I was so young."

"They gave me a day's notice—told me to catch your plane. I had to drop everything and leave immediately. With only a profile and this photo, they told me to concentrate on being palpably angry—very easy in the circumstances. They said you'd come looking. I had it wedged in a magazine and kept opening it up to look at you. I recall thinking, if they want me to seduce this lovely-looking woman for Queen and country, how lucky am I? Very naive. I had no idea how much you would come to mean to me. Not a clue. You'll be amused to know, I've carried it with me ever since."

Kreyna pulled the arms around her tighter. "You won't ever stop wanting to kiss me, will you?"

"Not a chance."

Bella Books, Inc.

Women. Books. Even Better Together.

P.O. Box 10543
Tallahassee, FL 32302

Phone: 800-729-4992
www.bellabooks.com